By Alan Dean Foster

Published by The Random House Publishing Group

The Black Hole
Cachalot
Dark Star
The Metrognome and Other Stories
Midworld
Nor Crystal Tears
Sentenced to Prism
Splinter of the Mind's Eye
Star Trek® Logs One–Ten
Voyage to the City of the Dead
. . . Who Needs Enemies?
With Friends Like These . . .
Mad Amos
The Howling Stones
Parallelities
Transformers: Ghosts of Yesterday
Transformers (tie-in novel)

THE ICERIGGER TRILOGY:
Icerigger
Mission to Moulokin
The Deluge Drivers

THE ADVENTURES OF FLINX OF THE COMMONWEALTH:
For Love of Mother-Not
The Tar-Aiym-Krang
Orphan Star
The End of the Matter
Bloodhype
Flinx in Flux
Mid-Flinx
Flinx's Folly
Sliding Scales
Running from the Diety
Trouble Magnet

THE DAMNED:
Book One: A Call to Arms
Book Two: The False Mirror
Book Three: The Spoils of War

THE FOUNDING OF THE COMMONWEALTH:
Phylogenesis
Dirge
Diuturnity's Dawn

THE TAKEN TRILOGY:
Lost and Found
The Light-Years Beneath My Feet
The Candle of Distant Earth

TRANSFORMERS

A Novel by

ALAN DEAN FOSTER

Based on the Screenplay by
Roberto Orci & Alex Kurtzman
from a Story by Roberto Orci &
Alex Kurtzman and John Rogers

BALLANTINE BOOKS • NEW YORK

A Del Rey Books Mass Market Original

Copyright © 2007 by Hasbro. All Rights Reserved.

Published in the United States by Del Rey Books, an imprint of The Random House Publishing Group, a division of Random House, Inc., New York.

TRANSFORMERS and the distinctive logo thereof are trademarks of Hasbro, Inc. Used with permission.

DEL REY is a registered trademark and the Del Rey colophon is a trademark of Random House, Inc.

ISBN 978-0-345-49799-4

Printed in the United States of America

www.delreybooks.com
www.transformersmovie.com
www.hasbro.com

OPM   9 8 7 6 5 4 3 2 1

To Yuri Zhovnirovsky and Pam Kostka,
on the occasion of their marriage
and their somewhat unconventional honeymoon,
with gorillas and in friendship

A million years isn't much, as the galaxy spins. Stars are older. Nebulae are older. Drifting shards of unidentifiable matter and splinters of subatomic particles and wave-form properties we don't even have names for yet are considerably older still. For human beings, though, a million years is a very long stretch indeed. It's a small step back in time, but one that extends way past our first feeble scratchings as a civilization, before we could be counted as even moderately intelligent creatures.

There are other entities Out There, however, for whom a million years is a simple, measurable, comprehensible passing of time. Beings made of sterner stuff both mentally as well as materially. Intelligences straightforward yet vast, to whom our petty everyday concerns would be of no more concern than are those of an ant to a strolling human. Sometimes these beings pause to contemplate the universe. Sometimes they raise monuments and works that would stun into permanent silence the most imaginative among us. Sometimes they embark on and bring to fruition good works.

And sometimes . . . sometimes they are not nice.

*   *   *

The symbol had not been wrought by the hand of man. Its design was simultaneously infinitely complex, astoundingly beautiful, and clear-cut. Any human sculptors would have been proud to have acknowledged it as their work. Etched into the side of an immense metallic cube, its straight lines and sharp diagonals, its whorls and curves and stylish embellishments, shone beneath the light of distant stars as it tumbled through space.

The symbol was not an isolated example of its type. A second one decorated the metal surface to its right, another to its left. A different symbol gleamed above it and still another kind below. The slowly spinning cube was covered with such metal inscriptions.

Thousands of them.

There was nothing to indicate why the cube had been created. Nothing beyond surface aesthetics to indicate what its purpose might be, if indeed it had one that extended beyond the mere visual. That it was the product of an immensely advanced intelligence would have been apparent to any sentient being who happened to set eyes upon it. That it represented the supreme power, the ultimate heart of an immensely sophisticated world whose utterly nonhuman inhabitants had all but destroyed themselves in an interminable war between darkness and light, between truth and lies, was perceptible only to those for whom it represented and focused their very life force itself.

Cast out from a world awash in death, catapulted into the emptiness of interstellar space by a convulsion greater than any that had preceded its creation, it now wandered aimlessly across the great glowing spiral of the galaxy as those who had battled over its control fought on even in the absence of that for which they had originally warred. Great cities were obliterated and laboriously rebuilt, whole cultures were swallowed and reborn, as the war dragged on and on—without purpose, without meaning, without end.

For time interminable the artifact tumbled through nothingness—and then a strange thing happened. Out in the vast reaches of interstellar space a minor but significant galactic anomaly occurred. Purely by chance, the great reflective mass of the cube encountered an errant solidity. The glancing collision with this wandering chunk of spatial debris caused the cube's course to be altered. The adjustment was tiny by galactic standards but substantial by those employed for local measurements. Instead of continuing onward through endless emptiness, the cube's course was nudged slightly downward into the more crowded region of the galactic plane. Its new path brought it unexpectedly close to a sun. Around this sun orbited planets and planetoids, asteroids and comets.

The cube ought to have been captured and swallowed up by the gravity well of one of the system's giant gaseous spheres, or by its star. Instead, its altered arc saw it fall within the gravitational influence of a much smaller, far less impressive planet. Unseen and undetected it circled that world, its orbit degrading slowly and gradually, until finally it slammed into the planetary surface with considerable force but far less impact than had the numerous comets and asteroids that had preceded it. Its arrival gouged out no crater and left no scar on the land. No telltale shocked quartz marked its resting place. Its journey through the galaxy had come to an unexpected end.

The cube's arrival was not noticed, but its purpose was

not forgotten. Expelled but unvarying, every thousand local years it sent out a call to those of whom it would always be a part. And every thousand years that automatic, questing electronic shout went unanswered.

Until those to whom its control had been denied at last came looking for it.

The polar gale that howled over the floes and bergs tore through the rigging of the trapped ship like wind-whipped pieces of steel wire. No sleek China clipper, no imposing and heavily armed warship, the ice-heavy vessel bore the stubby, workmanlike lines of a craft designed to carry people and cargo slowly but efficiently from one harbor to the next. It was not fast and it was not pretty, but it could cross difficult seas and bash its way through persistent storms that would force ships far more pleasing to the eye to heave stern-to and turn back.

It could not, however, defeat the ice.

That localized, private, and terribly debilitating battle was left to its tired but resolute crew. With axes and picks and an occasional dose of dynamite they chopped, gouged, and chipped away at the ice pressure ridge that had not only trapped their ship but lifted it up above the waterline. Skittering along the exposed wooden deck, a coil of cold wind wound tight as a tiny tornado danced its way from bow to stern. It swirled around legs swaddled in heavy furs and leather, stung exposed cheeks with an additional dose of Arctic chill, and as if reluctant to leave stole away with the front page of a newspaper that had been inadvertently left lying outside exposed to the elements.

The fragile sheet of crumpled newsprint that was swept over the railing to vanish forever into the white dawn was full of news about the situation in Europe and South Africa, circa last month—more precisely, it bore the date 27 October 1897. Every man aboard was conscious of the time that was passing while they remained marooned in the ice. Every man aboard worked as hard as he could to free the ship lest they miss not so much the coming century as wives and children and sweethearts.

Miniature icicles dripping from his thick beard, a husky figure strode among the men who were hacking at the ice that gripped the vessel's imprisoned hull and refused to let go. Isolated by the responsibilities of command, buried deep within his warm, protective greatcoat, Captain Archibald Witwicky alternately praised those members of the crew who were working hard while also doing his best to keep up the morale of others whose strength and spirit were beginning to flag.

"Put your backs into it, lads, or we'll be chopping ourselves a path all the way back to the States!" Lifting his gaze, he squinted at the gunmetal-gray sky and low scudding clouds. The cold wind whistled in his ears, mocking his efforts. *Chill and ill,* he thought grimly. *Damn this early cold snap!* Even though the weather had been promising at the time, he knew now that he ought to have turned south a week ago. There was nothing for it but to carry on. Weather was ever immune to hindsight.

Huddled together on the slick ice near the ship's uplifted stern and out of the wind, the expedition's huskies began to howl. First one, then another and another raised their muzzles and began to bay. Mournful, querulous cries offered a warm-blooded counterpart to the uncaring wind.

Working nearby, one of the sailors rested his ice axe on the frozen ground and turned to squint into the haze. He was careful not to stare too long. It was well known that some Arctic explorers who had been afflicted with snow blindness never recovered from it.

The dogs' howling grew louder and more anxious.

"Don't see nuthin'," the sailor muttered, "but there must be somethin' out there."

Ice crystals forming a snowy crust in his eyebrows and beard, his companion nodded knowingly. "Dogs don't waste energy howlin' midday for the fun of it." Turning, he followed his mate's gaze. "Ice bear?"

Shielding his eyes against the white of the ice, the other man kept trying to see through the wind-driven snow. "In this weather a bear could be close and we wouldn't see it until it were right on top of us. Unless mebbe . . . hey!" He took a couple of steps forward.

Without warning the dogs suddenly broke ranks and sprinted off into the haze. Expressions of surprise were joined by frustrated curses as those of the crew near enough to see what had happened raised the alarm. Cursing under his breath when he learned what had happened, Witwicky picked up his rifle and a nearby lantern and gave chase, taking the nearest of the crew with him. They could not afford to lose the dogs. In an emergency they could be hitched to sleds to travel overland in search of help. In the most dire straits, they were also an important source of food.

Running on ice and snow was the Devil's own obstacle course: slippery, deceptive, full of snow-filled cracks and crevasses hundreds of feet deep. One of the pursuing sailors went down, hitting his knee hard. He was promptly up again and hurrying to rejoin his fellows. That his leg was injured was likely, but he was too numb from the cold to feel any pain.

Whatever it was that had drawn the dogs away from the comparative shelter and safety of the ship's side was not immediately discernible. Having stopped and gathered in a circle around the object of their interest, they stood there barking and squealing. From the unholy racket they were making Witwicky could not tell if they were angry, expectant, or afraid. But then he was a sailor's sailor, not a musher. The only dogs he knew well were back home, warm and safe with the rest of his family. The ones on the ship were as alien to him as the habits of the local Esquimu.

Forcing his way through the circle of wailing, agitated dogs, one of the sailors who had accompanied the captain knelt and began pushing snow from side to side.

"Whatever it is has upset them," the man contended, "it's below the ice."

"*Nothing's* below the ice," Witwicky muttered as he looked on. "This area is frozen solid and frozen deep."

A second sailor considered the possibilities. "Could be a recent carcass, fallen into a melt hole and swallowed up. Bear, caribou, mebbe a walrus."

His fellow seaman glanced briefly over at him. "But if it's frozen in, how the Divvil can the dogs pick up the smell?"

As they were debating alternative explanations there came a roar like nothing any of them had ever heard, not even at the height of a nor'easter at sea.

There was no warning. One minute they were on hands and knees scrabbling at the snow; the next the surface beneath them simply parted as if smashed open by a gigantic cleaver. One sailor nearly fell through, only to be caught at the last instant by his companions and pulled to safety. A lead sled dog was not so lucky. Its terrified whines shrank with distance as it slid downward and disappeared.

A devoted dog being more valuable than a questionable man, an anxious Witwicky had put his rifle aside to reach out and make a grab for the wide-eyed husky. For an instant he had it, a fistful of thick fur clutched firmly in one gloved hand. And then he didn't. He'd lost his grip—along with his footing.

Fortunately for both man and dog, the fissure was no more than thirty feet deep and the wall tolerably slanted. Still, it was a swift slide downward, and both landed hard when they hit bottom. While he had lost his hold on the husky, sheer determination had allowed the captain to maintain his grasp on the kerosene lantern clutched tightly in his other hand. As he hit bottom the lantern's metal base clanged against the surface underneath. Somehow it stayed lit.

Clanged? he thought. That wasn't right. Metal striking ice made a much duller sound.

Dazed but otherwise unhurt, he rose slowly to his feet. Body and lantern and dog all seemed to be intact. Instead of running off, the frightened husky cowered close by, whimpering against his legs. Tilting his head back, Witwicky hastened to reassure the frantic shouts that were raining down on him from above.

"I'm okay, lads! Nothing damaged but my dignity. I've taken worse falls on the hills in New Hampshire!"

His ready and hearty response brought forth sighs of relief and not a few chuckles. Having reassured the crew, he set about reassuring himself—and promptly failed. His eyes widened as he looked down at his feet and saw what had produced the unexpected sound of metal lantern striking unknown surface.

He was not standing on ice. He was not standing on rock. Beneath his feet and revealed in the glow of the lantern was the unmistakable gleam of metal. But it was metal unlike any he had ever seen. As an experienced ship captain he knew iron well, and steel. He was familiar enough with bronze and copper and tin. But this was new to him. As he paced the surface below his feet and studied it more closely he thought he could make out a shape. He had no idea what to expect. An abandoned iron lifeboat, perhaps, or some strayed cargo. A boiler lost overboard in a storm and somehow drifted to this spot.

He certainly did not expect to see a hand.

It was huge, and he was standing in the center of its upraised palm. Gripping the lantern tighter than ever, he raised it above his head. Was that something else, not underfoot but shining from the ice wall directly opposite? He took a step closer—and stumbled hurriedly back, gasping in shock.

The face that stared back at him was proportionate in size to the gigantic hand on which he was standing. Its mouth was open: perhaps in surprise, perhaps in a scream. Despite the obvious eyes and mouth the visage was only vaguely human. Mouth, eyes: these he recognized. But there was also much that was inhuman and bewildering. Projections of unknown provenance, appurtenances of purpose mysterious. Taken together it was all very foreign and—frightening.

He took courage from the fact that whatever it was, it was dead—or at least unmoving. Archibald Witwicky might lack any number of qualities, but courage was not among them. Advancing slowly, he reached out and wiped at the ice with a gloved hand. Frost melted beneath his warmth or was caught and swirled away by the breeze that now filled the open fissure. He looked harder, closer. There was some kind of symbol, embedded in the shape . . .

Pulling his small pickax from his belt, he started chopping at the ice. If he could get a better look at the symbol, he reasoned, he might be able to identify it, and if he could identify it he could possibly determine its origin. Though his was a scientific expedition, the universal laws of salvage at sea still applied to anything he and his crew might find. The value of the strange metal alone might be enough to reimburse those science-minded individuals and institutions that had underwritten the mission. He had no doubt that the metal's provenance, if it could be discovered, would also be of considerable interest to the government.

Ice flew in chips and then small blocks, as if it had been imperfectly frozen. All the better for him, then. As he dug deeper the outlines of the symbols grew clearer. They remained unrecognizable, though. Maybe a variety of Russian, he mused. Though their tsar had sold the province of Alaska to the Americans, Russian fur traders were still to be encountered throughout the Arctic. *Had they been up to something here?* he found himself wondering. Again and again the pickax descended in smooth, measured strokes. He was settling into a rhythm now. In the absence of sufficient food his muscles were powered by excitement. Thoughts of biscuits and hot coffee back on the ship lent added impetus to the work.

From beneath the point of his relentless ax a light suddenly burst forth, bright and intense as the sun that had not been seen in days. It was replete with signs and symbols the stunned captain had no time to appreciate.

Dropping the ax, he screamed and staggered backward, clawing at the burning pain that seared his corneas. His hands ripped away his spectacles and sent them flying across the floor of the fissure. Hearing his screams, the newly anxious men clustered around the rim of the fissure and shouted frantically downward.

Witwicky did not answer them. Dazed and trembling, he straightened and dropped his hands from his eyes. On the floor nearby, his glasses lay open and miraculously unbroken. Had he picked them up they would not have done him any good. Their formerly clear lenses had been imprinted with a fantastic array of minute and completely unintelligible symbols that were utterly alien and incomprehensible to anyone on Earth.

But that was not why they were now useless to him. The imprinting was far too small to be detected by the human eye. They were of no use because Witwicky's corneas and pupils were gone, obliterated in a single blinding surgical flash, leaving behind only a whiteness as pure and harsh and unforgiving as the snow that continued to drift down into the open, forbidding wound in the ice . . .

The world is patched with all manner of deserts. There are the cold deserts of the Arctic and Antarctic, the rocky plains of Mongolia and western North America, the high plateau of Tibet, and the altiplano of Bolivia and Chile. But those that are most familiar to people, those that individuals see in their mind's eye when they think of the word *desert,* are those composed of sand and gravel and heat.

The CV-22 Ospreys that came screaming over the dune sea were probably flying in formation too close to one another. With no one around to chastise them, however, their crews felt free to indulge in a game or two, played at gallons of jet fuel per second.

Certainly four of the men in the lead craft felt no particular compunction to adhere minutely to regulations that had been compiled by desk jockeys back in the Pentagon. Military life was hard enough without having to live every moment of one's waking life exactly according to the book. Consequently, the interior of the rumbling aircraft was presently rockin' not to the officially approved tracks of Stars n' Stripes radio but to the irresistible beat of a choice snatch of Reggaeton hip-hop.

That William "Wild Bill" Lennox had risen to the rank of captain was almost an accident of military history. Though only in his thirties, coincidence had combined with competence to raise him from the ranks to his present exalted and unexpected status. His comparative youthfulness allowed him to identify, if not exactly empathize, with the owner of the stereo that was snapping out the thump.

Hailing from East Oakland, California, Technical Sergeant Epps had yet to encounter anything in Qatar tougher than his old neighborhood back home. Swaying and singing along with the music, he clung to the compact player as if it were a brick of aphrodisiac. Lennox caught his attention.

"Who sings that song, man?"

Still swaying, Epps responded without looking over. "Daddy Yankee."

"Right." The captain pursed his lips. "So why don't you let *him* sing it, and we won't give him *your* fire missions."

A pained look crossed the tech sergeant's face. "Don't

mock my gift, bro. One day I'll win *American Idol* and you be wishin' you knew me when."

On the other side of the fuselage, Chief Warrant Officer Jorge Figueroa looked pained. Though not much older than Epps, both his background and temperament were radically different. Not to mention his tastes in music. As he listened to captain and sergeant argue the merits of Reggaeton versus North Jersey back and forth, he muttered under his breath.

"Sixteen *months* of this. Can't wait for a lil' taste o' home." A smile of remembrance played across his lips as his voice rose. "Plate of Mama's alligator *étouffée*."

Epps's face screwed up in a grimace. "Make note to self: at all costs, avoid dinner at Fig's mama's place."

"Fig" Figueroa met the other man's gaze. "For real, Epps—gator tail's got the most succulent meat." His smile returned, broadened. He was tasting it in his mind, swirling the roux around his tongue. "Add a little sauce piquant, a little extra cayenne, some fried okra on the side . . ."

Breaking off the music debate, Lennox glanced over at him. "So what you're tellin' us is that you can't wait to get home so you can eat some of Mom's homemade lizard ass."

A doleful Figueroa shook his head. "Why you gotta ruin it for me? This is my *heritage* we're talkin' here." He lowered his voice, mumbling softly. "Tell you one thing, man. Gator beats camel *any* day of the week."

"Maybe so," Epps chimed in, "but you can *milk* a camel."

Seeing that the warrant officer was taking the gentle jibing all too personal-like, Lennox decided it was in-

cumbent on him to change the subject. "Hey, hey—
weekends. Remember those?"

Putting out a closed fist, Epps dapped his superior.
"Heard *that*."

Figueroa sighed resignedly and turned to the captain.
"What about you, Lennox? First thing you're gonna do
when you get home . . . ?"

The captain turned wistful, didn't hesitate. "Hold my
little girl for the first time. Imprint. Stare into her baby
blues. Start teaching her how to say 'Daddy.'"

A chorus of drawn-out, gently mocking "awwws"
filled the interior of the aircraft. Setting aside the music
player, Epps dug into a pocket and pulled out a photo. It
was scratched and bent and sand-scored. One corner was
missing, but it was still perfectly viewable. From within
the square, three little girls looked back at the viewer.

"Enjoy it, my man," he told Lennox. Or maybe it was
a warning. "Once they start talkin' back, they own you.
Be like all 'Daddy, Daddy, my My Little Pony needs *a
new hairbrush* and a My Little Pony *purse* and, oh, the
new My Little Pony Butterfly Island Adventure playset,
and . . .'"

An irritated Lennox interrupted him. "You through?"

A grinning Epps put the picture away, eyed his fellow
soldiers, and commented with the voice of experience.
"He don't know what he's in for."

There was a slight jolt and the quartet went silent as
they prepared for touchdown. Smoothly, the wings of the
CV-22 swung from horizontal to vertical. In helicopter
mode it settled gently to the tarmac below. Troopers
emerged, Lennox's small group among them.

Younger than his comrades, Sergeant First Class Donnely caught up to them as the men made their way off the

landing pad. A hand brushed a few grains of the omnipresent sand from his red hair. "Hey, anybody know if my Celtics won?"

Epps replied before Lennox could respond. "Naw, they got thrashed."

Dejection slid down over the previously ebullient Donnely's face as he adjusted his glasses. "You couldn't just say, *No, they lost.* You're rude, dude." He looked crushed. "I had five hundred on those bums to cover."

Striding alongside, Lennox had to shake his head in disbelief. "A thousand miles from nowhere and he finds a way to call his bookie."

Like any warrant officer, Figueroa had an explanation for everything. "Fly boys have special privileges. Air force *supplies* bookies. Right, Epps?"

"*Hell* yeah. 'Cause unlike army, we can actually *count* past ten, and understand the *nuances* of a point spread." One hand described a shape in the air. "Missile spread, point spread: not all that much difference, y'know?"

Their general laughter drew the attention of Mahfouz. Not Qatari and hailing from a poor immigrant family, he and his wandering clan had not shared in the general flood of oil and gas money that had inundated the country. He immediately sidled up to the captain.

"Lennox, you cool! Did you bring chocolate?"

The captain shook his head. "Sorry, kid. Already ate it."

"No, you lie!" The boy began dancing and hopping in front of the advancing officer. "Give it to me, or I will call down the wrath of Rakan and Jalila upon you!"

Lennox had to smile. "Kids and comic book heroes: some things never change." Reaching into a pocket, he extracted a Snickers and tossed it to the eager youngster. "Give us a hand with the gear. And let's hustle, okay?"

Mahfouz grinned as he peeled the wrapper from the chocolate. "Lennox man, you think I'd miss HBO tonight?"

It was cooler inside the Joint Operations Center. Infinitely cooler. Normally it was also relaxing, but not now. At least, not for the air force staff sergeant who was staring intently at his console. A readout had materialized that he was unable to identify. The sergeant didn't like unidentifiable readouts. They tended to portend trouble, or at the very least a curt reprimand. Still, he had no choice but to announce it.

"Inbound unidentified infiltrator, ten miles out and closing."

Within seconds the watch commander was at his side, peering down at the same readout. He could make no more sense of it than the sergeant seated in front of the monitor. He could, however, react to it. The console's omnidirectional mike picked up his formal warning.

"Unidentified aircraft, you're in restricted Qatari and U.S. military airspace. Squawk ident and proceed stat east out of area."

There followed what might have been a response, but it was lost in a wash of unintelligible static. Bad comm unit, the watch commander wondered—or a deliberate and calculated attempt to stall for time? In such situations he was not allowed time for extended contemplation and analysis.

"Raptors One and Two: snap to heading two-five-zero for intercept. Bogie is in the weeds ten miles out and not squawking."

The Raptors on patrol located the intruding craft almost immediately. The massive MH-53 Special Operations Command helicopter below them made no attempt to conceal itself—or to alter its course. The much faster F-22s thundered past overhead. As they did so, the pilot of the lead fighter addressed what he hoped was the most opportune frequency.

"Unidentified aircraft, we will escort you to U.S. SOC-CENT air base. If you do not comply, you will be brought down. We will use deadly force. Repeat: we will use deadly force. There will be no second warning."

Moments later, after he had locked in his fighter's weaponry on the low-flying chopper, the huge helicopter began a slow descent. Relieved, the pilot settled back into his seat and spoke again into his pickup mike.

"Tower—Bogie's coming down. It's an MH-53, tail ID number AF4. Be advised: it's one of our Pave Lows. Still no response to repeated queries. Its transponder and comms may be out. Advise."

In the operations center the chief research tech promptly entered the declared craft identification into his computer and was almost as quickly rewarded with information. The trouble was that though there was a wealth of detail, none of it made any sense. Not in light of the most recent input to the relevant file. Frowning, he looked over at the watch commander.

"Sir, says here AF4 was shot down three months ago. In Afghanistan."

The watch commander's brow furrowed. Shot down or not, the question remained as to how an AF4 could make it from the Afghan theater all the way to Qatar while avoiding Iranian airspace. Even more tellingly, perhaps it had not avoided Iranian airspace. Either way, the ident they were getting from the patrol didn't make any sense.

"Gotta be a mistake. Too many things don't add up. Get a reconfirm from intercept." Turning, he headed upstairs. Not that he doubted the veracity of the two well-trained pilots, but he fully intended to see this mystery arrival for himself.

It was growing dark out. When the sun went down in the desert, it went down fast. In the distance, the lights of numerous wells flaring off natural gas imparted a slight and unnaturally rosy glow to the belly of the atmosphere. The captain broke off helping his friends with the unpacking to answer the insistent ring of his cell phone.

"Lennox," he responded curtly. He was tired, hot, and in no mood for bureaucratic chitchat. Not with darkness and the prospect of a good night's sleep so close at hand. Probably it was typical military stuff that could wait until morning. But he did not rank high enough to just ignore the call. When its subject was explained to him, he was glad he had answered.

"Captain," the voice on the other end informed him, "I'm pleased to report that we have a secure home-front connection for you." His spirits leaped immediately and the day's fatigue vanished. "Please hold and respond to the incoming link."

Working fast, he dragged his laptop from the pile of luggage and snapped the cell phone's connector into the appropriate receptacle on the computer. As soon as his login was accepted, his wife's face appeared: larger, clearer, and in far more achingly beautiful detail than would have been available on his phone's sharp but tiny screen.

"Hey there, baby girl," he murmured softly, working to repress the lump in his throat. "How're my ladies?"

Thanks to the wide-angle camera pickup in the kitchen back home, he could see that Sarah was feeding the baby as she addressed the pickup. "Missing their guy," she told him. It was a great connection, and there was very little time-delay between picture and voice. "It's official now. She has your laugh."

Lennox felt he would bust with pride and break out crying all at the same time. He could have cared less about the consequent ribbing such an outburst would bring from troops working nearby, but he didn't want to do anything that might upset his wife. His baby girl's first laugh. Another of life's precious moments missed, and here he was sucking sand halfway around the world. No point in laying that dejection on Sarah, though. It was hard enough him being so far away without her worrying about him any more than she already did. So for her benefit he did his best to sound upbeat when he replied.

"She laughed? You sure it wasn't just spit-up?"

His wife's giggle sent both joy and pain shooting through him. "No, it was a for-sure laugh. Her first real one, yeah."

"C'mon—must've been gas."

She shook her head and grinned mischievously. "What happened was, I was telling her about the night we got locked out of the house, how instead of going to the neighbors to ask for a key her daddy decided to build a campfire in the backyard, and nine months later—"

"—Whoa, *hey*," he interrupted her hastily, feigning distress. "I thought we'd wait till she was at least two before we got into the R-rated stuff."

Sarah's eyes were dancing with the memory. "I started laughing when I told her the keys were in your jacket the whole time, and that's when she laughed, too. But I think it was at you more than with you."

A sly smile spread across the officer's face. "Ever think maybe I locked us out on purpose?"

She pursed her lips in a challenge. "Ever think maybe I slipped those keys back in your pocket?" From half a world away her bubbling laughter lifted him higher than a kilo of khat. "Still coming home soon, baby?"

For once in the course of his seemingly endless deployment Lennox did not have to fake an encouraging response. "We're due for a rotation. Colonel assures me no bull this time. I'm right at the top of the list." Across one ocean and a couple of continents he tried to make eye contact with his daughter. "Hear that, Annabelle? You're gonna meet your daddy any day now . . ."

The picture broke up, shattering into confused pixels as static filled the laptop's screen. "Sarah . . . ?" Fragments of the music that was her voice crackled back at him from the computer's speakers. There was no indication of panic on her part. He was not calling from the corner fast-food market, and she was familiar with such unforeseen interruptions. But that did not make them any easier to take, he reflected unhappily. For either of them.

A few quick work-arounds showed that he was not going to be able to get the connection back. Reluctantly, he closed the rubber-armored clamshell as the *thump-thump* of heavy rotors began to fill the night air. Epps wandered over and the other troops paused in their unloading to look up as the big chopper settled neatly to the tarmac not far away. Lennox reflected that it was one of the better night landings he had witnessed. Whoever was piloting the copter knew how to handle their instruments.

Unexpectedly, as it touched down it was immediately surrounded by a flotilla of armed Humvees. Lennox's interest in the arrival suddenly doubled. He was startled to see that the encircling vehicles' heavy machine guns and grenade launchers were fully manned and aimed at the chopper. What the hell was up?

Spotlights swept across the helicopter as its blades continued to slow. One high-intensity beam settled on the cockpit to pin the pilot in its unrelenting glare. He was wearing a tan flight suit, a mustache, and a blank expression. That was strange, Lennox found himself thinking. Whatever the circumstances prompting the confrontation, with a dozen heavy weapons aimed in his direction you'd think the guy would wave, make a face, give the Humvee gunners the one-fingered salute, or *something*. Instead he continued to just sit there, staring straight ahead as if paralyzed. Except that paralyzed pilots couldn't bring an aircraft as complex as an MH-53 gently to ground.

Inside the tower the anxious watch commander picked up a pair of binoculars and promptly focused them on the big helicopter's tail. "AF4," he muttered to himself. "All the way from Afghanistan, without us getting a copy of a flight plan. And why come here? Why not head for a closer base in Pakistan? Something's definitely not right." Raising his voice, he directed it toward his headset's pickup. "MH-53 pilot, shut down all systems and have your crew step out *now*. Nothing personal, but just to make base security happy, show no weapons as you come out."

Lennox and the watch commander up in the tower were not the only onlookers unsettled by the chopper pilot's subsequent lack of response to this order. The troops manning the surrounding Humvees were equally ill at ease. Nervous fingers hovered close to well-oiled triggers. As MPs working overseas they had been trained to respond to a whole gamut of exotic possibilities they would never be expected to have to deal with back home, but indifference was not among these.

"Hey . . ." The gunner in the nearest Humvee suddenly pointed.

Inside the chopper's cockpit, the man in the tan suit disappeared. Well, he didn't exactly disappear. To the gunner it looked as if he suddenly turned into a bad television picture, a sort of three-dimensional electronic frizz. Then he, and the visual static that had taken his place, vanished completely.

The penetrating, disquieting, ear-tingling shriek of a high-pitched energy pulse filled the desert night air, rising rapidly in intensity. Somewhere, something inorganic was screaming. It originated from within the helicopter.

Within the SOCCENT operations center the image on every screen and computer monitor suddenly turned to electronic mush. Readouts went berserk. Even the center's chronometers went crazy, with no two telling the same time.

"Systems failing," a tech declared, his own voice rising sharply. "Radar's jammed." Involuntarily, he turned to look over his shoulder. With the apparent failure of his instrumentation, the only sensors he had left that he could trust were his own eyes and ears. *"It's coming from the chopper."*

His gaze now fixed unblinkingly on the copter that had become the center of everyone's attention, Lennox found himself backing slowly toward the big tent where he and his men and the helpful Mahfouz had been stacking supplies. Behind him, Donnely had his hands to his ears, trying to shut out the earsplitting electronic squeal. It didn't trouble the music-manic Epps nearly as much. The tech sergeant's hearing was already damaged.

In front of them the sodium-vapor arc lights illuminating the landing pad began to grow brighter, brighter, pulsing—and then they exploded, a simultaneous flash that left drifting echoes lingering on everyone's pupils even as the tarmac was plunged into darkness. Fighting to blink away the effects of the unexpected flare, the captain struggled to clear his vision. The chopper was still there, only—it wasn't. That is, there was definitely still *something* there, but it no longer looked like a chopper. It was changing, shifting, metamorphosing even as he squinted and stared in its direction.

It had feet, and arms, and a head. It also had a name: Blackout. But Lennox could not see or sense that, and the machine that had made itself out of the chopper did not choose to identify itself. The captain was not sure of what he actually *was* seeing, because what his eyes told him did not square with reality. It made no sense, no sense at all.

Then there came a thunderclap, a moving wall of air knocked him off his feet and backward, and he could not see anything at all.

The blast blew out every window in the control tower and sent those inside staggering backward or knocked them hard to the ground. Shattered glass cut and scoured exposed flesh, sending drops of blood splattering across the cleanly vacuumed floor. Instruments shorted out and the monitors closest to the windows crackled and went dark. So did every light inside the building, until the emergencies came on. A still-functional speaker began to call plaintively for a response from those who had been stationed inside, but none was forthcoming.

In response to the rising whine of the general alarm, soldiers poured out of barracks and other buildings in time to see a series of energy blasts vaporize an entire row of neatly parked C-17 cargo planes, shattering fuselages and wings with unnatural precision. Men and women ran for cover or dove behind anything standing and solid. Screams and shouts of confusion punctuated the periodic explosions. Making everything worse, fire and smoke combined with the darkness to reduce visibility to near nothing.

Inside the command center, those who had not been deafened by the electronic shrieking and subsequent detonations found their attention drawn upward as the roof was ripped from its support beams by an unseen force. Reactions ranged from utter panic to stunned fascination as a gigantic hand reached down and in. Technicians and support personnel rushed to scurry clear of its descent. Metal fingers probed consoles and walls, seeking and eventually finding what they were looking for. Punching into one bank of still-functioning consoles, giant smooth-surfaced digits ripped out a handful of cables. These somehow came alive, snapping upward like snakes to wrap themselves around the massive metal forearm. Actinic light flared as one cable after another melded itself to the huge downthrusting limb while electronic shrieks and howls continued to reverberate through the violated command center.

Dragging himself out of the rubble of the destroyed ceiling, the watch commander found himself staring at a still-intact screen. It should not have been active, but it was. Something had broken or bypassed the code that controlled the drives locked into the console that was purposely isolated from every other system in the tower. Files were being run. Files that should not have been active or generally visible. He was not even authorized to view them himself. During one pause he was able to read a title.

PROJECT ICE MAN—TOP SECRET SCI—SECTOR SEVEN ACCESS ONLY

What the hell was Sector Seven? If it was so secret he had never heard of it himself, it certainly shouldn't be visible or being run now. Feverishly, he struggled to pull himself clear of the rest of the restraining wreckage. Something across his legs was still holding him back. At least, he told himself, he could still feel his lower limbs. Movement on the other side of the room drew his attention, and he yelled across to a senior airman. The soldier was cautiously picking his way through the rubble while careful to avoid the enormous metal limb that remained shoved into the room.

"It's going after the deep files," the watch commander yelled, "accessing off-site information! Cut the hard lines, cut the hard lines!"

A moment passed before the airman indicated that he could hear his superior officer's shouts, and that he understood. Nodding sharply, he began hunting through the debris. Several moments passed before he found the fire axe still secured to the wall. Using a chunk of concrete to break the case, he removed the axe, drew it back over his right shoulder, and rushed forward. He was a big, husky guy and when he brought the axe head down hard it smashed right through the coil of critical cables. Sparks flew and lights flared—but the essential link was severed.

To the relieved watch commander the electronic shriek that followed the shearing of the connection sounded almost like a howl of outrage.

Amid the chaos that was rapidly overtaking the entire base, Lennox and his team found themselves racing through the camp's motor pool. As he ran, he found himself wishing that for once one of his fellow soldiers had screwed up and left the keys in the ignition of a parked Humvee. No such luck. They ran on, hoping to intercept someone riding a working vehicle.

Flanked by two lines of parked Abrams tanks, they sped out beyond the last one in line—only to find themselves running directly between the rampaging monolith's towering legs. Lennox looked up and stared. The interloper was some kind of robot or robotic automaton, he immediately decided. Human-like in its general appearance, appropriately bisymmetrical, but in many respects strikingly and ominously different. Too different. The monster did not look like anything he had seen at the movies lately. A foot rose and descended nearby, shaking the ground as it crushed an unhooked trailer to scrap. This was no cinematic special effect, he realized, and it was most definitely not some perverse manifestation of reality TV. Not even the PR flaks on contract to the Pentagon could dream up something like this.

Neither he nor any of the men with him was carrying anything more lethal than a sidearm, but the fast-thinking Epps had grabbed up a thermal imager before they had fled the unloading area. *Leave it to Epps*, Lennox thought even as he ran and dodged, *to be the one to reach for the latest electronic gadget instead of a rifle.* He tried to keep an eye on what his friend was doing but was too busy dodging elephantine robot feet.

Behind him Epps dove to avoid being squashed, then he rolled and swung the thermal imager straight up. Even as he took the shot he was unsure what it would show, but since the sky above him was completely blotted out by the amok machine, he felt optimistic that whatever it revealed would prove useful. Then he was on his feet again, running to catch up to his buddies.

Lennox was not the only one to take note of the thermal imager. Alerted to its presence when Epps snapped the picture, Blackout's targeting system located and homed in on the tracking device. Weaponry was unleashed.

At the sound, Lennox tackled Mahfouz and brought him to the ground as something shot past overhead to explode beyond them. Epps ran wildly in and out between pallet-loads of supplies and parked, useless vehicles. Figueroa was there, too, trying to unlimber the scatter-shot he had strapped onto his back. Lennox saved him the trouble. Relieving the warrant officer of the cylindrical burden, the captain unlocked the launcher, raised the muzzle, and fired. With the vista before him consisting entirely of looming, oncoming metal he correctly concluded that speed was more important than aim.

The spray of phosphorus-magnesium flares the launcher spit forth lit up the night like the coda of a D.C. fireworks display on the Fourth of July. All that was missing were the final bars of the relevant Tchaikovsky overture. Several of the wildly spinning flares actually struck the oncoming monster—and astonishingly, brought it to a halt. The robot took a couple of giant steps backward.

In the midst of all the flame and fire and confusion no one saw the thing that disengaged from the mechanoid's back to drop to the sand. Turning a swift circle, it surveyed its chaotic surroundings. Like its cohort it, too, was made of metal and strange alloys, but unlike the much bigger bipedal mechanism to which it had been clinging it did not look in the least humanoid. Taking its shape from several much smaller creatures that were native to the region and had already sensibly scurried underground, its powerful mechanical limbs began to dig it into the ground. Just as no one saw it arrive, none of the base personnel saw it go.

Having succeeded in reaching the camp's perimeter, Lennox felt that he and his men had at least managed to escape the worst of the confrontation that was ripping the heart of the base to shreds. Neither he nor his comrades saw the arachnoid metallic skull that emerged from the sand behind them. Glistening lenses scanned the darkness, effortlessly differentiating between sand and sky. They quickly hit upon and locked onto five heat signatures moving fast toward the eastern horizon. Dropping back into the sand, the horrific head vanished. From the place where it had emerged a curving line of mounded sand arose and sped off rapidly to the east.

Skorponok had located the indicated target and was on the hunt.

Some high schools are named after famous scientists, others after important historical figures. Some are renamed for local sports heroes or helpful philanthropists. A few are given the names not of people but of important events in history, or even animals.

Tranquility High School was simultaneously blessed and cursed with the anonymity of its nomenclature. In truth, the student body tended to be as bland and middle-class as its name. Except for the occasional opposing cheering section at Friday-night football games that once referred to their opponents as "the Fighting Transvestites," it's difficult to make much that is untoward out of a name as vanilla as *Tranquility*. It was named, of course, for the town in which it was located—though student advocates liked to insist that it was named after the site of the first moon landing: Tranquility Base. Or as one frustrated wag on the school paper referred to it, prior to her being permanently dumped from the staff, Free Base.

Inside one classroom, Captain Archibald Witwicky was gazing out of an ancient newspaper clipping that was presently being displayed on a laptop screen. Beneath his stern formal seaman's portrait a considerably less re-

strained caption screamed, ARCTIC ADVENTURER AL-
LEGES ICE MAN FOUND! The clipping was in service of
an ad on eBay selling a pair of old spectacles that had belonged to the captain. Spectacles that had been recovered
under circumstances not detailed in the accompanying
sales pitch. Had the exact details been known, it was
likely the glasses would long since have been sold. Those
details, however, had perished along with the much-
vilified captain himself.

None of which was known, of course, to the present
owner of the spectacles, who had put them up for auction
online. The glasses were important to Samuel Witwicky
because they had belonged to his great-great-grandfather.
According to the advertisement he had carefully composed, they were being put up for auction along with a
number of other relics by one of the captain's own
descendants—i.e., him. This was true, insofar as Sam
had been able to ascertain. He did not really want to
sell his great-great-grandfather's glasses, but he needed
the money. For something more important than a remembrance of a relative he had only read about but had
never met.

After casting a quick glance toward the front of the
classroom to make sure Mr. Hosney was not looking in
his direction, Sam checked for progress on the sale. The
relevant software informed him coldly, BIDS PLACED: 0.
With a sigh he looked up from the screen and across the
room. The girl on whose outline his gaze fell was
Mikaela Banes. She was a screensaver made real: beautiful beyond description, mesmerizing of voice and gesture, and utterly, utterly, out of his league. As if that
weren't enough she was seated beside her current para-
mour, one Trent DeMarco. Mr. DeMarco was fashioned

of muscles, jaw, and attitude: all jock, all the time. Unfortunately, Sam had concluded resignedly, there were at present no state or federal laws that he had been able to discover to prevent creatures like DeMarco and his ilk from reproducing their kind.

Score one for the devolutionists, he muttered silently to himself. If ever there existed an irrefutable argument against intelligent design, it was seated across the room alongside Mikaela Banes.

From the front of the class the voice of doom (or at least of terminal boredom) trumpeted forth. "Mr. Witwicky," the social studies teacher boomed out in the voice of a football announcer calling a 9–6 game in the fourth quarter, "you're up."

Leaning slightly over from his seat at the desk next to Sam's, his best friend, Miles, softly snapped his fingers in front of the glowing laptop screen. "*Sam*. Dude—Earth. Now."

Closing the laptop's clamshell, Sam gathered himself and his backpack along with a cardboard chart whose title spelled out in neat if undramatic letters MY FAMILY GENEALOGY. Embarking on a march no less painful than that endured by the prisoners of war at Bataan, he slowly made his way from his desk to the front of the room. Along the way he was showered with derisive laughter from teenage girls who had not yet succeeded in suppressing the germane giggle gene that usually faded in women once they reached adulthood, along with assorted handy objects of shame such as crumpled papers and the occasional carefully molded spitwad. Reaching the front of the room having lost blood only from his face, and that from embarrassment, he carefully propped his cardboard visual aid against the blackboard and turned to face the usual assortment of friends and heck-lers. The latter outweighed the former by a distressingly large margin.

"Uh, yeah," he began unpromisingly. From behind his desk, Hosney looked on with a mixture of subdued ex-pectation and pharaonic patience. "So, for my family ge-nealogy report, I picked my great-great-grandfather Captain Archibald Witwicky—one of the first guys ever to sail north of the Arctic Circle."

Deep within the bowels of the class, Trent DeMarco leaned over toward Mikaela Banes and whispered a deri-sive comment with practiced smarminess. The beauteous Banes responded to this characteristically juvenile at-tempt at wit with a slight smile, though whether from tolerance or out of genuine amusement it was impossible to tell. Turning to open his backpack, Sam made an ef-fort to ignore them both. He even managed to disregard the rubber band that DeMarco, with an athlete's skill, fired in his direction. It stuck in his hair. Briefly roused from the stasis of teacher's Purgatory, Mr. Hosney nearly detected the latex launch.

"Quit it," an irritated Mikaela hissed at DeMarco.

"What?" The team's star tight end feigned innocence. He was not good at it.

An acquiescent Sam plucked the rubber band from his hair. Determined to get something for the old junk that had been left to him, if not via eBay then in person, he maintained his composure as he laid out an assortment of old navigational instruments. Battered, broken, miss-ing parts, and badly worn, they had thus far proven of little interest to collectors. Collectors wanted gear that was in pristine condition, not stuff that looked as though it had been left outside—well, outside in the Arctic—for years and years. He had promised himself that once he had used them to (hopefully) get a good grade, he would give them a couple more weeks on eBay before dumping them at a secondhand store for whatever they would bring. Family sentiment was all very well and good, but it didn't get you wheels.

"So, like, here are some of the tools of a nineteenth-century seaman." He ignored the anticipated flurry of giggles and continued without pausing. "This here is a quadrant. Worth about seventy-five bucks today. This one is called a sextant, used for fixing a ship's location by taking sightings at sea. A steal at fifty bucks or best offer even though it's missing a part. Look great on your desk at home." As he spoke, his hand moved from object to object. "This is obviously a portable compass. Yours for eighty. And these were his actual glasses, worn on the actual expedition, actually in the Arctic. Price on these is negotiable."

A dry-voiced Hosney peered over his own glasses at him. "This isn't 'Show and Tell,' Mr. Witwicky, or even the Shopping Channel. It's the eleventh grade. Need I remind you that this presentation constitutes a significant portion of your final grade in this class?"

Normally intimidated by Hosney's typically disapproving tone, Sam uncharacteristically chose that moment to speak up and defend himself. "I'm not just trying to make a couple of bucks here, Mr. Hosney. There is a serious purpose behind it. I'm selling this stuff to put toward my car fund. Getting a car will expand my horizons and allow me to experience the world at large, thus greatly adding to my education." Turning back to his fellow students, he indicated his collection. "These are also on eBay if you wanna tell the folks—I take Pay-

Pal." His hand danced over the meager display. "They'd make really cool gifts. Like the compass, for Columbus Day . . ."

Hosney inhaled dangerously. "Sam . . ."

"Right," the youth responded quickly. "Anyway, I guess years of suffering through bouts of recurrent hypothermia froze Captain Archibald's brain, and he ended up going blind and crazy. He was put in a psycho ward, where he spent all his time drawing weird symbols and babbling about a giant ice man." A few "oohs" and "aahs" came from students too enervated to do anything other than actually listen to him. Encouraged, he pressed on.

Turning, he pointed to a blown-up copy of the newspaper clipping he was using to promote the sale of the old instruments online. Below the captain's picture was another photo, this one of some of the crude symbolic sketches with which the old explorer had been obsessed during his institutionalization. Though easy to see in the surprisingly sharp old photograph, they made no sense to Sam, or Mr. Hosney, or anyone in the class. Just as they had made no sense to the doctors who had attempted to treat Archibald Witwicky. Just as they would have made no sense, in fact, to anyone.

On Earth.

As Sam prepared to continue, a most miraculous event took place: the bell rang. The last bell. *Ask not for whom the end-of-the-school-day bell tolls,* a blissfully relieved Sam mused: *it tolls for me.*

As his classmates promptly imitated rush hour on the Tokyo subway in their concerted mob sprint for the door, a rising Hosney manfully tried to make himself heard above the familiar delirium.

"Thank you, everyone! Might be a pop quiz tomorrow. Might not. Sleep in fear tonight. Bye." As he resumed his seat behind the desk he cast a jaundiced eye on the classroom's other remaining occupant. "Saved by the bell, Mr. Witwicky. Enjoy it for now and mark it well. It is an occurrence that will not follow you through life." He let out a jaded sigh.

Sam lingered, on the cusp of desperate curiosity and fear. "So, if it's okay to ask—what's my grade?"

Leaning forward and looking to his left, Hosney took a moment to appraise the carefully crafted cardboard chart and spare a glance for the exhibition of banged-up old instruments. "I'd say a solid B-minus."

"B-minus?" Sam blurted it out as if he had been shot. Which in a manner of speaking was exactly the case. He gestured desperately in the direction of sextant and spectacles, compass and quadrant. He'd spent hours cleaning them up, polishing what could still be polished. Maybe he should have added the dirty clothes and the empty can of Brasso to the display. "What about all the visual aids?"

"Interesting exhibit," Hosney conceded, "but poorly utilized. You would have done better to emphasize the historical context as opposed to potential monetary reward." Turning away, he bent to study the stack of papers piled up in front of him. "I wasn't really feeling it. No—passion."

Sam was beyond worrying about whether he gave offense. He had really worked hard on the presentation and now . . . "No passion? I'm all about passion!" With Hosney displaying all the interest of a dozing mollusk, Sam grew desperate. "Can you just do me a favor? One favor. Look out the window really quick? Please!"

Swiveling slowly in his seat, like an old construction crane badly in need of lubrication, a reluctant Hosney complied.

"See that man sitting in the car?" Sam pleaded as he pointed. "The one straight ahead, at the inside curb?"

Hosney squinted through his glasses. There was indeed a man sitting in a car parked at the curb. This meant nothing to him. Turning back, he eyed his—suddenly passionate—student expectantly.

"That's my dad," Sam informed him. "When I turned sixteen last year he said if I saved two thousand bucks and got three A's, he'd help me buy half a car. I've locked in everything else, it's all good to go, but I need at *least* an A-minus in your class."

Hosney turned unexpectedly reflective, staring off into space as though a genie might appear and whisk him away from the four-walled torpor in which he found himself imprisoned.

"Ah, I remember my first car. A 1970 Gremlin."

"Don't you still drive that?" At the teacher's fiery glare Sam hastened to recover. "What I *mean* is—*please,* Mr. Hosney. My future—my freedom—the furtherance of my education—is now solely in your merciful hands. Think back, Mr. Hosney. Think back—and try to remember."

Hosney met his gaze. Not teacher-to-student, this time, but man-to—well, not to man. But close.

"I hate begging, Mr. Hosney," Sam finally whispered into the continuing silence.

Wondering what could be keeping his son, Ron Witwicky sat in the car and checked his watch. Sam was a far from faultless progeny, but he was commendably punctual. When the glum-faced youth finally came jogging down the slope of grass outside the school and climbed in, Ron eyed him evenly.

"So?"

His son was silent for an unusually long time—almost two seconds. Then, unable to conceal the erupting grin any longer, he held up the cover sheet from his final report of the last class of the day. A big A– had been written boldly across the front.

"Last class, Dad. End of quarter. You owe me half a car."

His father's expression did not change, but if possible he was even more gratified by the grade than was his beaming son.

When he was much younger Sam had delighted in pressing his face to the glass of the car window and staring at storefronts as they whipped past. Drugstores and boutiques, cafés and garden centers, fast-food outlets and real estate offices: all shooting past the family car in a blur of bright colors and what were back then incomprehensible letters as he waited eagerly to catch sight of the one tourist shop in Tranquility that sold embroidered clothes, gimcracks, T-shirts, and—specialty candy. Today he was still looking for candy, but of a radically different kind.

As the sign in front of the local VW-Porsche dealership loomed larger ahead, Ron started to swerve in its direction—only to veer at the last moment back into the northbound lane.

"Got a surprise for you, Sam. You're *not* getting a Porsche." He broke out in gentle hysterics. Okay, so maybe the gesture and its follow-up inclined toward child abuse—but he still couldn't quite stop laughing.

Sam pressed back in his seat, sour-faced, sour-voiced.

"That is just so—so—*wrong*. Teasing your own flesh and blood, your biological descendant, the bearer of your family name. What's happened to you, Dad?" He peered over at his father. "You used to be so—so—*paternal*."

His father returned the look. Fully intending to respond seriously, he took one look at the piteous expression on his son's face and cracked up all over again.

Neither Ron, buoyant in his present glee, nor Sam, sunk in a transitory funk, happened to notice that they were being followed at a discreet distance by a battered, dented, intensely yellow '75 Camaro.

The garish sign out in front of the car lot identified it as BOLIVIA'S AUTO RESALE. Gazing morosely at the train wreck of a selection on offer, Sam was hard put to decide if the name referred to the owner's patrimony or to the country from which the vehicles on display had been imported. The venerable machines packed too closely together facing the street were a long, long way from those shining on the lot of the Porsche dealership they had passed. Most of them were a long, long way, he decided as his father slowed down, from even the now-sanctified Mr. Hosney's archaic Gremlin.

Standing out front on one side of the main driveway was a man in a clown suit. The suit had seen better days, and so had its occupant. His amateurishly applied face makeup was melting in the hot sun. Sam knew just how he felt: he was melting inside. Employing both gloved hands, the clown held up a sign that read CHEAP WHEELS 4 U. As Sam and his dad pulled into the lot, the clown flipped over the sign. The reverse declared, I'M NOT CLOWNING AROUND!

Oh God. Sam's stomach sank to somewhere in the vicinity of their car's transmission. "Here? Nonono, you said you'd buy me half a car, not half a piece of crap." He gestured, a bit insanely, at the clown's sign as it receded behind them. "That's what it should say, 'Cheap Crap 4 U.' Crap on wheels. Crap that . . ."

Having heard just about all the crap he was prepared to tolerate, Ron turned to his son. "When I was your age," he began sternly, "I would've been glad just to have had four wheels and an engine. You oughta count yourself lucky. You're gonna get one with a roof, and windows, and maybe even a radio."

"A *radio*?" Sam was beside himself now. "You mean so I can, like, listen to *The Lone Ranger* and *The Shadow*?" Straightening in the seat, he would have been shocked to learn that he had unconsciously adopted a teaching pose not unlike one favored by Mr. Hosney. "Dad. Lemme explain something to you. 'Cause you're like an ancient person and even though that isn't your fault I need you to try and understand this: the right car says to girls, *Get to know me. Touch me.* These cars say, *Run! Run away from the spaz! Run like the wind!* A car needs to say, *Want something to drink, baby?* not *The Pepto-Bismol's right there, in the cup holder.*"

As always, Ron had a ready reply. "On the contrary, I think they say you're the guy who knows the value of a hard-earned buck, accumulated after much diligent and honest labor by father and son. Remember: no sacrifice, no—"

"—no victory," Sam finished for him. It had been his grandfather's favorite saying, and now it was his father's. "I know, I *know*. The old Witwicky family motto." Deflated by tradition, defeated by reality, he sank back into his seat and stared glumly at the dash. He should have been looking at the cars in the lot, but he couldn't bring himself to do so. They hurt his eyes too much.

His father's next comment as he parked the car was not encouraging. "Maybe you'd be happier with a new—Schwinn."

Sam refused to dignify the suggestion with a response. Sullen if not exactly acquiescent, he opened the door and climbed out as Ron exited from behind the wheel. They were met immediately (confronted was more like it, Sam felt) by the lot's owner. Professional welcoming smile plastered from ear to ear, the man approached to greet them, open hand extended to a willing but wary Ron. At that moment the owner noticed the condition of his clown and whirled to yell in the direction of one of the yard's mechanics.

"Manny! Get your cousin outta the damn clown suit! He's havin' heatstroke again, scares the white folks!" The instant smile (just add money) was back in place in less time than it took the mechanic to put down his power wrench.

"Hiya, gentlemen, hiya. Bobby Bolivia." He pumped Ron's hand. "Like the country, 'cept without the diarrhea." His head bobbed, powered by relentless enthusiasm. To Sam's surprise, no wires were visible. "At your service."

Ron finally freed himself from the welcoming grip. "Nice to meet you. My son's buying his first car."

Though sans makeup, Bolivia's eyes bulged wider than those of the clown. "And you came to *me*? Well, that practically makes us family. Call me 'Uncle Bobby B.' " Reaching out, he extended an arm and wrapped it around Sam's shoulders. Sam flinched but, trapped, decided it was useless to try and escape. A momentary vision of immolating himself in front of the Porsche dealership was discarded as pleasingly dramatic but of decidedly short-term efficacy.

"I've been doing this a long time, kid." Struggling to identify the unique odor emanating from Bolivia's mouth, Sam finally gave up. Just like the old Japanese horror movies said, there were some things that mankind was not meant to know. "That first enchilada of freedom's just waitin' under one of these hoods," Bolivia informed his unwilling prisoner. "See, drivers don't pick their cars, nossir. *Cars* pick their *drivers*." With his free hand he traced an imaginary arc across the cosmos. "It's a mystical bond between man and machine, for *real*. A relationship no woman can hope to match. Would I lie to you in front of my mama?"

Holding Sam's shoulders in a death grip worthy of the current World Wrestling Entertainment champion, he spun the listless youth around and pointed toward the house that occupied the lot next to the shop. On the front porch an old woman sat rocking slowly in her chair.

"See that lady on the porch? Mama, wave!" When the old woman failed to respond, Bolivia raised his voice. "MAMA, WAVE!" She did not bother to look up.

Bolivia's smile never wavered, but his tone grew dark. "I *know* you hear me, Mama. Don't make me throw a rock!"

She finally responded, albeit nonverbally, the index finger of her withered right hand rising, ascending: commenting pithily.

Bolivia whirled his by-now-nearly-moribund young customer around once more and proceeded to escort him through the heaps of metal that pockmarked the lot.

Some, a discouraged Sam decided, might once have been called cars. Ron followed, scrutinizing each minivan, each semi-fossilized coupe with the studied air of an English lord shopping for a new Rolls. Sam ignored them one and all, his eyes barely focusing, his brain on autopilot, thoughts of squiring the beauteous Mikaela Banes around town receding like the memory of a half-remembered haiku.

And then he stopped. Slipping free of Bolivia's grasp, he retraced his steps, darting in among the ranks of junkers and discarded soccer-mom mishaps. Despite himself, despite what his father had told him about not showing any interest in any one particular vehicle when they went shopping for cars, he found himself staring.

Camaro. Classic. Bright yellow. *Really* bright. Like, bright enough to generate its own reflection. Okay, so the color was a bit out of control. There was a thing called paint. Camaro. He found himself wondering what kind of engine, dirty and unmaintained and probably in need of a serious tune-up though it doubtless was, sat under the hood. Assuming there *was* an engine. Black racing stripes. Cheap-looking racing stripes; a Pep Boys' ten-dollar attempt to look cool, but still—black racing stripes. He heard a voice saying as much.

"Least it's got racing stripes." The voice was his.

He wasn't the only one staring at the car. Bolivia gaped at it, then frowned, and finally gave vent to his confusion. "Where'd this one come from? I don't remember anybody rolling this out on the lot." Turning and raising his voice, he yelled toward where the lot supervisor was wiping down the hood of an Oldsmobile that had barely outlived the demise of its marque. "MANNY!" He indicated the Camaro. "What the heck's this?"

Ambling over, the lot supervisor stared hard at the bright yellow car, scratched the back of his head, sniffed, did everything but mutter *Ah, shucks!.*

"Maybe came in with that bunch of other trades last week," he finally suggested. "You know, the ones that came off that eighteen-wheeler from—"

"Thank you, Manny." Bolivia hastily turned the manager around and hustled him off in the other direction, muttering harsh words in his ear. In the lot owner's absence Sam tried the door. It was unlocked. A sign of lax security on the dealership's part or—he was wasting his time checking out something that wasn't worth stealing. He slipped inside the car and behind the wheel. The cushion felt good, comfortable, the seat back providing just the right amount of resistance against his spine. He didn't even have to adjust it: it was just the right height and the ideal distance to the wheel.

His initial delight at finding that the door opened and closed smoothly and that no loose springs were going to puncture his butt vanished as he studied the dash. His expression fell.

"Gee, an actual eight-track! The girls will swoon." He looked imploringly out the window at his father. "The cassettes for this antique are bigger than my iPod. Where's the hand-crank?"

Ron smiled back comfortingly. "Think of the fun you'd have picking them up on eBay."

Bolivia wasn't gone long. Returning, he saw his customer seated securely behind the wheel of the mystery car. As soon as he ascertained that the youngster wasn't spitting up curses or his lunch, the dealership owner didn't pause to ask questions. Okay, so maybe the actual provenance of the car still needed to be determined. A detail. In the interim, he began improvising.

"Fits ya, doesn't it? You look swell in there, kid. Great engine in these old Camaros, lemme show ya . . ."

Moving around to the front of the car, he bent to open the hood. Then he struggled to open it. Neither muscular forearms nor the application of severe language budged the hood so much as a millimeter. As the lot owner fought with the recalcitrant sheet metal, Sam found himself distracted from the drama by a glint of light on the steering wheel. It drew his gaze to an emblem. Covered in grime, its outlines became clearer when he used a little spit and elbow grease to wipe away the grunge. He frowned as he studied it, trying to make sense of what he was seeing. Whatever it was, it certainly wasn't the familiar Chevy chevron. Some kind of customizer's mark, he finally decided.

Ron had been studying both the car and his son long enough to come to a conclusion. Looking toward Bolivia, he uttered the magic words.

"How much?"

From a pocket Bolivia extracted a grease pencil about the size of a horse's foreleg, made a show of thinking hard (if only for appearance's sake), and replied as he scrawled a figure on the dirty windshield. "Well, uh, considering the semi-classic nature of the vehicle, the timeless lineage, the custom racing stripes—five grand."

Ron nodded once, briskly "We're not going above four. For anything."

"*Four?* For a Camaro? The body alone's worth that." He peered sharply down at Sam. "Kid, outta the car . . ."

Leaning out the open window, Sam gazed imploringly back at the lot owner. "But you said cars choose their drivers."

Bolivia was unrelenting. The trap had been baited, the trap had been sprung, and now it was time to see if the trapped quarry could free itself. He was prepared for the forthcoming struggle, having participated in many thousands of them.

"Yeah, well," he responded casually, "sometimes they choose one with a cheap father." Turning, he waved toward a half-gutted Pacer. "Now, this one here's a beautiful—"

He was cut off in midsentence as he started toward the antique section. As he turned around, the Camaro's passenger door swung open and slammed into the other car, nearly crushing his legs and the large spherical hind portion of his body to which they were attached. Thrown off-stride, he struggled to regain his balance, doing his best to recover mentally as well as physically.

"Uh, no problem with that door. Loose hinge. Can hammer that out *easy*. Shows you how easy the door works. Some of these older models, you know, the hinges are so rusted up they have to be replaced." He smiled at the Camaro. "This baby, they swing like silk." He yelled at his lot manager. "Manny! Go get the sledgehammer." In the same breath he gestured toward the far reaches of the lot, wanting to get as far away from the offending Camaro and as close to the necessary paperwork as possible. Before these two left, he was determined to have the father's name writ large and clear on a bill of sale. And if they were finding themselves less and less enamored of the mystery Camaro . . .

"Now, lay your eyes on *that* one," he began as he turned up-lot.

As he gestured, he pushed hard on the Camaro door that had seemingly swung open by itself. As soon as it slammed shut, the car's horn started blaring. No, not blaring, Bolivia decided as he flinched. It was a sonic *explosion*.

Maybe it was the volume, maybe the timbre, maybe something about the combination, or maybe a certain something they couldn't hear. Like a sound that was pitched too high for the human ear to detect. Whatever it was, the resulting concussion blew out the windows of every other car on the lot. Bolivia's lower jaw headed in the direction of southern Brazil as he gaped at the vitreous devastation. His cherished, beautiful, dollar-generating lot looked as though it had just suffered through a ten-second hailstorm. Sunlight sparkled and flashed from millions of glass shards.

It was actually quite pretty.

"Oh, nonononono," Bolivia moaned, digging at his cheeks with the fingers of both hands. "MANNY, GET OUT HERE!"

A stunned Ron was already shepherding his son toward the customer parking area. Something wasn't right here, and it had nothing to do with the condition of the vehicles they had been looking at. Father and son moved fast, but not fast enough to escape the pursuing Bolivia. Even in the depths of despair in which he now suddenly and unexpectedly found himself, he could not let a potential customer get away.

"Nono, wait! Okay, okay!" He paused to catch his breath. "It's your lucky day. Not mine, but yours. We got some kinks to iron out around here and a little cleanup to do and I ain't got time to dicker for a '75." He took a deep breath and winced, as if his heart hurt him. Which was not far from the truth. "Four grand and it's yours."

Sam looked over at his father. As a child, he had once seen several cheaply reproduced paintings at a yard sale of cats with impossibly oversized black eyes. They had been looking upward; open, beseeching, all but crying in the absence of tears. He now did his best to mimic them.

It worked. Or maybe his dad was just tired. Ron nodded his assent.

Sam tried not to actually leap off the oil-stained pavement. *"Yes!"*

Having left his collection of eight-tracks at home (not!), he hesitantly tried the radio (he had to remember to turn the knob and not push it) as he slipped behind the wheel and turned the key in the ignition. To his surprise, that of his dad, and not a little of Bolivia's, the sound that emerged from multiple concealed speakers was both loud and clear. Turning up the decibels to a level just short of city statute–busting, he prepared to shift the car into drive.

Ron leaned into the window, his expression dad-earnest. "Make me one promise. If ever, for any reason, and I'm not pre-accusing you of anything here, you think you shouldn't be driving? Call me and I'll pick you up. Wherever you are, whatever I'm doing. No questions asked."

"Promise." Sam smiled back: one of those rare son-to-father smiles that was deep and genuine instead of merely condescending. "Thanks, Dad." He sat up proudly. "I'll write you a check when I get home."

Ron Witwicky stepped back from the window of his son's old-new car. "You don't have a checking account, but that's all right. You can give it to me later." He smiled, managing a passably good imitation of a Jersey wiseguy. "If youse tries ta stiff me, remember dat I knowse where youse live. Now go find your adventure."

Though Ron Witwicky felt that it was a little bit early in the stage of ownership to be wasting rubber, he held his peace as his son peeled out of the parking lot and succeeded in doing so without hitting anything except the car's accelerator. In the excitement of the moment neither of them had thought to query Bolivia about fuel, so Ron could only hope there was more than a pint of gas in the Camaro's tank. As Sam roared up the street, one of the car's mufflers fell off, clanging and banging loudly as it rolled toward the curb. Ron shot a glare in the lot owner's direction. The brazen Bolivia was unabashed. Having just sold a car he wasn't sure he'd ever owned, he was hardly about to apologize for its condition.

"What d'you expect for four g's? For *five* grand we'd a checked that sorta thing." Letting out a snort, he turned back in the direction of the main office, muttering to himself. "Next thing you know they'll be asking if I had the *brakes* checked."

W III W

The capital of the United States is Washington, D.C. Its broad boulevards and geometric street plans were designed and laid out to accommodate horses and carriages. When horseless carriages came along, they brought with them traffic that the attractive avenues had not been intended to handle. As vehicles powered by internal combustion engines grew larger in size and greater in number, the beautiful streets were often overwhelmed. And at rush hour, the sound and fury of growling cars and harried pedestrians all jockeying for position on the same too-narrow roadways and sidewalks created a confusion not even the fastest computers could untangle.

One of those pedestrians was in search of a car. A taxi, to be precise. Her name was Maggie Madsen. She was brilliant, confident, and, in the eyes of the stuffy political denizens of America's capital, would have been considered attractive instead of simply brazen had she lost the green that streaked her hair and the diamond stud that sparkled on her nose. That didn't stop the cabdriver from picking her up, of course. The taxi pulled out into traffic—and promptly stopped.

"Twelve Hundred South Hayes Street," Maggie told the driver. "I'm in a *crazy* hurry."

As a recently resettled refugee from a brutal conflict in a far-off land, he was hardly about to be thrown into a tizzy by an anxious commuter. He gestured out the front windshield. "Observe, miss lady, the traffic, and note please the time of day. I have learned an appropriate term for this condition. Another passenger helped me rehearse it until I got the pronouncing correctly. It is called 'impenetrable congestion.'" He smiled pleasantly into the rearview mirror. "I assure you that I will make as rapid progress as the gods allow."

It was a perfectly understandable response from a D.C.-area cabdriver. Eloquent, even. Eloquence, however, would not get her to her intended destination in time. Digging her cell phone out of her purse, she speed-dialed someone who was not a god but who might still be able to help her.

On a lower floor in the local offices of the Rand Corporation, Glen Whitmann answered his desk phone. This entailed setting aside the wireless mouse he had been manipulating. Before he answered the call he employed the mouse to hurriedly blank from his screen the multiple video clips of the current contenders in the Miss Black America beauty contest. He had been studying these one at a time, compiling a lengthy list of mental notes while imagining himself in the position of sole judge and jury. Using his tongue, he shoved into his left cheek the mass of partially pulped Fruity Pebbles he had been masticating. The result was a visage that bore more than passing resemblance to a bespectacled meerkat. Fortunately, there was no one in his immediate vicinity to take notice—or, worse, snap a picture with a cell phone.

"Y'ello," he addressed the desk phone's pickup.

Sequestered in the back of the unmoving taxi, Maggie

let out an impatient breath. "About time! Glen, it's me."
She took another look at the traffic ahead: a solid wall of
sedans, vans, delivery trucks, and government vehicles.
There were glaciers in Greenland that moved faster. "I'm
in a cab, traffic blows. I'm gonna be late. Serious late.
Can you patch me into traffic control?" Cradling the cell
phone against her cheek, she worked the laptop's keyboard in anticipation of his compliance.

Alone in his cubicle, Whitmann sat up a little straighter
and snuck a fleeting look outside. No one had paused at
the portal to eavesdrop. "Again?" he muttered into the
phone. "You're always 'serious late.' How'd you ever
land a job at a think tank without knowing how to set
your *alarm*?"

Got no time for this, Maggie thought crossly, indifferent to her friend's rebuke. "I wasn't oversleeping. I was
hiding in a bush. Ditching my landlord 'cause I owe so
much *rent*. Can you get with that, Glen?"

Progressively, the mass of Fruity Pebbles recommenced
its downward descent in pursuit of the digestion that
awaited it. In its absence, Glen Whitmann hoped to make
his feelings better understood. "Mags, don't do this to
me." He checked the walkway outside. Still empty.
"They almost traced us last time."

She would have yelled into the cell phone except that it
might have alerted the cabdriver. Though from the look
of him and the cadence of his English it didn't appear as
though he was inclined to make trouble, even if he happened to comprehend the import of what she was saying.
Anyway, she didn't have time to worry about it. In that
respect, at least, she was being honest with her friend.

"*Glen.* Get your face out of the Fruity Pebbles and *help*
me. If my signal encryption brief isn't turned in by four,

I'm out. I'm fired, it's over. I'm broke, behind in my rent, and I'm crashing at *your* place."

Usually Whitmann was easily intimidated, especially by Maggie. Not this time, he vowed. Leaning back in his chair and chewing the Styrofoam-like pellets, he replied easily. "Nope. Not gonna happen. Grandma doesn't like my gaming buddies coming over. Wouldn't stand for me living with one. Wouldn't live with one herself. And unlike game weapons, hers are *real*."

"Hate you." Stonewalled and outmaneuvered, Maggie took a deep breath. When she resumed the conversation her tone was carefully nonconfrontational. "Okay. How about this? I'll have lunch with you all next week."

Instantly reengaging, Glen straightened in his chair. "In public? And say my name?"

A sigh came from the phone. "Okay."

He was not finished. "You'll talk to me, pretend I'm smooth?"

"Yesss." The sighs issuing from the speaker were growing deeper and more resigned.

"We see a cute mutual acquaintance, you'll introduce me to her?" Glen held his breath.

"Fine! You want a pint of my blood, too?"

He was already working his keyboard. "You know I don't like hot drinks. Get ready." On his computer's screen appeared the legend ROUTE TRAFFIC PREEMPTION SYSTEM TO REMOTE SERVER.

In the backseat of the cab the screensaver on Maggie's laptop suddenly gave way to a complex, multihued street grid covering the entire metropolitan D.C. region. Punching a couple of keys, she brought up the name CONSTITUTION AVENUE. The grid view zoomed in to center on her present position. Grunting softly as if to say *About time,* she finished by hitting a single key.

Immediately every traffic signal in front of the cab went green. She leaned toward the driver.

"See all the pretty lights? That means warp speed!"

Having survived war and famine in a far-off land, the driver had learned long ago that it is a wise man who accepts miracles without question. Though he no more comprehended what had happened than he understood his mother-in-law, he obediently gunned the engine.

Maggie flung the door open before the cab came to a full stop, nearly decapitating a stray cat in the process. Arms loaded, she charged the entrance to the nondescript building only to be held up at security until she could produce the necessary identification. Racing through the structure, she reached her intended destination only to be informed while passing the desk attendant that "Some guys're here from the Pentagon to see your group."

Maggie had no time to mumble a response, as she was focusing on hitting the elevator call button with the heel of her right shoe. A pair of black suits arrived before the doors to the elevator cab could close.

"Maggie Madsen?" Both agents flashed badges. Before she could react, the man nearest her gestured to his right. "Defense Intelligence Agency. You need to come with us." Gently but firmly his counterpart took her elbow and guided her away from the elevator doors.

She struggled to hold on to her armful of material. "Guys, if this is about the traffic lights, I acted alone. All me, my fault. I only wanted to make a presentation on time, honest."

Moving to her other elbow, the first agent joined in accelerating her forward. "Just come along with us, please."

All that effort to get to her office, she reflected, not to mention an illegal insertion into a local government agency, and here she was being herded back outside. She was startled to see that she was not alone. One by one she and her sunglassed escort were joined by the rest of her research team. Anxious glances were exchanged, but no explanations were forthcoming.

There was an idling helicopter sitting on the front lawn. Maggie sensed that it had not been placed there for decoration. "What's up?" she asked Alice from Statistics.

"I dunno." The other woman looked equally bewildered. "They came and picked up the whole team. Nobody's volunteering anything and they won't answer any questions. It's just—"

"I know," Maggie broke in. " 'Come with us, please.' At least they're being polite."

The somber-faced statistician was not reassured. "Firing squads can be polite."

Once the entire team and a portion of its escort had been piled into the waiting craft, it took off immediately. Maggie was luckier than most. With everyone packed in tight, at least she was next to a window. Washington stuttered past below, the view familiar and unchanging until they began to shed altitude. At least they now had an answer to the question of where they were headed. There was no mistaking the building toward which they were descending.

An escort was waiting for them as they touched down on one of the multiple interior landing pads. An armed escort, she noted. Unusually, the soldiers did not look relaxed, were not chatting casually to one another about how the area sports teams did the night before or who had managed to do what to whose girlfriend or boyfriend or why the latest pay hike hadn't come through. That was more than unusual, she thought. That was bad.

She had been inside before but never in this section. Though it was easier to lose one's way in the Pentagon than in any other building in America, she had always prided herself on finding first her destination and then an exit. But having entered from the middle instead of from a street outside, she quickly found herself completely adrift. A marine sergeant led them down corridor after corridor. What was going on? What was this all about, and why wouldn't any of the escorting agents answer her questions or those of her colleagues? She had long ago come to the conclusion that whatever was afoot, it had nothing to do with her illicit manipulation of downtown D.C.'s traffic controls.

Utilizing a long stride to come up alongside her and her colleagues, an army lieutenant colonel began methodically handing out documents. The pages were crisp, the folders containing them brand-new. Maggie did not waste time trying to read hers. She had a feeling that whatever information they contained was soon to be explained to them anyway.

"The information you're about to receive is classified," the unsmiling lieutenant colonel was saying. Now, *there* was a big surprise, she thought. "You are not to discuss its contents or the details of anything you hear here today with anyone beyond the perimeters of this building, including immediate family. The nondisclosure form you're about to sign is classified. The fact that you're even here is—classified. As far as anyone on the outside is concerned, you are not here right now and the meeting you are about to attend will never have occurred."

Maggie nodded slowly. In the course of her work she had been subject to similar strictures before, but the relevant admonitions had never been delivered quite so somberly. "So asking any more questions would be out of the question?"

Turning to face her, the colonel replied without hesitation. Also without so much as a hint of amusement. "That's classified."

A few more responses like that and she would be in danger of losing her natural good humor, she felt as they turned a corner. Her growing concern was mirrored in the faces of her equally baffled associates. If she had no idea what was going on, some of them were not even sure where they were. For some, it was their first excursion into the bowels of national security.

The briefing room was spacious, overlit, and crowded. It was soon filled with anxious whispers. Making a quick headcount she estimated that there were seventy or so people present, divided evenly between uniforms and suits. Despite her typically eclectic attire, she would be accounted one of the latter. As she and her colleagues jockeyed for space among those already present, an immaculately dressed civilian entered from a side door at the far end of the room and proceeded to an empty dais. Instead of an armful of documents or an expensive portfolio case, he was carrying coffee in a paper cup. Those who were seated rose in recognition of his arrival. That didn't stop him from draining the last of the coffee and tossing the cup at a nearby wastebasket. He missed.

The statistician standing close to Maggie murmured in

astonishment, "That's John Keller—secretary of defense." Maggie wanted to reply that she knew who he was, except that she was equally startled by his presence. The importance she had already attached to the forthcoming extraordinary briefing had just doubled.

Settling himself in behind the podium, the secretary scanned the suddenly attentive crowd, waiting for the conversation to die down of its own accord. Leaning slightly to his right, he whispered to a nearby aide.

"A lot of them look—young."

The aide nodded sympathetically. "They're the top subject matter experts, sir. NSA's recruiting right out of high school these days." A pause, then, "It's the abilities that are important, sir—not the age."

"I know," a reluctant Keller replied, "but under the circumstances and given what we're likely to be dealing with here, a little maturity would be—welcome."

"Maturity is not a function of age, sir," the aide reminded him, quoting a favorite childhood book before stepping back.

Straightening, Keller eyed the now-silent and -expectant crowd. There was nothing to be gained by delaying any further.

"Please, those of you who can find a chair, be seated. I'm John Keller." He knew he did not have to identify himself further, especially to this group. "Obviously, you're wondering why you're all here. I'll keep it simple. That's all we have time for anyway. These are the facts: at zero nine hundred local time yesterday the SOC-CENT Forward Operations Base in western Qatar was attacked. There was no warning and insofar as we have been able to determine, there were no survivors."

Uneasy murmurs filled the room. The secretary's terse

announcement affected even those who customarily professed disinterest in the daily news. Keller noted the effect his words had produced and gave them a moment to sink in. He took no satisfaction in it.

"The rest of the world's going to hear about it in half an hour. You're hearing now. Post-assault analysis has identified the objective of the attack as an attempt to hack the deepest reaches of our military network. We aren't sure exactly what information the attackers were after, but we do know that thanks to quick-thinking and brave action on the part of our on-site personnel, the attempt was stopped during the assault. Which leads some of the more pessimistic and forward-thinking among us to assume the attempt will be made again.

"No one has claimed responsibility, no group, no Internet site, no country. So far our only real hard lead is this." He gestured at another aide, who was standing off to the side of the podium. The aide did something with a remote control.

Muted from its original volume, an unearthly shriek filled the room. It took Maggie less than ten seconds to shift from startled to appalled to intensely curious. Digging her phone out of her purse, her mind racing, she hurriedly entered several short bursts of text, making notes as fast as thoughts occurred to her.

Keller went on. "That's the signal that hacked our network. NSA's working at full capacity to analyze it and intercept any attempts to send it at us via the Net or any other medium. I hardly need to tell any of you what the implications of this are for national security." Leaning forward, he tried to meet the eyes of as many of those in the audience as possible. "But we need your help to find out *who* did this. You've all shown considerable ability in the area of signals analysis and its related disciplines or you wouldn't be here. I want to add that service in this matter *is* voluntary. Anyone wants out, now's the time." He nodded to his left, tersely.

"There's the door. Anyone wants to leave or feels they have no choice but to go, aides will be waiting outside to escort you back to your place of work, and no marks of any kind, positive or negative, will appear on your records."

It was dead silent in the conference room. Nobody moved. Near the back, someone tried to stifle a cough. The secretary repressed a gratified smile. "Thank you. We're on a hair trigger here, people. The president has dispatched full battle groups to the Arabian Gulf and Yellow Sea. This is as real as it gets." Turning to leave the podium, he paused a moment, added a heartfelt, "The clock is ticking. Godspeed and good luck."

The babble of excited conversation that immediately filled the room was energetic but muted. Pushing her way through the crowd and ignoring the queries that were cast in her direction, Maggie struggled to catch up to the departing secretary. He was already out in the corridor, he and his aides and escort heading south and moving fast. An average employee might have been discouraged by all the security. Maggie was anything but average. Or maybe it was the fact that she was sufficiently nihilistic not to give a damn. Seeing the green-haired missile making a beeline for the secretary, an aide tried to intercept her. She juked right, then left, and went right around him until she was striding alongside Keller himself. Preoccupied, he barely glanced in her direction.

"Uh, Mr. Defense Secretary, I'm Maggie Madsen— work at Rand, algebraic cryptanalysis, code breaking. I apprenticed under one of your deputies, Ben Tharpe. Put myself through MIT doing a little modeling—strictly tasteful. Mostly. Anyway, why am I telling you this?"

"No idea." Keller finally looked over at her. Possibly it was the line about modeling that intrigued him. Or maybe he was just being polite. "Ben approve of that diamond in your nose, Margaret?"

Reaching up, she quickly popped it out. "Actually, it's not *Margaret*. I *hate* that. It says *Maggie* on my birth certificate and whenever anyone calls me Margaret I tend to—never mind, sorry. I got a little impulse-control problem, no filter. Like I probably shouldn't say your bushy eyebrows are kinda throwing me right now . . ."

Defense secretary, entourage, and Maggie turned a corner. "What's your *point*?" Keller inquired coolly. The attractive young woman was an interesting distraction. One he did not have time for.

Swallowing, she continued. "Well, I thought right off that the signal sounded like modulated phasing. Like when you plug in a modem, only a hell of lot faster and more sophisticated."

"Yes," Keller said dryly, "I know what a modem is."

Unmindful of the sarcasm, she continued. "Well, so, if what I heard was right, and it's just a preliminary guess, mind, it was not just fast. It was faster than anything out there. What I'm trying to say is, it was faster than anything that's even *possible*."

He nodded. "I assure you it is possible, because it happened. The playback you heard was reduced in volume but real time; no acceleration, no compression. Perhaps one of your team is going to find out how it was accomplished. Oh, and for the record, since you saw fit to make a point of the irrelevancy, it's only your brain we're interested in here." His stride lengthened as hers slowed, and in a minute he and his staff had disappeared around yet another corner, leaving her to come to a halt in his wake. As soon as they were all out of sight she rolled her eyes and slapped her forehead in self-rebuke.

"Real smart, Mags. Just brilliant. Eyebrow thing went over real well with the *secretary* of *defense* . . ."

Rising from the superheated dunes far out in the desert a hot desiccating wind tickled the dune crests, spraying sand downslope in neat sine curves. It was not the cause of the eruption of sand that occurred near the center of one dune, however. That fountaining owed its existence to the abrupt emergence of a mechanical skull, arachnoid in design and callous in expression. With eyes far more perceptive and sensitive than those fashioned of simple organic compounds, it scanned the desert spread out before it all the way from the infrared to the ultraviolet.

The eyes paused to zoom in on the blackened carcass of a demolished tank. Huddled against its lifeless metal bulk were several bipedal heat signatures. One signature was tending to the injured upper limb of another smaller, slimmer shape. All this was of negligible interest to Skorponok. What mattered was the purple-tinged outline of the device held tightly in one biped's hand. It was a recording device. A thermal imager. Primitive in design and construction, but perfectly functional. Fixing the bipeds' position, the metallic horror plunged back beneath the sand.

Donnely and Epps stood studying the picture on the imager's screen. It showed the underside of something huge, bipedal, and surrounded by some kind of electrified aurora that ought to have interfered with the automaton's own internal command and control systems but self-evidently had not.

Epps shook his head as he replayed the view and examined it from multiple angles. "Never seen a weapons system like this. Looks something like a power loader, but bigger than even the experimental jobs I've heard about. Thermal shows this weird aura around what might be an exoskeleton. Like whatever's generating it is cloaked by some kinda otherwise invisible force field."

" 'Force field'?" The skeptical Donnely let out a snort of derision. "But that's impossible, right? 'Cause there's no such *thing* as 'invisible force fields,' 'cept in comic books and science-fiction novels." When his buddy failed to reply, Donnely added uncertainly, *"Right?"*

Lennox had come up behind them and was looking over their shoulders at the screen. "Look at that thing! We got nothing like it in Skunk Works. Leastwise, nothing I've ever seen. Or heard about. Hell, we don't even have *rumors* about something like this."

Epps rolled his eyes. "Oh, man—I signed on to repair little computers in Florida. My recruiter definitely did *not* tell me about all this extracurricular activity." He gestured at the screen. "One thing's for sure: we ain't gonna make this thing go away with no piece of off-the-shelf antivirus software."

From where he was seated cleaning his weapon, Figueroa looked over at his companions. "My mama, she had 'the gift,' y'know? She saw things. I got that gene, too. And that thing that attacked us? The feeling I get from it is that this ain't over."

Donnely snapped back at him, "Yeah, like you really need 'the gift' to figure that out. So since you got 'the gift,' how 'bout you use your magic voodoo to get us the hell outta here?"

Setting aside his weapon, the warrant officer started to rise. "Y'know, specs, you are a lot smaller than me."

Removing his glasses, Donnely also stood. "That is true. But I'm also very determined to shut you up."

As the two men started toward each other, Lennox stepped between them. Frustration lent force to his voice. "*Easy! Listen up.* That thing came in stealth, hit the antenna farm, shut down all communications in and out. Wiped out all evidence it was ever here." Pausing to let that sink in, he added, "My guess is it didn't want anyone to know what it was."

Donnely and Epps exchanged a glance. "When I took the picture," Epps declared, remembering, "I think it saw me. I mean, it looked right at me. That's assuming what I was looking at were actually its imaging sensors and not some kinda smart-ass visual decoy."

Lennox's tone turned grave. "If you're right about it wanting to keep its appearance secret and it saw you use the imager, then it would be reasonable to assume it's still looking for us. Before the party resumes, we need to get this imager and its contents home to the Pentagon right away." He eyed Epps. "You tried sending it electronically again?"

Nodding, the technical sergeant gave vent to his continuing frustration. "We're still in a dead zone. Nothing electronic coming in, nothing going out. No satellite, no base e-mail: nothing." Looking over a shoulder, he nodded eastward. "If we can get out of these dunes and close to Qatar City, there's Wi-Fi all over the place and I can grab a signal." He looked back at Lennox. "Otherwise it's carrier pigeon time."

The captain made a face. "Hand delivery it is, then. I

know we dropped a lot of stuff hightailing it off the base. What's left of our gear?"

Donnely spoke up, trying not to sound too discouraged as he reported. "Not much. Half the weapons. Some flares. Radio's fried. Like Epps said, phones are dead. Can't get a hookup with aerial surveillance." He looked at Epps. "Just like he said, we can't talk to anybody and they can't bitch at us. What we need is a Humvee."

"Or a couple of racing camels." Lennox turned to face Mahfouz. Having accompanied them on the retreat from the base, the youngster had been listening silently to the soldiers' conversation. "Kid, you've spent plenty of time visiting us. I think it's time to return the favor. How much farther to your village?"

Pushing hair out of his eyes, the boy turned and pointed. "Very close. Over next hill."

"Piece o' cake." Lennox looked at his tired but resilient companions. "Ain't that right, Fig?"

"Piece o' cake, sir," the sergeant responded as he dumped sand from his right boot.

"All right, then." Lennox started off in the indicated direction, scooping up equipment as he went. Other officers would have distributed their portion of the load among noncoms and enlisted men for them to carry. Not Lennox. Though he had come up through the ranks and wore double bars on his shoulders, inside he was still as much of a grunt as anyone in the service. Not only did he not mind the weight of his share of the surviving equipment, he welcomed it. In a firefight, he would not have to go looking for it.

"We're losing time," he barked. "Let's go—five-meter spread, stay parallel, keep up. Anybody sees any metal funk, sing out. I don't care if it's a used C-cell rolling downhill, I wanna know about it."

As the others stirred themselves to fall in, Figueroa lifted something hanging from the chain around his neck and gave it a quick kiss before tucking it back beneath his shirt. Lennox spied the gesture.

"What's that?"

Hefting his weapon, the warrant officer passed him. "Medal of Saint Christopher. My man." He gently patted his shirt, where the metal disc lay flat against his chest. "He'll keep us safe, bring us home."

Lennox nodded appreciatively, glanced back the way they had come. In the distance and sharp as paint against the blue of the desert sky, smoke rose from the vicinity of the base. "One metal versus another."

Coming in fast off the carrier standing out in the Gulf, it was understandable that neither of the two patrolling Black Hawk helicopters spotted the spread-out line of desert-hugging men. They did, however, look good on CNN as a backdrop for the somber-faced secretary of defense as he addressed the bird's nest of upthrust microphones clustered in front of him.

"At this time," he was saying solemnly and with a professional straight face, "we can't confirm whether there were any survivors, but our prayers are with the families of the brave men and women who were stationed at SOCCENT Forward. A full investigation of the disaster is proceeding. As soon as any information is confirmed, it will be released to the general media.

"Given the seriousness of this ugly and unprovoked attack, the gravity of the offense, and the casualties apparently suffered, the president and the Congress have concurred with the Joint Chiefs that all American bases domestic and worldwide should now go to DEFCON Delta, our highest level of military readiness."

Even as the reporters present scribbled notes or checked their recording devices, they marveled at the straightforward, no-nonsense speech. Completely devoid of the usual political overtones, it reflected a bipartisanship not heard in some time. More than anything else, the seriousness of the situation and the threat to the nation was underlined by the secretary's failure to mention the name of either political party.

The judicious display of bipartisanship did little to comfort Sarah Lennox. Safe in the secure confines of her home, she broke away from the TV as the secretary started to take questions from the mob of reporters. Ignoring the noise from the set, she picked up the baby, who had started crying. Holding her daughter close, she headed for the kitchen to warm a bottle.

"Shhh—Daddy's okay—Daddy's okay . . ."

If she said it often enough, she thought, she might come to believe it herself.

IV

When he could not find refuge in daydreams, Sam always pumped up his music. To their credit, his parents' tolerance extended to letting him actually crank it up to a level that was almost acceptable. Which is to say, loud enough to cause the water in his salamander's terrarium to vibrate like the road pools in the movie version of *Jurassic Park*. What the salamander thought of its owner's taste in music was not known.

At the moment, Sam Witwicky's attention was focused only marginally on the music that blared from the iPod mounted between twin speakers and more on the handwritten list of goals he had tacked to a wall. Picking up a pen and crossing off number one, "Get car," he stepped back to study the remaining objectives.

"Get new car stereo"—"Get new paint job"—"Get female passenger." Reaching out, he proceeded to circle number four. On his bed, a shorthaired Chihuahua sporting a collar speckled with faux diamonds stared at him out of contemplative eyes. The dog's name was Mojo and despite his diminutive size, he had plenty of it. One bandaged leg trailed a little bit behind the other.

The persistent canine gaze finally caused Sam to turn. *"What?"*

His tongue lolling out of the right side of his mouth, the quietly panting dog stared blankly back at his master.

Putting down the pen, Sam turned away from the modest list of goals and walked over to his dresser. From the assortment of bottles and cylinders dumped on its top he selected a half-empty tube of hair mousse. No more or less greasy than any other overpriced petroleum product guaranteed to turn nerdy wimps like himself into sleek rock-hard visions of irresistible male pulchritude, its repeated use tamed but did not transform his hair. Its application was followed by aromatic splashes of midpriced cologne across face, shoulders, chest, and—in a gesture fraught with hope if not probability—his underwear.

Thus fragrance-fortified, he moved to his computer. A couple of quick keystrokes brought up his eBay auction page. A quick check of the box alongside the photo of the aged, damaged spectacles revealed the discouraging and by-now-familiar legend, BIDS PLACED: 0. Shaking his head, he found and opened a small pill bottle, removed one pill, and fed the dog his daily dose of painkiller. With his mind focused on other matters, he absently shoved the bottle into a pants pocket.

"I know you get wasted on these things and can't always control yourself," he told the expressionless Chihuahua, "but if you whiz on my bed again you're sleeping outside, and I don't care *what* Mom says." Leaving that dire and impassioned warning in his wake, he headed for the door. Pausing only for an instant to make sure that his master was indeed leaving, an eager Mojo followed.

Working outside in the front yard Judy Witwicky could hear through an open window, though not presently see, the television. At the moment it was delivering yet another news bulletin detailing the escalating tensions around the world that had been kindled by the attack on the American base in the Middle East. These sorts of things happened all the time and the media always jumped on them and blew them all out of proportion, she believed. If you paid serious attention to each and every one, you'd go crazy in no time. Devoting to the dire warnings no more attention than she felt they deserved, she clipped and fussed at the row of rosebushes. Nearby, her husband was laying down the last of the precast stone path he had picked up at Home Depot.

Emerging from the front door, Sam sprinted between them, racing toward the driveway. Initially hot on his master's heels, Mojo caught the scent of something in the grass and stopped to sniff.

Sitting back on his haunches and looking up from his work, Ron followed the course of his energetically bounding son with the kind of patience fathers acquire only through years of practicing tolerance in lieu of actually committing filicide.

"Sam Sam Sam—it's called a 'path.'" With a wave of his hand he indicated the hard work he had just concluded. "The nice stones make a nice path." Knowing more than enough to read the implied warning in his dad's words, his impatient offspring reluctantly backtracked. With great deliberation, Sam retraced his approximate trajectory by making his way along the carefully placed stepping-stones.

"See?" his father continued, pleased. "That so hard? When you own your own grass, you'll understand. When you've spent years pruning, and grooming, and mowing, and fertilizing . . ."

A choice comment revolving around fertilizer immediately sprang to Sam's mind. Sensibly, and wishing to live to see eighteen, he squashed it, choosing instead to address his mother.

"Mom, seriously, could you stop putting jewelry on Mojo? He's got enough self-esteem issues as a Chihuahua without you pimping him every day."

His mother looked up from her roses and frowned. "You know I don't like for you to use that term," she scolded him.

Ron chipped in helpfully, "Maybe you should put him back in the dryer, hon."

A pained expression on her face, Judy Witwicky looked back at her husband. "It was an *accident*! I didn't know he fell asleep in the laundry basket. You know how hard he is to see sometimes." Reaching down, she picked up the little dog and cuddled him close. Legs flailing wildly, the frantic Mojo struggled to escape, but to no avail.

"How's your little leggy-weggy, huh, tough guy?" She looked over at her son. "Did you give him his pill?"

Continuing exasperation underscored Sam's response. "Yeah, I gave him his pill. We're turning him into a junkie. Any day now we're gonna get a visit from the dog division of the DEA." He flashed an electric smile. "By the way, roses are lookin' *awesome*. Colors really complement your hair."

"Don't BS me," she riposted. "Home by eleven. The 'Hair' will be waiting up for you. And drive safe."

The warning and the caution trailed in Sam's wake as he slid into the Camaro and slammed the driver's-side door behind him. The turning of the key in the ignition produced a loud grinding noise that was followed by a gush of black smoke from the tailpipe as the car roared off down the street. Involuntarily inhaling, she alternately coughed and gasped as she looked over at her husband and shook her head sorrowfully.

"Good God, you're cheap, Ron."

Miles Lancaster was Sam Witwicky's best friend. This was not enough to distinguish him in any way, shape, or form except in Sam's eyes. At the moment Miles was sitting on the stoop of his house, waiting but not patiently. Excitement rose within him at the sound of an approaching engine. It faded as soon as the vehicle generating the growl hove into view. Reluctantly, peering around to see if anyone else was looking on, Miles rose and walked over to the idling car.

A proud Sam revved the engine. Audible above the undeniable throatiness there sounded a persistent pop, the internal combustion engine equivalent of a chronic respiratory infection. Miles winced but said nothing.

"Listen to those ponies purr, huh?" Arm resting on the door and propped jauntily out the window, Sam grinned up at his friend. "What d'you think?"

Miles could only stare. How could one not? The—color—had imprisoned him. "It's—yellow. *Real* yellow."

Sam shrugged it off. "Dude, it's old school."

The color was not only blinding, it was numbing. Miles tried to turn away from it, failed. If he stared at it too long, like at the sun, he wondered, would it make him blind? "But it's—yellow."

"Why you gotta dis my wheels?" Turning away, a disappointed Sam stared straight ahead, out the dirty windshield. "C'mon, man, say something upbeat. I just got it. Don't judge it until you've taken a ride."

Managing to regain control over his outraged optic nerves, Miles relented slightly. "Can I drive?"

"That's not what I meant by 'upbeat.' Get in the car, Miles."

As soon as his friend did so, Sam peeled away from the curb. For several minutes as they cruised out of town, Miles said nothing. Though he did not say so out loud, he had to admit that the car sounded better than it looked. When he finally spoke up, his words were circumspectly vehicle-neutral.

"Can we stop at PETCO for a box of crickets?"

Sam looked over at his passenger, a tolerant expression on his face. With the superior air inherent in one-who-possesseth-da-wheels, he declared seriously, "Dude, you're way too old to have a pet toad."

Miles's response was a mixture of desperation coupled with a plea for understanding, the kind of understanding only a best friend could supply. "What can I do? I've had A-Rod since I was eight." There was a suggestion of rising hysteria in his voice. *"He won't die."*

The lake was always busy on a weekend, especially this time of year. Though a number of families were present, their little kids underfoot like the pesky vermin they were, the section of beach and shore where Sam parked was the one favored by far more superior subadults his own age. Excepting the music, the clothing, the fast food, the subjects under discussion, the slang, the excess of consumer electronics, and the makeup favored by the majority of the girls, the scene would have looked familiar to Norman Rockwell.

Come to think of it, maybe not.

Miles did not so much exit the Camaro as slide surreptitiously out of the front passenger seat. If he was lucky, no one would notice how he had arrived. Sam eyed him reproachfully and would have added a choice word or two except that his attention was distracted.

Not far away Mikaela Banes was emerging from the water. Oblivious to the fact that he was gawking like Goofy in a Disney cartoon, at that moment Sam would have gladly traded Botticelli's *Birth of Venus* for a photo of Mikaela striking a similar pose. That is, he would have if he had known who Botticelli was, and if any all-powerful entity had been capable of or inclined to make such an offer.

She was wringing out her hair. A perfectly prosaic activity that in Sam's addled brain was transformed into the quintessence of unconscious eroticism. As she walked past where he happened to be rooted to the lithosphere, he mumbled a fractured "Hi," attempted to coolly toss and catch his car keys, dropped them, and promptly banged his head on the protruding side mirror in his hurried attempted to recover both keys and poise and straighten up.

"Smooth," Miles observed from nearby. "Real clutch move."

His attention fixated on the retreating Mikaela, Sam didn't hear his friend. Sweeping past him, she was embraced by a cluster of girlfriends. This flock of giggling, preening adolescent swans slowly drifted off in the direction of Trent DeMarco, his friends, and his gleaming Escalade. She was cool, Mikaela was. Her girlfriends were cool. And justice be damned, it had to be admitted that DeMarco and his jock buddies were cool. He, Sam Witwicky, was manifestly not cool. For him life, at that moment, could not possibly be any worse.

Life begged to differ.

Noticing Sam watching, DeMarco stepped away from his expensive toy and called out, with great deliberation, "Hey, bro! Sorry 'bout your grandma. She died and left you that car, right?"

His entourage laughed appreciatively at their alpha male's perceived wit. Of them all only Mikaela did not reflexively join in.

"I like it," she stated unexpectedly. "It's old school. Everyone has different tastes." Her gaze shifted to the suddenly unsmiling DeMarco. "And not everyone has rich parents."

"Yeah," he mumbled, not in the least defensive. "Yeah, that's right." Acknowledging her observation without really agreeing to anything, he sauntered over toward Sam. At the approach of the hulking tight end, Miles suddenly discovered he had urgent business elsewhere.

Though DeMarco towered over him, Sam held his ground. Not that he wanted to. What he wanted to do was run like hell. But he couldn't. Not with Mikaela right there, watching. And he had to protect his car. Trent studied the smaller boy, aware that he could crush him like a bug. Since he knew it, and Sam knew it, DeMarco magnanimously chose not to do so. For the moment, anyway.

"Thought I recognized you in class. Aren't you the dude who joined the last-minute tryouts for the team last semester?"

Sensing that, at least for the moment, DeMarco had something other than homicide on his mind, Sam did his best to look casual and shrug off the implied indictment.

"Oh, that? Yeah, that was me. That was just—research. I wasn't really trying out. I'm—working on a book."

A predatory smirk spread across DeMarco's face. It was unpleasant, reminiscent of the smile of a sunning crocodile. "A book, eh? On what? Sucking at sports?"

Something snapped inside Sam. Momentarily, reason deserted him. "No, actually. On the link between football and brain damage."

DeMarco's humorless smile vanished and he took a menacing step forward. Unexpectedly Mikaela was there, blocking his advance.

"Stop it."

Glaring at her, DeMarco turned and stalked back to his Escalade. Swinging open the driver's-side door, he put a foot up on the chromed step. "Let's get out of here. Stupid lake's full of rugrats. I know where there's a raging frat party. This sucks." He nodded brusquely toward the water. "Kiddy stuff." His attention returned to Mikaela. "Let's go."

"I am not your *dog*," she snapped at him. "You can't just load me up and go."

Several of DeMarco's sycophantic teammates let out mocking "oohhs." Compelled to react, his voice dangerously low, he growled at her. "Don't pull that with me. You're not being funny." He indicated the interior of the SUV. "Get in."

She held her ground. "Or what?"

"Or I'm gonna leave your ass here." For a second time he nodded in the direction of the lake. "You wanna hitch a ride back with some loser mommy and daddy and their puking little kids?"

"I'll save you the trouble," she shot back, " 'cause I'm leaving *your* ass." With that she whirled and stomped off up the access road, heading in the direction of the main highway, ignoring the suddenly anxious and confused cries of several of her friends urging her to come back. She ignored them all. For a long moment DeMarco followed her with his eyes. Then he grunted and slid in behind the big SUV's wheel. As he revved the engine the rest of his entourage piled in, laughing and squealing. Kicking up grass, dirt, and a couple of discarded soda cans, the Escalade peeled out of the parking area and was gone.

Her expression furious, Mikaela stalked up the road, her mind focused on her anger. Both the confrontation and its climax had been unexpected. Almost as unexpected as the sudden and inexplicable coming to life of the Camaro's antique but high-fidelity radio as it began to play the Cars' "Who's Gonna Drive You Home?" Tracking the retreating Mikaela's receding form with his eyes, Sam barely noticed the music. But Miles did. Emerging from the cover of nearby trees, a strange expression on his face, he stared at the car as he rejoined his friend.

"Hey, man, what's up with your radio?"

A slight dreaminess in his voice, Sam replied without looking as he paraphrased the lyrics. "I'm gonna drive her home—tonight."

Mikaela was rapidly vanishing into the distance in the direction of the main road. "What?" Miles wondered aloud as he questioned his friend's competence—not to mention his sanity. "Stay away from her, dude. Yeah, she's hotter than Jorge's mom's tamales, but she's an evil jock concubine. Leave her alone. Let her hitchhike. If the apeman finds out you gave her a ride, he'll take you apart like a box of takeout from Colonel Sanders." He kicked at the grass. "Anyway, there's nothing to worry about. I give her two minutes on the highway and she'll have a ride."

Walking around the front end of the Camaro, Sam slipped into the driver's seat.

"Maybe not. It's too early for families to leave the lake and it's the weekend. No commercial traffic out here," Sam told his friend. "It's like ten miles to her house." He shoved the key into the ignition. "I'm never gonna get another chance like this."

"Okay then, just throw her in the back," Miles entreated, caving abruptly as the Camaro started up. "I call shotgun." He hopped into the passenger seat.

"Uh, yeah. About that." Hands gripping the wheel of the idling car, Sam looked over at his friend. "Miles, *out*."

The other teen stared back at him. "Oh no. Oh no, dude. C'mon now. You can't bone me like this. Don't leave me here." He indicated their surroundings, lake and trees and—*families with little kids*. "It's *creepy* out here."

Sam's sudden swing from declamatory to desperate was truly piteous to behold. "Please, Miles, I'm begging you in the name of all that's holy, begone!" He could no longer see Mikaela. What if someone had already picked her up? "If our friendship has ever meant *anything* to you, *get out*."

For a moment Miles did not move. Then he jammed a hand down on the door handle and exited. Stepping back as the Camaro tore up grass, he yelled after its receding driver.

"You better come back for me! Son of a . . . !"

Sam did not hear the last of his friend's angry diatribe and probably also missed its beginning. Scanning the road ahead, he let out a sigh of relief. Mikaela was still there, already coming into view just in front of him. She was plainly still angry, still stomping more than walking as she approached the entrance/exit to the lake parking area. She was as beautiful, as tempting walking away from him as she was coming toward him, he reflected distractedly.

"Okay," he murmured firmly to himself, "be cool. Be—supercool. Be liquid nitrogen, man." Slowing, he pulled up alongside her as she continued to march in the direction of the distant town.

"Uh, hey, Mikaela? It's Sam. Witwicky." *Cool, so cool. Not too close,* he warned himself. *Don't run over her foot, you freaking idiot.* "Hope my putting De-Marco in his place didn't get you stranded." With as much subtlety as he could muster, he circumspectly raced the engine.

She replied without looking over at him. "He's a jerk!"

Her eloquence was threatening to undo him. "Won't get any argument on that from me. So, I was, like, wondering if I could ride you home . . ."

Panic, instant and overwhelming. A bead of sweat appeared on his forehead. It immediately gave birth to another. "I mean," he corrected himself frantically, "*give* you a ride home. 'Cause I was just leaving anyway and wondering if you wanted a ride. Or not, y'know. Whatever. I understand."

She took another couple of steps, then stopped. It was hot. Town was a long way away. This mumbling Witwicky person was here, alongside her, with a car. She glanced over at the Camaro. Kind of a car, anyway. The next vehicle to come along might be a truck, piloted by the usual leering driver.

As options were clearly being weighed, Sam waited

silently in the idling car. Hopeful. Tense. Trying really hard not to sweat and failing miserably.

Her reluctant, resigned sigh ranked right up there with the most beautiful sounds in the universe.

Later, as they cruised back toward town, her voice rose above the thrum of the Camaro's engine as the car coasted down the hillside road. Sunset muffled the light but did nothing to mute her continuing rant.

"I cannot *believe* I'm here," she was saying.

"You can duck down if you want," Sam suggested helpfully. "It won't hurt my feelings."

She flicked her eyes at him. "Duck down? Are you crazy? Not with you, in your car. *Here,* in this situation." Leaning back against the headrest, she implored the heavens. "This serves me right. God, I've got such a weakness for hot guys!"

So this is what Grandma Lee meant when she used to talk about someone making her feel knee-high to a caterpillar, Sam mused as he mumbled a response. "Yeah, that, that *is* a weakness."

"I'm just so sick of this place," she rambled on, as if he weren't there. "It's so *boring.* It's so white-bread. I can't *wait* to go to college and get out of here!"

"Yeah," he murmured, feeling that whatever he might say could not be any worse than sitting silently behind the wheel like some mute driving robot. "College could be—cool."

For all the attention she paid to his comments he might as well have been writing them down on a pad instead of vocalizing.

"'Cause there *seriously* better be more to life than *this,*" she snapped. It was at that moment that it occurred to her that she was not entirely alone in the car. There was, albeit incidentally, a driver. "Sorry about all that. I was just venting." Her forehead wrinkled perfectly as she frowned. "Are you wearing cologne?"

Liquid nitrogen man panicked. "No! No, I don't wear cologne. I mean, I'm wearing—a little aftershave. And, uh, some guava lip balm." Quickly he rolled down his window. "Is it bothering you? Don't worry—I'll waft it."

"Yeah," she urged him thoughtfully. "I'd lighten it up a little." Finding the ensuing silence even more boring than the most inane conversation could possibly be, she prodded him. "So, are you like new this year?"

"Um, no." Though he wanted to look at nothing but her, he kept his eyes glued to the road ahead. "We've actually met before. In fact, we've been at the same school since first grade."

"Oh, really? Hmm. Do we have a class together?"

"Math. Gym. History." Hands gripping the steering wheel in a death grip, he stared straight ahead, afraid to look in her direction. "I sit next to you in homeroom." When she did not respond, he saw no hope for it but to continue. "Also, we were lab partners in Biology Two, remember? We hacked up that fetal pig? You threw up on me?" Still nothing. He was losing her. As if there had ever been anything there to lose. Yet even in the face of apathy and ignorance he knew he had to keep trying.

"Mr. Hosney's class today? I was standing in front of you for like five minutes? I did a really great presentation on my great-great-grandfather, the Arctic explorer dude?"

With cosmic tardiness, a glimmer of recognition dawned somewhere beneath that perfect hair. "Sam—right." It seemed as if, oh bliss, oh wonder, she was about to say something more, perhaps even something personal—only to be interrupted by a peculiar chirping noise coming from the backseat.

"What's that sound?"

Sam winced. "My friend forgot his crickets. They're for his toad. He's had it so long he can't get rid of it." Cringing, he awaited the anticipated verbal flaying, doubtless to be accompanied by lashes of derisive laughter.

She surprised him. "A pet toad. Oh, cool." The revelation that the sound arising from the rear seat emanated from insects destined for captive amphibian consumption had not fazed her a bit. A flicker of optimism sprang back to life within him.

And then, just when he was willing to allow himself a modicum of hope that the ride back to town might end in something other than total disaster, the engine sputtered. And died. Eyes widening, he gaped at the dash in horror and disbelief.

"No . . . nononono, not now." Involuntarily, he shot her a look. "New car, still working out the kinks."

Unbidden, the Camaro finally rolled to a stop not far from the edge of a bluff overlooking the town below. Unsolicited, the radio sprang to eager life, the car's speakers crooning Barry White's "I'm Ready for Love." Grabbing at the knob a frantic Sam turned it off, only to have it snap back on and belt out a vigorous version of "Sexual Healing."

"Uh, I know how this looks," he stammered helplessly. "I would *never* try something like that on you, Mikaela. I mean, not that you're not worth trying something like that *on,* but I wouldn't do it to you—I mean, I'd *do* it to you, but . . ."

Shaking her head tolerantly, she gazed at him as if he

had suddenly morphed into a large, gangly, badly manipulated string puppet. Which was not all that far from how he was feeling at the moment.

"Just pop the hood," she told him.

Pop the hood? What was she going to do? Hunting beneath the dash for a pull release, he found none. Was it possible that a car this old didn't have an inside hood release? By the time he thought to mention the possibility she was already out of the car and around front, bending low and fiddling with the Camaro's nose.

She had no more luck with it than had the bemused owner of the used-car lot who had sold Sam and his dad the car. He told her as much.

"It's stuck or something," he explained. "The guy who sold it to us—to me—couldn't get it open, either. I guess there's a latch that needs work, or something els—"

The hood gave a metallic *click* and swung up, to reveal in the fading daylight not the grease-streaked, grime-choked hunk of half-rusted iron he had expected to see but the gleam of polished chrome, serpentine coils of wire-wrapped nonstock hoses, shining cables, and a full panoply of glistening components that were as alien to Sam as the workings of his mother's laundry room. A similar degree of surprise was reflected in Mikaela's startled observation.

"Whoa—nice headers! Check out the compression setup. You have a high-rise double-pump carburetor. This has the makings of a stealth street racer. Impressive, Sam."

He should have kept his mouth shut. Instead he blurted, "Double-pump?"

Another *guy* would have jumped all over his transparent ignorance concerning things automotive. Instead Mikaela just explained, simply enough so that even a ten-year-old would have understood. "It squirts the fuel in so you can go faster."

"Oh yeah, right. I'm into horsepower." His comeback sounded unconvincing even to him. Thankfully she didn't call him on it. Either she was being polite and compassionate, or else she was so thoroughly engrossed in the particulars under the hood that his presence was nothing more than a noisy (and smelly) distraction. As she leaned farther in, he forced himself not to lean farther back for a better look.

"Cool—your distributor cap's loose. Might be able to hand-tighten it." She started using her hands, digging in and twisting, putting her back into it and apparently careless of her nails. Already knowing no bounds, Sam's admiration for her promptly doubled. He bent over alongside her, trying to see what she was doing. If he couldn't instruct, then maybe he could learn.

"How d'you know the whole—distributor thing?"

She explained while continuing to work with the cap and its attendant wires. "My mom tends to fall for romantic, yet tragically irresponsible men—like my dad. He was a serious grease monkey. Loved my mom, loved cars, loved working on both."

Sam hesitated. " 'Was'?"

She turned immediately evasive. "Yeah. He, uh, kinda left."

"But you seem so, uh, not mechanical. If you know what I mean."

Reaching up, she wiped sweat from her forehead with the back of one arm before redoubling her efforts to tighten the distributor cap. "Yeah, well, I don't broadcast it. Guys don't like it when you know more about cars than they do." She shook her head. "Inherent peculiarities of the subspecies, like they say in science."

Sam had always been quick to see an opening. For a change, he didn't waste this one. "But if Trent's driving you nuts, why d'you care *what* he thinks?"

This time she did glance back at him. "Hey, I have issues, like everyone. I guess I'm kind of a superfreak of contradictions. When they look at me everybody only sees the frosting, not the cake." Straightening, she wiped her hands before slamming the hood shut. "That ought to do it, at least until you can get a mechanic to look at it." She turned and smiled at him. "I think I'm just gonna walk."

The knee-high caterpillar analogy having not gone away, Sam fell back into it without so much as a blink. "Oh, yeah," he mumbled. "Sure. Walking's—walking's healthy."

He followed her with his eyes as she headed off down the road leading back toward town, everything he had ever dreamed of in his short life collapsing into the distance along with her. In her absence there was only the car left to talk to.

"How can you do this to me *now*?" he moaned. Since the car wasn't answering (hardly surprising), he tilted back his head and implored the sky. "*Please* don't let her just walk away."

The engine roared to life. A startled Sam's eyes got very wide very fast. An instant later the independent-minded radio once more came to life, blasting out "Baby, Come Back" through its surprisingly pure speakers.

A little way down the road a surprised Mikaela turned and looked back. Not having seen what had just transpired, she was a good deal less astonished than the car's owner. Forcing himself to look away from the Camaro, Sam turned to see if she had noticed the music.

Not only had she noticed, she had reversed course and was walking back. Retracing her steps. Coming toward—him.

Or maybe, he cautioned himself, having been disappointed entirely too many times before, she was just still curious about the car.

He didn't remember much about the rest of the ride into town. He was sure they'd talked, though for a thousand dollars he could not have recalled any one specific subject. He did, however, remember people turning to look in the car's direction. Some of the expressions reflected curiosity, some amusement, and one or two showed open disdain. He didn't care. He was riding through Tranquility in *his* car and his passenger was *Mikaela Banes* and the rest of the peons could whisper among themselves and think what they liked. On that afternoon, he would not have traded places with anyone on the planet.

Even with her to supply directions and guide him, it took some time to wind his way into her neighborhood. For one thing, the whole driving business was new to him. And naturally, he had never been to her house before. Assuming it would be as classy as a certain one of its occupants, he was surprised to find himself in a dumpy part of town. It wasn't really what you'd call a slum, he thought as he cruised slowly between the rows of unimposing homes—just beaten down. Following her directions he pulled up to a house that was as mundane as those that flanked it. There was absolutely nothing to distinguish the building, either individually or from its equally humdrum neighbors. As soon as he stopped she pivoted in the passenger seat, turning to face him.

"So, thanks for the ride. And thanks for letting me vent." She nodded in the direction of the hood. "I'd get your oil pan checked—I think there might be a small leak. And I'd get your pistons lubed."

He swallowed hard, trying not to think of lubricating pistons. "Yeah. Cool. Thanks for the advice." He wanted to stop staring at her but found that he had no more control over his eyes than he seemed to over the car. For a moment it looked as if she wanted to say something else, something more. But the feeling was only fleeting, and then it was gone. Opening the door, she turned to leave. Partway out she looked back over her shoulder at him.

"You think I'm shallow, huh?"

"Shallow?" He smiled. She was leaving, so what the hell, he thought. "No, I think—I think there's a lot more to you than meets the eye."

It was difficult to decide what lifted his spirits more: his new car, or the smile she gave him then. Leaving the smile shimmering in her wake, she stepped out and headed for the house. Solitary but not abandoned, he sat there alone behind the wheel, letting the memory of that smile permeate his soul as deeply as any ecclesiastical blessing. Then he slapped the steering wheel and put the Camaro in gear, pulling cleanly away from the curb.

"I love my car—I looove my car!"

He kept repeating the phrase, over and over, even above the jaunty counterpoint of the radio, all the way home.

Monitoring every radio and television signal and Internet communication on the planet was not a job for a couple of hackers squatting in a basement. While the National Military Command Center was located largely underground, it could not by any stretch of anyone's imagination be described as a basement. Row upon row of uniformed personnel sat quietly at multiple stations, their eyes fixed on numerous individual readouts, their sensitive headphones conveying to them the slightest of broadcast sounds even as both video and audio signals were being recorded for later deep study and analysis.

At a station set slightly apart from the rest, Maggie Madsen sat listening to the shrieking signal that had served as the electronic score to the attack on the SOCCENT base in Qatar. She had played it over and over, to near exhaustion. As a consequence, a growing numbness had manifested itself, but sadly not revelation. Worn out and frustrated, she pulled the headset off and laid it aside. The analyst posted closest to her station took advantage of the break to lean toward her and ask a question.

"What d'you think? Encrypted Mandarin? Amharic? Or maybe some obscure African language like !Xan or Twi?"

With half of her mind focused laser-like on the seemingly insoluble task at hand, she used the other to formulate a reply. "No, no. This is nothing like Bantu-derived dialects or anything else African, or for that matter like anything the Chinese have been using. It's no more like a Xingiang dialect or Tibetan than it is the King's English. This is—something else."

To the disappointment of the analyst, who had been considering following his query about the signal with one involving dinner and maybe a drink afterward, she slipped the headphones back on and once more activated the playback. For the thousandth, or maybe the two thousandth time, she concentrated on trying to distill a comprehensible pattern from the wild, high-speed shriek.

The four supercharged engines of *Air Force One* generated shrieking of a different kind, though as it cruised in circles high and wide over the eastern seaboard the sound they produced was not noticed within the heavily soundproofed interior. On either side of the much bigger plane, fully armed F-22s kept effortless pace. The fighter escort was rotated every few hours so that fresh pilots were always in the air, always on watch.

Inside the 747, a miniature version of the command center buried deep belowground near the capital monitored communications from all over the planet. On one screen an air force general with two stars on each of his epaulets was addressing the chief communications officer.

"Battle Group Truman is nearing the Arabian Gulf. Review in one hour for POTUS."

"Yessir." The major at the station acknowledged the information as succinctly as it was delivered.

As the day wore on, more messages were received,

more directives exchanged, more orders passed. Adjusting her shirt slightly, an air force staff sergeant walked through the cabin where so many communiqués were being exchanged and made her way to another part of the big plane. Following a brief formal exchange with the Secret Service agent stationed there, she was allowed entrance.

Inside the president's airborne stateroom, a single figure sat on the wide bed. She did not smile at the figure's stockinged feet, having encountered them on numerous previous occasions.

"Yes, Mr. President?" she asked politely by way of announcing her arrival.

Engrossed in a thick printed file, the figure on the bed did not look up. "Think you can wrangle me up some Ding Dongs and a glass of milk?"

"Right away, sir." Only when she was once more outside the room and beyond hearing range of the agent stationed at the door did she allow herself to mutter, "I did not survive West Point for *this*."

Keeping further opinions to herself, she strode past the Secret Service cabin. Within, other agents were busy at work or catching up on sleep. Agents were good at that: you slept when you could because you never knew when the next catastrophe might announce itself.

No one was using the small boom box nestled under one seat. By the same token, no one noticed when its outlines began to shift and flow like silver-tinged oil, or when it astonishingly sprouted short legs and tiny feet. Unseen and unobserved, it lifted itself and scuttled crablike behind the shoes of the agent seated nearby.

Only when it was well out of sight did it transform completely. The four-and-a-half-foot-tall Decepticon had assumed a terrestrial designation most accurately translatable as Frenzy. With its narrow body, and legs like steel sticks, it looked like some giant insect stepped straight out of the Carboniferous era. Silently, it scuttled off behind a row of unoccupied seats.

Near the middle of the plane the staff sergeant paused for a moment to join other presidential aides. Some were sipping coffee or tea; most were chatting amiably. The sergeant announced her arrival with a roll of her eyes.

"Yesterday it was Ho Hos. Today, Ding Dongs. The Republic is safe. What's tomorrow hold for us, ladies?" Laughter accompanied her as she made her way through the room. "Anybody looks for me, I'll be in supply for a few minutes."

The tiny elevator carried her down into the belly of the plane. Exiting, she worked her way back through ranks of cabinets and storage freezers. The last in line yielded a Circle K counter's worth of snack food, the presidentially requested Ding Dongs among them. Hauling out a box, she started to remove several of the individually wrapped cakes, only to drop one and see it tumble across the floor to disappear beneath another cabinet. It immediately rolled back into view. With a sigh, she bent and picked it up.

She did not notice the reed-like legs that had kicked it back out from beneath the cabinet.

Recovering the wayward snack, she dusted it off, put it on a plate with the others, and returned to the elevator. Only after the elevator had started up did Frenzy step out into the dim light of the storage area. Skittering along the floor, the Decepticon paused before a locked access panel labeled P.O.T.U.S. ONLY. Digits fashioned of an alloy not forged on Earth probed the edges of the panel: testing, feeling, analyzing. Then they ripped it off.

Revealed in the light of the storeroom was an open terminal. A small sound of satisfaction, a muted, modulated electronic shriek, issued from the intruder. Maggie Madsen, among others, would have recognized it immediately as a greatly subdued and twisted version of the scream that had accompanied the assault on the base in Qatar. The terminal winked to life and a single small readout announced matter-of-factly, CONNECTING TO PENTAGON SECURE NETWORK.

Somewhere in subterranean Virginia, the deputy director of operations paused before a certain usually innocuous monitor station. Something on the screen had caught his eye. As the incoming transmission announced itself, a similar report caused Maggie to sit bolt upright and press her headphones even more tightly against her head. What had drawn the deputy director's attention was a small pop-up identical to one that had appeared on her console.

FOREIGN SIGNAL DETECTED

Alert, completely awake, and no longer bored, her fingers flew over the keyboard before her. On the screen a pair of sound graphs appeared side by side, followed almost instantly by a single word: MATCH. Her eyes widened. Without turning, she raised her voice to a yell.

"THEY'RE HACKING THE NETWORK AGAIN!"

Within the storage room on board *Air Force One,* the probing shriek continued to emerge in a steady and unbroken aural scream-stream from the Decepticon called Frenzy. New words scrolled across the small readout.

SEARCHING SPECIAL ACCESS FILES. The shriek modulated slightly—digging deeper, demanding, insistent. At last the file heading the robot was seeking appeared on the readout. PROJECT ICE MAN—TOP SECRET SCI—SECTOR SEVEN ACCESS ONLY.

Inside the lower Pentagon the detected shriek screamed from every open speaker as Maggie typed furiously. Expression grim, the deputy director had rushed to her position and was now leaning over her right shoulder, staring at her monitor. Others clustered nearby, straining to see.

"Run a trace route!" he ordered her. She ignored the command. Not because it was a bad idea, but because she was way ahead of him.

"I've been trying, but it's locking me out! The probe includes some kind of mobile, continuously adaptive firewall that responds differently to each trace attempt. The freakin' thing adapts every time you try something new." Her fingers pounded away at different keys, continuously trying new combinations in the desperate hope that something would work, that something would slip past the probe's remarkable defenses. "It *learns*."

Concurrent with Maggie Madsen's frantic efforts at the Pentagon, a new window insert appeared on the small monitor within the storeroom terminal on *Air Force One*. TRANSMITTING LOCAL SYSTEM CORRUPT TO PENTAGON NETWORK. This announcement was followed by a continuous line of streaming destinations.

U.S. CENTCOM, U.S. STRATCOM, U.S. SOCOM, U.S. . . .

On one of the screens at Maggie's console a normally placid data stream suddenly went insane. Without hesitating she turned to the tight-faced analyst closest to her.

"Are you or anyone you're linked with running a systemwide diagnostic?"

"No." He was taken aback by the intensity in her voice. "Do we need to?"

Standing up, she shouted at the top of her voice. "IS ANYONE IN THIS ROOM RUNNING A SYSTEMS DIAGNOSTIC?"

Startled by her accusatory exclamation, not to mention its volume, everyone looked up from their consoles. A few abandoned their positions to join the crowd that was now fighting for a look at her main monitor. Staring at the console, she sat down hard.

"Oh my God—cut the hard lines!"

The deputy director gaped at her. "What? Are you kidding? I can't just do that. What've you got?"

She ignored him, waving her hands at her console as if she could somehow reach inside and tear apart the offending data streams with her bare hands. "If you can't do it, then get *some*one who can! They breached the national defense firewall. I think they're planting a virus!"

The deputy director stared at her. "A virus?" he echoed dumbly.

She leaned forward. "Wait a minute, wait a minute. They're not just inserting—they're *taking* something, too! They're planting and they're taking, and I can't make any sense out of either one." Whirling in her seat, she stared up at him. *"Cut the hard lines!"*

To his credit the deputy finally recovered from the initial shock her words had induced. He yelled into his headphone pickup. "Code Red! We have a full security breach. Cut all server hard lines *now*! Initiate full physical isolation!"

On board *Air Force One* the small secondary terminal was blinking out straightforward percentages: 75% . . . 90% . . . TRANSMISSION COMPLETE. Next to it a secondary readout declared FILE FOUND—PROJECT ICE MAN. TYPE SPECIMEN DISCOVERED 1897. FIRST ON SITE WITWICKY, ARCHIBALD, CPT.

Whoever actually cut the hard lines deep inside the Pentagon deserved more than a medal. At the moment, the names of the pertinent individuals were not important. Only the results of their desperate efforts mattered. The deputy director exhaled sharply as he made the announcement.

"All connections have been cut! Server isolation is complete."

Even a bot can be distracted. Frenzy's frustration as the terminal connection it was utilizing suddenly vanished was so absorbing that it failed to notice the arrival in the storage area of a Secret Service agent and a flight deck specialist. They, however, were not similarly preoccupied. They immediately noticed the broken lock that had fallen to the floor.

Instantly the agent brought his wrist communicator up to his lips. "Break in sector two. Repeat: break in sector two."

Seconds later a second agent was pounding down the stairway at the other end of the room, gun drawn. Emitting an electronic hiss, Frenzy spun behind the first two arrivals as they advanced. Impossibly thin, impossibly sharp metal discs shot from the Decepticon's upper torso. Both men went down as the agent at the other end of the room crouched and opened fire.

Electronic predictors faster than anything on Earth were able to note the dispersal of the individual bullets in the enclosed space and their trajectory. They were easily blocked. More discs spat from the whirling mechanoid.

When a line of heavily armed agents charged into the storage area from opposite ends all they found were three bloody, motionless bodies riddled with metallic discs. That, and a boom box on a food preparation table playing easy listening . . .

It was late, and dark, and all through the Witwicky house not a creature was stirring, provided one discounted the occasional twitch of a slumbering Chihuahua's bandaged leg and the chamber music chirp of Miles's crickets from inside the box set on Sam's open windowsill. A visitor might have wondered why, after singing steadily for most of the night, they suddenly went silent.

Out in the driveway, an old but brightly colored Camaro suddenly came to life, its engine rumbling softly. The sound was deep enough and near enough to wake the vehicle's owner. Sitting up in bed, Sam blinked once, rubbed at his eyes, and turned to the window—just in time to see his now-beloved new car backing smoothly out of the driveway. Half asleep and half hysterical, he fell out of the bed, yelling at the presumed someone in the car.

"Hey, that's my car. *Thief!*"

It was impossible to watch the car and throw on shoes and clothes at the same time, so he concentrated on the latter. Yelling at the car thief wasn't going to do any good. Sam made no attempt to mitigate the noise as he pounded down the stairs. He couldn't take the care to move quietly. If he woke his parents, so much the better, but he could not spare the time to rush into their bedroom and rustle them awake. Every second he delayed, his car would be that much farther away.

Outside, he picked up the first bike he saw and gave chase. He was just in time to see the Camaro heading south. Fortunately it was not speeding. Plainly, it had been taken by a smart thief. Smart enough to know not to exceed the speed limit and thereby draw the attention of some patrolling cop. That kind of caution might work in *his* favor, Sam knew. Pulling his cell phone from an inside jacket pocket, he dialed with one hand while steering with the other. The response was gratifyingly fast.

"911 Emergency."

"My car's being stolen," he yelled toward the phone. "Like now, like I'm on my bike chasing him *right now*. I'm behind him and I can still see him. Get the cops!"

"Yessir. Appropriate steps are being taken even as we speak, sir. Sir, do *not* approach the stolen vehicle," the operator warned him. "The driver could be dangerous."

Sam gaped at the phone. "Ya *think*? Get me some help!" He looked up to get his bearings—just in time to see that the Camaro had braked at a stop sign, almost immediately in front of him. He didn't *slam* into the rear bumper, but he did hit it hard enough to end up on the ground, the bike lying on its side and spinning its front wheel. The car took off again. Only slightly bruised, determined, and undaunted despite the 911 operator's warning, he picked up the bike, climbed on, ascertained that it was still functional, and resumed pedaling madly. Throughout it all he had never let go of the cell phone.

As if to remind him of that fact, and of his resolve, the emergency operator's voice sang reassuringly out to him from the tiny speaker. "Sir, sir—we're trying to trace your call. Are you all right? Sir?"

At the speed he was going he needed both hands to steer. "Cops. Now," he barked at the phone before sliding it, still on, back into his jacket pocket. He didn't need to make small talk in order for the police to be able to trace him. He did need all the wind he could spare to keep pedaling.

In smaller communities, industrial and commercial centers are not as far from residential areas as they are in a great metropolis. Still, the chase had covered enough ground so that by the time the Camaro busted the lock on the gates to the old cement factory and materials storage yard, Sam was pretty well winded. It was a relief when the Camaro entered the yard and finally slowed down. Hopping off the bike, he stowed it carefully out of sight and followed the car on foot. Disappearing briefly behind a slow-moving train, the Camaro emerged a few moments later. For the first time since the car had awakened him and pulled out of the family driveway Sam had a good look at the front of it.

There was no one in the driver's seat.

As he tried to digest this impossibility, arguing that surely he had not seen correctly, that it had been a trick of the darkness, the car cruised slowly around the corner of the abandoned factory. He followed with care, making sure to keep out of sight while bearing in mind the emergency operator's warning. The driver could be dangerous—except that there was no driver. That, he reflected a little unsteadily, could also be dangerous. To his state of mind.

It got worse when the car, its outline muddled by distance and darkness, appeared to change its shape and *stand up*.

Oh boy, he thought. Had Mojo secretly been storing his pain pills in his cheeks and spitting them out later into Sam's evening soda? Huddled behind a crate he looked on as the dark, now-vertical silhouette removed something from its torso. Without warning the object emitted a light as overpowering as it was unexpected, temporarily blinding him. Shielding his eyes, he tried to identify the light source. All he could tell was that it had regular, precise outlines. Some sort of symbol . . .

Before he could get a better look or analyze it further, it leaped upward and vanished into the night sky.

Ohh-kayyy, he thought as he fumbled wildly for the cell phone. Not your average car theft, then. Nono. Though he aimed the phone's built-in camera as carefully as he could, it was just too dark and his "car" too distant and hidden for him to get a clear shot. That didn't stop him from babbling urgently into the phone, however.

"M-my name's Sam Witwicky. My car—I thought it was stolen, but it's *alive*. Or at least self-animated, or something, I dunno. I don't know how, but it's alive. These could be my last words on Earth, so lemme just say—Mom and Dad, if you find a copy of *Busty Beauties* magazine under my bed, I was only holding it for Miles, I swear, I . . ." His expression contorted. "Oh God, *I can't lie, not now*—it's mine! I'm sorry! I—"

His ongoing confessional was interrupted by a sound. Not in front, but behind him. There was nothing of the mechanical about it. It was a long, low growl, mean and ripe with anticipation. Heart pounding, he turned and looked behind him.

There were two of the rottweilers, and each looked big as a bear. At least, their teeth did. Snarling and spitting, they were coming straight toward him, a pair of black four-legged Sam-seeking missiles flashing gaping jaws. Choking out a cry of terror, he rose and ran for his life.

Long chains unfurled like kite strings from the dogs' heavy leather collars. Fortunately, the chains were bolted to a wall. Fortune, however, was not Sam's companion tonight. With a snap and a *bang,* first one restraining bolt and then its companion tore free of the aging concrete.

His gym coach would have looked on in disbelief as Sam executed the greatest vertical leap of his life up onto a pile of crates. The ascent didn't stop the dogs, but it did slow them down for a moment. So did the barbed-wire fence Sam scrambled over, ripping his clothes as he cleared it. Without pausing for breath, the dogs tore through a nearby hole under the fence. One was close enough to snap at one ankle. Teeth caught his pants and not his leg, but it was enough to send him sprawling into the dirt. As his cell phone went flying he rolled over fearfully, fully expecting far more personal possessions to follow the piece of torn denim.

It was at that moment that the Camaro reappeared. Spinning doughnuts around the prone Sam and honking furiously, it confronted the startled dogs with mass, light, and complete confusion. One tire ran right over the errant cell phone, reducing it to a handful of crushed circuitry. Whimpering now, faced with a phenomenon they did not understand, the dogs turned tail and fled. Scrambling to his feet, Sam fervently desired to follow them. But while the car was now between him and the retreating dogs, it was also between him and the distant exit. Fighting not to cry, he turned to the roaring, wheel-spinning machine.

"Please," he begged, "don't kill me! Take the car, whoever you are. Whatever you are. It's all yours. Just don't kill m—"

Red, blue, and white lights pierced the settling dust as the sound of wailing sirens closed on the yard. The police! Pivoting, Sam accelerated in the direction of lights and noise, nearly running up onto the hood of an arriving cruiser. Guns drawn, what seemed in the darkness like a whole company of cops piled out of the arriving vehicles. They held their weapons steady and ready.

And every one of them was pointed at Sam.

"Freeze!" one sergeant commanded him. "Hands! Up!"

Sliding slowly off the hood of the cruiser, Sam hastened to explain. "Not me! Not me! Wrong guy! My car! Mine! It's . . ."

Turning, he pointed at the Camaro. Or rather, he found himself pointing at the spot where the Camaro had been idling only a little while ago. It was gone, and with it his rationale. He could think of nothing to say as he was spun around and dumped facedown on the same hood he had only a moment ago embraced as a savior.

It was early morning in the Global Response Center of the National Military Command, but a visitor would not have known it from the flurry of activity that had continued through the night and had filled the room since the previous day. Along with the very best techs representing all services, the secretary of defense was there, as were the directors of the NSA and CIA, a number of especially tech-knowledgeable generals and admirals, and a wide assortment of grim-faced support personnel.

Maggie was there, too. At the moment she was just

looking on, analyzing people for a change instead of sounds, sights, and algorithms.

The admiral who was speaking nearby wore a name tag that identified him as Bingham. It meant nothing to her. Within the circles she moved in she often encountered officers from every branch of the service, but rarely of such exalted rank.

"*Air Force One* made an emergency landing," the admiral was saying. He looked very unhappy. "Three fatalities on board, all support personnel. About the only good thing you could say about the entire incident was that the president remained unaware of any difficulty. He is presently being shifted to a secure location from which he can safely direct ongoing activities."

He seemed like a nice enough admiral to Maggie. More importantly, he had the virtue of being right there, right now. She moved closer. "Um, if I could just mention—"

Ignoring her, the center's deputy director responded to the admiral's account. "Whoever did this finally managed to infiltrate our defense net—which is the same thing they tried to do in Qatar. Only this time, it worked. They got in before we could intercede."

"What'd they get?" The secretary of defense, she thought, was admirably composed under the circumstances.

The deputy director shook his head dolefully. "We still don't know, John. Shutting everything down as fast and aggressively as we did scrambled all kinds of software. The techs are still sorting things out, trying to get everything back up online. They're going slow. Nothing gets rebooted unless and until we can be sure it's in a guaranteed safe mode. Also, instead of bringing everything back up with the usual cross-platform integration, we're trying to keep the most sensitive material and programs isolated from one another. That way, if there's another breach it will only affect a small portion of the total data. Plus, we can then concentrate all our defenses on it."

"What about the intrusion?" Keller asked him. "The virus—if it is a virus, as we understand it."

The deputy director looked dejected. "We're still trying to break it down. It's a brand-new kind of infiltration. None of our people has ever seen anything like it before. I'm told that it has similarities to a spider-bot, but that both its core and the way it propagates are different. Way different. We're not sure what it's going to do when it fully activates but I'm told that if and when it does, penetration is widespread enough to cripple the entire system."

The secretary of defense coughed softly. "That would put us back to Pony Express days. Can we stop it before it detonates?"

The deputy director took a deep breath. "Every time we try to insert an antidote, an antivirus, it analyzes the threat, mutates a countermeasure—and speeds up. Almost as if it draws strength from every attempt of ours to neutralize it. It's like it's not a virus anymore—it's *become* the system. Infiltration has been so thorough that if we find a way to shut down the intrusion, we'll end up shutting down the system ourselves." He spread his hands helplessly. "Same result as if we do nothing. It's not exactly a technical term, but the best word I can find to describe it is *fiendish*."

"Well, whatever happens," Keller muttered, "the one thing we're *not* going to do is 'nothing.'"

Bingham had listened long enough to the deputy director's perception of the basic situation. It was not reassuring. Technical chat was all very useful and good, but it was not going to protect the citizens of the United States.

"This is obviously the first phase of a major strike against the U.S. The Joint Chiefs have known for years that the first step would be to try and take down our communications capabilities. It may be only a test, to see if this kind of attack can succeed. Or," he added portentously, "it could be the first stage of an all-out assault. If our defenses can't talk to one another and we cannot coordinate a defensive strategy, then we're as helpless as a duck in a decoy factory." He glanced at each man in turn.

"According to the latest intelligence, Russia and North Korea are the only countries with the potential to mount something like this. As you know, we are reacting accordingly." He drew himself up. "Whatever happens next, appropriate countermeasures will be taken before our ability to do so is rendered inoperative. In this we have no choice."

A persistent noise caused all three men to turn. For once, the sound that distracted them was not an indecipherable electronic shriek or the announcement of some new outrage against the American military establishment. It was a laugh, sharp and close at hand. Settling on its source and taken aback by the bravado behind it, Bingham frowned.

"Didn't see you there, young lady. You would be who?"

Maggie met his gaze without flinching. "I'm the one who detected the hack."

"It was you?" Keller was startled: no one had told him. Or maybe they had tried to and failed. He had been somewhat busy the past twenty-four hours.

"Yessir." Now surrounded by the three men, she did her best to stand a little taller without making the effort obvious. "I was just trying to point out that whoever we're dealing with hacked the national military firewall in *ten seconds*. Even a brute-force frontal attack with our best supercomputers would take twenty *years* to achieve penetration like that."

"I'm not sure where you're going with this, young lady," Bingham told her, "but if the assault is so impossible then maybe you can explain why the latest surveillance imagery taken by our spy aircraft—all satellite communications are down—shows North Korea doubling its level of naval and air force activity."

She tried not to sound bitchy when she replied. "Maybe they're afraid of an attack of some kind. Maybe it's nothing more than a precaution. Isn't that what we're doing? Maybe they're just reacting to *our* maneuvers."

Bingham responded with a crooked smile. "*Maybe* isn't a word we like to build our national defense posture on."

When challenged, Maggie's response was always to counterattack. It frequently got her in trouble. "Well, I kinda hope it's not a word you'd go to war over, either—man." Aware that she was verging dangerously close to the debate society equivalent of self-asphyxiation, she cut off that line of discussion.

"Admiral. General. Major. *Sir.*"

Fortunately for any future career prospects, her initial impression of Bingham had been correct. He really was a very nice admiral. Unexpectedly, he smiled tolerantly down at her.

"How nice to be young," he observed, his expression deadpan.

"We're listening, Ms. Madsen." Keller gave her his full attention. "All ears. Fill 'em."

She turned to the deputy director. "Look, *you* said it. The signal pattern's evolving, changing. Mutating. It's learning. Everybody needs to move past the notion that simple Fourier transforms are at work here and start thinking quantum mechanics. We're not dealing with the usual speeds here—we're talking instantaneous cyber-cognizant adaptive algorithms."

The deputy director shook his head, not believing. Not wanting to believe. "Come on, there's nothing on Earth that complex, capable of that kind of evolution. There's nothing that can simultaneously process so many complex adaptations across an entire program."

"Yeah there is," she shot back. "An organism. Like maybe the still-theoretical DNA-based computer. I know it sounds crazy, but—"

"Okay." Bingham cut her off. "I've heard enough." He turned to go.

Having committed herself, Maggie saw no option but to press her case as far as she could take it. "Look, let my team study the signal pattern—assuming there is one. You can let us do it or you can stand there looking down your noses at me, but you don't have time for both so *choose*."

Keller eased himself between her and the increasingly intolerant deputy director and the preoccupied retreating admiral. "*That's enough*. We have senior analysts for that kind of work, Margaret, and given the sensitivity of—"

"*Maggie*," she interrupted him, making no effort to keep the irritation out of her voice. "I *told* you—it's on my birth certificate."

Keller paid no attention. "Now, if you find proof to support your theory, I'm available and happy to hear it. But if you don't work a little harder on that brain-to-mouth filter, I am taking you *out,* and you'll find yourself back evaluating water flow statistics for the lower Potomac." Turning, he joined the deputy director in following Bingham toward the exitway.

Maggie watched them go. She would have been really upset and angry, except she didn't feel she could afford the time . . .

There were enough military police and civilian police vehicles surrounding a parked *Air Force One* that morning to mount an invasion of a small third-world country. But they were only at an air force base in Oklahoma. Forensics specialists swarmed the interior of the plane, hunting for clues to the inexplicable. Three people had been murdered, their thoracic arteries severed by razor-sharp metal discs, and no one on board had the slightest clue how it had been done.

What the bevy of experts was looking for, though none of them could imagine it, was presently scuttling across the damp tarmac. It halted beside one of the many parked police cars. Except that this particular machine was not a police car. It only *looked* like one of Oklahoma's finest's law-enforcement vehicles. Having adopted the name Barricade, it was—like the crawling spider-thing—also a Decepticon.

Barely audible bursts of precisely modulated sound passed between the cruiser-that-wasn't and the insectoid-thing. What would have sounded like pure noise to a human was actually complex communication, too rapid and advanced for any primate brain to comprehend.

"The virus will activate soon," the insectoid-shape that had taken the name Frenzy declared. It was sufficiently advanced to express satisfaction.

The passenger-side door opened on the transformed police cruiser, and a sonic reply issued from the nearest speaker. "It is all well and good that the intrusion goes according to plan, but what about the Cube?"

Flexing metal legs, Frenzy hopped effortlessly up into the empty front seat. Their attention wholly focused on one another, on their work, and on the giant plane parked in their midst, none of the humans was looking in the direction of the "empty" car.

"They isolated the relevant network," Frenzy replied in response to Barricade's query, "but not before I found this."

A thin metal wire extruded from the body of the multilegged Decepticon and jacked into a port on the dash-mounted "police" computer. It took only a second for the designated data to transfer. Had the handover of information taken place at humanoid speed, the name WITWICKY, ARCHIBALD, CPT. would have been among the words that would have appeared on the car's computer screen.

Staying alive, the computer and its monitor ran a complementary search/scan of their own. Almost instantly, the name Frenzy had provided was matched to several newspaper articles from 1897. The unfortunate captain's face was among the graphics that made a split-second appearance. So were several photographs of symbols that were alien to anything on Earth—but not to the disguised police cruiser and its spidery passenger.

The search continued, going worldwide, seeking any match, any bond, any link. It found one—on a basic eBay page. Ignoring the accompanying image of the young human, both machines focused their attention on a pair of battered, badly scored spectacles. The extraordinarily primitive dual-lens artificial sight-correcting device interested them not in the least. But the symbologic code that had been burned microscopically into the two lenses interested them very much indeed.

Conveniently, the simple coded page provided the physical locality at which the owner of the page and the spectacles resided. It was all too easy. While neither Barricade nor Frenzy was of a mechanoidal type programmed to express thankfulness, they were both quite capable of appreciating the apparent minimal amount of resources that were going to be required to recover the object of their search.

"Shall I summon the others?" the insectoid-shape hissed electronically.

"Not yet." Being of a higher order of competence, it was left to the morph that presently held the form of a police cruiser to make the applicable decision. "This world's defensive mechanisms are crude and of an extremely low order of individual intelligence, but those who direct them possess, in their singularly primitive way, some slight degree of competence. And the devices themselves can be deadly. We cannot risk exposure until we know the location of the Cube. For now it is best that we sustain the masquerade and remain in disguise."

"Understood." At that, the smaller Decepticon chose an appropriate mechanism that was part of the police car, transformed, and fused itself with the dash, becoming nothing more than another component of the cruiser. Behind the wheel a human figure began to take shape. The uniform it wore was that of an Oklahoma police officer. The faux cop had a light tan and sported a short, neatly combed, distinctive mustache. Up close, the swath of decorative lip hair looked almost like a miniature antenna . . .

Out of ideas, out of breath, and out of patience, an exhausted Sam sat in a chair inside the main Tranquility police station while the duty cop grilled him. The youth was about fed up but too fatigued to do much more than shake his head at the stream of nonsensical questions. His father stood nearby, not happy with the situation but unable to do much about it. Prior to the start of the interrogation Sam had been allowed the traditional one phone call, and it had been to his dad.

The questions being asked seemed perfectly sensible to the officer who was asking them. It wasn't the first time he had been required to deal with this kind of teenage weirdness. Experience told him that he already knew the answers.

"So your car was driving by itself."

Who did this guy think he was? a tired Sam mused. Serpico? Or was he acting like this for the benefit of the inevitable concealed camera that was undoubtedly recording the entire interview?

"Yes—*yes*. That's what I *said*." Sam's exhaustion was exceeded only by his exasperation. "Could I *be* any clearer than how *crystal clear* I'm being right now? I don't know how else to say it. The car, it, like—transformed. It *stood up*."

The cop smiled disdainfully. "Wow. Stood up? That's so—*neat*. All by itself? No help from a crane? A car that stands up. I gotta get me one of those. Think how useful it would be for police work. You could check out second-story windows without having to get out of your car, lord it over the bad guys, and parking would be a snap. Except you'd have to watch out for all those NO LOITER-ING signs." Turning, he opened a drawer, reached inside, and took out a small, widemouthed clear plastic cup. Lines and numbers were inscribed on the side. He tried to hand it to Sam, who drew back in distaste.

"Fill 'er up, chief," the cop ordered him. "We'll see what the lab comes up with. Maybe some better answers than you're giving me. What're you rollin'? Goof balls? Wowie sauce? Crystal? Whippets?"

Tired as he was, Sam had enough energy left to be in-sulted. "I'm not on anything!"

"Oh yeah?" The cop was grinning in a way Sam didn't like. "What's this, then? Found it in your pocket."

Triumphantly, he held up a pill bottle. A bottle half full of prescription pain pills. That they were for someone named Mojo had intrigued the interviewing officer only that much more. He made a show of examining the worn paper label.

" 'Mojo,' huh? That what you ravers are calling it these days?"

Aware that he must be sounding a little desperate, Sam tried to explain. "They're my dog's painkillers!"

"Oh yeah, right." The smirk on the cop's face grew wider. "I suppose the next thing you're gonna tell me is that your pusher is a poodle and this interview should be conducted by a K-9 unit."

A defeated Sam stared straight ahead. That his line of sight happened to intersect with the holster on the cop's belt was not lost on his interrogator. The man stiffened slightly.

"You lookin' at my piece, Fifty Cent? Wanna reach for it? Think you're fast? See what happens, c'mon."

Aware that he was starting to feel more than a little stoned even in the complete absence of any ingested recreational pharmaceuticals, Sam peered up at the cop.

"Are *you* on drugs?"

Ron had seen and heard about enough. Until now he had stood by quietly, not interfering or protesting, just listening and waiting for the interview to be over. But he did not like the turn the dialogue was taking. Arrest or no arrest, that was his son alone in the chair, and the cop was provoking him. He stepped forward.

"Look, that's it. He's had a hard night. Read out some charges and make a formal arrest. Otherwise I'm taking him home."

The cop looked displeased. This wasn't the way these kinds of interviews worked out on TV. "We'll run all this through the wire, see what turns up," he announced threateningly. Then he turned back to Sam. "But before you go, there's something you need to see." Smiling tolerantly at the increasingly impatient Ron, the cop picked up a remote and pointed it at the television mounted on the wall opposite.

Static cleared, and a program began to play. A girl appeared on the screen. She was attractive but austerely dressed. "This is your brain," she began solemnly as she held out an egg. She cracked it in a pan heating on a stove. "This is your brain on drugs."

Trapped and unable to escape, Sam pulled at his lower eyelids. *This is your pain on slugs,* he recited to himself, fighting to retain his sanity.

Thankfully, it was the standard unembellished public service announcement and ran only a few minutes. Sam stood morosely nearby while his father signed papers, and then they were allowed to leave. Ron didn't say anything until they were outside the station and halfway down the front steps.

"Wanna tell me what really happened?"

Sam hesitated, then looked up at his dad. "Remember right after we bought the car? When you said you'd pick me up, wherever I was, whatever the situation, no questions asked?"

Buoyed by his own concern and his son's exceptional memory, his father had no choice but to concede the point. "That—was the deal, yeah."

They continued on in silence, crossing the street and slipping into the family car, Ron behind the wheel, Sam in the passenger seat staring straight ahead. His father turned the key in the ignition.

"Dad, y'know how Great-Great-Gramps pretty much— flew over the cuckoo's nest? Think that kind of— difficulty—could've been passed down to me? Like—some kind of mutant Witwicky gene?"

His father smiled as he checked the street for oncoming traffic and pulled smoothly out away from the curb. "I don't see it, Sam. Besides, my father was perfectly— normal. And so am I." Reaching over with his right hand, he playfully tousled his son's hair. "Except on the days when your mother asks me to do certain kinds of work around the house."

Sam was not mollified. He did his best to smooth down the hair his father had disturbed. "We learned in biology that certain abnormal genes can skip a generation or two. Maybe that's happened in my case."

"As long as it doesn't affect your grades or your SAT score," his father quipped. "Or doing your chores. Too many kids these days seem to have inherited the chore-skipping gene." A coffee shop loomed ahead, on their side of the street. "How about we get something to eat? I'm willing to bet your abnormal gene doesn't prohibit the consumption of chocolate shakes."

Sam nodded agreeably. He hadn't thought about it while he had been held at the police station, but he really was famished.

"Okay." He managed a tired smile. "Better make mine a double."

VI

It was an old village. Once inhabited by the ancestors of Qataris who were now made wealthy by revenues from the sale of oil and natural gas, it had long ago been abandoned to the desert. A community of immigrants, many illegal, had claimed it as their own. The settlement was ignored by the authorities, who had more important security matters to attend to. The newly rich needed protection, and there was always the occasional fanatic who needed locking up.

The village could boast a well, in a part of the country where there was no need to pipe in expensive desalinated seawater. That precious liquid was reserved for the inhabitants of the gleaming new cities that hugged the white sand beaches of the Gulf. But where the desert gave up water, it would always attract some kind of life.

The place was not wholly isolated. Probably dating from the 1960s, a single telephone wire still connected the line of poles that marched in sturdy single file across the sand-and-gravel plain. It made an easy trail for the boy and his friends to follow.

One of the poles abruptly shuddered, even though there was no wind and the ground underfoot was steady. Nearby, an old wood-frame sign trembled and came crashing down. Gun muzzles rose, leveling in its direction. Plainly unsettled, the pair of vultures that had been roosting on the sign rose skyward and headed eastward, inland and away from the still-distant sea.

Captain Lennox eyed his men: a team of three, and the stragglers they had picked up in the course of their retreat from the devastated base. Had their footsteps been enough to cause the old sign to collapse like that? He was pondering other possibilities when the sand beneath Donnely began to vibrate.

Something gleaming, metallic, and snake-like slithered out beneath him. Exhibiting reflexes fast enough to bring tears to the eyes of the most demanding drill sergeant, the Irish-American sergeant whipped his gun downward and fired off a concentrated burst. Sand erupted in all directions, and the thing disappeared. *Gone?* Lennox wondered.

His question was answered an instant later as Skorponok exploded from the dry ground. Sand flew in all directions as the barbed metal tail curled around the startled Donnely's lower legs and yanked him off his feet. Flipping the soldier upside down in midair, it grabbed him anew and vanished back beneath the surface. The young sergeant hadn't had time enough to scream.

Lennox did. *"Move move move!"*

He and the remaining members of the squad broke into a mad sprint toward the village. They gained a moment or two before the metal scorpion shape erupted from the ground behind them a second time.

Inside the village boundary dogs appeared, barking like mad. Horses and camels reared and bolted in all directions, adding to the confusion. Rounding a mud-brick wall, Lennox howled at his men.

"You two, cover the road! Epps, take point! Fig, you're eyes in the back! Everyone, *watch the ground*! Try to stay off the sand and on the rock!"

Soldiers took up defensive positions behind the mud walls. Appearing out of nowhere, an older man ran toward them. Probably Yemeni, or maybe Somali, Lennox thought absently as he took the measure of the newcomer. Espying Mahfouz, the man swerved in the youth's direction. Their attention on other matters, Lennox and his colleagues ignored the reunion of father and son.

"Where have you been?" the man inquired anxiously in Arabic.

"At the base. It's gone, Papa. All gone! Something destroyed it, in spite of the Americans' weapons. It was killing everybody, blowing everything up. Not terrorists, I think. Something different, like out of Hell." Turning, he pointed toward where Lennox crouched behind an ancient whitewashed wall. "I didn't know what to do or where to go. These men saved my life, Papa!"

The bearded elder glanced over at the American captain. "Better you had stayed away from them and kept your nose in the Book!"

Despite his terror, Mahfouz was indignant. "I attend to my studies! Ask the mufti. And I do my chores. After that, my time is my own. And there is nothing in the Qur'an against taking chocolate from visitors."

Listening to the familial byplay had stimulated Lennox's far-from-fluent but moderately competent Arabic. Glancing occasionally at the deceptively quiet ground on the other side of the wall, he looked back and yelled as politely as he could, "Sir! In the name of the Prophet, praise be unto him—*do you have a phone?*" At that moment Skorponok exploded from the sand almost directly in front of the wall.

"Lay down fire!" Lennox yelled as he followed a beckoning father and son toward one unremarkable whitewashed building among many. Each soldier promptly let loose with whatever armament he happened to be carrying. The metal arachnoid shape responded with bursts of white-hot plasma that erupted against walls, sand, and the buildings behind, vaporizing everything with which they came into contact.

The interior of the old building had been competently fixed up and decorated with a raft of salvaged and scavenged materials. As befitted the detritus of a society suddenly become wealthy beyond imagining, some of the castoffs were practically brand-new. Such was the case with the cell phone that the father grabbed from a desk and passed to the frantic American officer. It was a standard commercial phone, and he dialed rapidly. When the international operator answered, Lennox had to shout to make himself heard over the staccato reverberations of the gunfire and explosions outside.

"A T and T," the voice declared in heavily accented subcontinental English, "how may I direct your call?"

"International to the United States," Lennox yelled. "This is an emergency Pentagon call, *class A!*"

"Your cell service does not include long-distance minutes, sir. Do you have a major credit card?"

Lennox had to force himself not to crush the slim phone in his fist. "*Listen carefully to me:* I need you to put me through *now.*"

"I will be most happy to connect you, sir. Preferably without the yelling, *and* with a major credit card."

Uttering an oath sufficiently universal in tone and nature that both accommodating father and son could easily understand the gist of it, Lennox whirled and raced back outside.

The prospect from the exterior of the house was not good. Bullets merely deflected off the scorpion-thing's metal hide. As Lennox dove for cover, Figueroa took aim with a grenade launcher and let loose. Sand and gravel flew in all directions. More accustomed to handling paperwork than RPGs, the warrant officer bawled in frustration.

"I hit it—I hit the son of a bitch, but the freak thing won't go down!" As Figueroa stood staring in disbelief at the rapidly recovering monster, Lennox sprinted up to him and spun him around. One desperate stare met another.

"I need a credit card!"

"Wha?" Figueroa blanked for a moment, then shook his head apologetically. "My wife cut 'em up, Cap. I thought I came out ahead on that one."

Crap! Leaving the warrant officer to reload in his wake, Lennox looked around wildly until he spotted Epps. Heedless of his own safety, the tech sergeant was still on point, firing furiously at an agile, dodging target that refused to succumb to the blazing crossfire.

"Come on, sucker!" Epps was screaming at the top of his lungs and blasting away madly as Lennox slid to a stop alongside him. "Tear your metal ass up!"

From the open cell phone held in a death grip in Lennox's left hand, a voice exclaimed rather sternly. "Sir, I appreciate that you are having some kind of difficulty, but there is no need for that kind of language."

"No, not you, not you!" the captain howled at the phone. *"Hang on."* Grabbing Epps by the shoulder, he turned him around to face him. "Your wallet! I need your wallet!"

To his credit, Epps barely blinked. "Back pocket!"

Yanking out the battered wallet, Lennox rolled to one side as balls of plasma hissed past overhead. "Hello!" he yelled at the phone. A waterfall of static crackled back at him. "Oh *no*. Do you hear me now?" While waiting for a response he fumbled through the surprisingly large packet of cards contained in the wallet, studiously ignoring the ones featuring nude women on the reasonable assumption that they had been issued by institutions other than major international banking concerns.

"Got it," he wheezed gratefully as a basic Visa fell into his hand. As fast and clearly as he could, he rattled off the numbers into the phone. "And *don't* tell me you don't take it."

"Of course we take it, sir." The operator's tone was calm and reassuring. "Would you like to hear about our Premium Plus World Service Package? Five hundred award points gets you a free shiatsu massage at the participating hotel of your choice—and from your continuing tone may I say that it is my personal opinion that you could definitely benefit from this special limited-time offer."

"Put the damn call through now!" He passed the phone to Epps. "Here! Pentagon!" As Epps swapped his weapon for the phone, Lennox set himself up and began unloading clip after clip in the direction of the relentless mechanical monstrosity.

It was equally frantic but considerably less noisy in the Washington, D.C., exchange room. With advanced communications down, multiple lines manned by studious, well-trained operators were busily being manually routed across the country and to every continent. One operator barely had time to murmur "Pentagon Emergency Line" when a frenzied voice on the other end howled "United States Air Force officer and team under hostile unidentified fire in Qatar, east of recently attacked SOCCENT base, relay position to National Military Command!"

As earth and stone erupted around him, Epps tried to shield the phone's pickup from as much of the destructive din as possible. Ominously, less and less of the clamor was coming from nearby as one soldier after another was taken out by a weapon the likes of which the tech sergeant had never encountered. Containing his fury, he concentrated on making himself understood over their only lifeline to the outside world.

"Troops in contact mission, unknown freakin' aggressor! Need gunships on station ASAP, everything you can send this way." A readout on the phone's miniature screen drew his attention. "*And* I got a low battery!"

Using more initiative than he had in his entire career, the panting staff sergeant snapped to attention opposite the secretary of defense. Thankfully, it had taken only a moment to locate Keller in the swirl of activity that filled the intelligence center. The soldier did not even wait for his arrival to be acknowledged. Having spent time under fire himself, he fully comprehended the urgency in the voice he had heard on the phone.

"Mr. Secretary, sir! We're presently tracking a special ops team under fire in Qatar. They say they're survivors of the attack on the base."

Keller frowned. "Forensics says there were no survivors."

Soldier and secretary locked eyes. "This sergeant I had on the phone says otherwise—sir."

Keller's expression tightened. "I appreciate your take on the situation, Sergeant, but we still need confirmation before we can act. Reactionary elements in the Qatari government are already threatening to throw us out if there's any more trouble. We can't just go in and shoot up another piece of desert unless we have a damn good unassailable reason. What's the nearest in-theater AWACS?"

As soon as the Predator reconnaissance drone crested the scrub-spotted hill its camera locked on the images of the firefight directly ahead. Banking sharply to its left, it began to circle the field of battle while keeping as much of it as possible sharply in focus. On board the AWACS plane airborne just off the Qatari coast, the drone's controller adjusted the unmanned aircraft's angle of approach even as he relayed what it and he were seeing back to Washington via the hurriedly launched new communications satellite.

In the intelligence center, the staff sergeant who had alerted Keller touched a finger to his earpiece to make sure he was hearing correctly before reporting to the secretary.

"AWACS has visual, sir. Coming online now. I can't vouch for the strength of the signal: it's a new satellite and we haven't had time to test—"

An impatient Keller cut him off. "Put it on the monitors. Whatever we've got."

The sergeant relayed the order. Oversized screens that had been full of statistics went blank, only to brighten with a flurry of thermal signatures. Most were clearly human. The other was . . .

Keller stared at the outline of what appeared to be a gigantic yet nonorganic scorpion. "What in God's name *is* that?" His reaction, if not his exact words, was echoed by everyone exposed to the real-time images that now dominated the room's multiple screens.

When the mud wall they had been shielding behind was disintegrated by successive bursts of plasma, both Epps and Lennox had to beat a hurried retreat in search of fresh cover. With buildings collapsing or being blown to bits all around him, the tech sergeant somehow managed to keep the cell phone in the vicinity of his mouth. It was hard enough to hang on to it, much less keep talking as he ran and dodged.

"Roger—hello? *Hello?* Oh *no*—do you hear me now—hear me now? Shit, *hear me now?*" Once again something intelligible crackled from the speaker. "*I got you, I got you . . .*"

Plasma touched down and blew a crater in the ground just to his right. Instead of sprinting in the opposite direction he held his ground. Move again and he might lose the signal for good.

"Roger that," he barked into the phone. "Seven-man team north of orange smoke, plenty of dust and fire signals." Another chunk of barren soil vaporized off to his left, and he flinched. "Whoa, almost lost my head! Attack directions west, you're cleared hot." His gaze shifted toward the cloudless, burning blue Arabian sky. "This will be danger close, but we got no choice. We're getting sliced and diced here!" The reply made him smile. Seeing the captain glancing in his direction, Epps shot him a thumbs-up and raised what was left of his increasingly hoarse voice.

"GOT A BEAM-RIDER INCOMING! LAZE TARGET!"

As the word was passed around, the surviving soldiers

fanned out, all trying to aim their laser designators at their attacker from different directions. The more options they gave the approaching aircraft, the more precise the strike would be. Which, considering their own inescapable proximity to the intended target, was a concern very much on everyone's mind.

The red beams that crisscrossed the scorpion-thing were instantly picked up by the designators in the cockpits of the two low-flying A-10s. In the lead fighter, the pilot acknowledged them gratefully. It was always useful when someone else marked the objective for you.

"Warthog One to base, we've acquired target."

All of the firing and killing Skorponok had unleashed had been in search of a single device. The deaths of so many resident organics were incidental and of no consequence. The Decepticon regretted only the amount of time and effort it was being forced to expend. The humans were determined fighters, but the negligible weapons they carried constituted little more than an irritating inconvenience.

Finally locating the apparatus for which it had been searching, the mechanoid took careful aim and fired afresh. The human holding the desired device went down, and the instrument spilled from his pack. Gratified, the Decepticon started toward the place where it lay unprotected on the sand. It was time to terminate the farce and move on to matters of considerably more significance.

"Hogs One and Two," the pilot of the lead fighter declared systematically, "locking on."

As the first to see the incoming missiles, Lennox had just enough time to yelp, "The heat's coming!" as he dove over a low embankment fronting a shallow gully and tried to bury himself in the sand deeper than the deadest pharaoh. Outraged earth erupted behind him as missiles from the Warthogs hit home. With the last clods and bits of sand and soil still raining down around him, he raised his head for a look.

The missiles had dug an impressive hole in the center of the village. But to his horror and disbelief, a by-now-all-too-familiar mechanical shape was angrily clawing its way out of the cavity.

"*No way.*" It was as much a curse as an expression of disbelief. Scanning the ravaged surroundings, he spotted the tech sergeant pressed up against a still-standing building and shouted in his direction, "Still not down, Epps!"

Staring back at his superior, Epps nodded his understanding and yelled into the phone. His message was relayed halfway around the world and almost instantly back again.

"Spooky, thirty-two: use one-oh-five shells. Bring the rain!"

A droning roar made him look up. Lennox did likewise, as did every one of those still able to do so.

"Oh crap," Lennox murmured—but not unhappily. Rising, he ran like hell. Not for cover, but away from the location of the scorpion-thing. Anywhere away from the scorpion-thing.

Lumbering through the superheated air, the AC-130 gunship unleashed a six-thousand-round-a-minute storm of sabot rounds at the metallic shape clearly visible on the ground below. Sand vaporized, rock disintegrated. A miniature artificial sandstorm engulfed the fleeing soldiers.

On the screens at the Pentagon the attack played back like outtakes from a bad movie. Like everyone else, an anxious Keller was mesmerized by the white-hot thermal signature that had overwhelmed the view from the circling reconnaissance drone.

"What happened? Did we lose them?"

Still standing alongside the secretary, the staff sergeant who had brought the initial news once more addressed his headset pickup.

"Warthog One and Two: do you have a visual on the soldiers? Over. Report on survivors, over."

In the absence of wind, it took a moment for the dust to settle. When it had cleared enough to see again, Epps peered around the building behind which he had taken shelter. Something was moving in the center of the hell that had been unleashed by the gunship. Their mechanical nemesis, still standing.

But . . .

It was stumbling around, clearly in distress. As he looked on, the tip of its metal tail fell off, seared from the rest of the body. Dipping its head, it dropped back into the sand and—disappeared.

"Man," he muttered to himself as he cautiously stepped away from the building that had protected him, "that is one *freaky* machine."

There was a rumble as one of the A-10s did a flyby directly overhead. Closer, another shape materialized out of the smoke: Captain Lennox. Officer and noncom exchanged exhausted, somber grins.

Soaring past, the Warthog's pilot returned his gaze forward. "Copy, base. We got 'em. Swinging around to do a count." The slow-flying antitank fighter banked sharply as its pilot brought it around for another look.

Completely winded, Lennox sank to his knees. Around them villagers began to emerge from hiding. Officer and noncom were inordinately relieved to see that Mahfouz and his father were among them.

The captain's respite lasted only until he remembered something else. Where was . . . ?

Figueroa was stumbling toward him, breathing hard. Part of his uniform was tinted a nonregulation red, the dark stain spreading fast. Forcing himself to his feet, Lennox raced over to his friend. Figueroa smiled back at him, started to give the thumbs-up, and collapsed. Seconds later Lennox was kneeling beside him. The stain—the stain was too broad, too big.

"Stay with me, oh man—*stay with me*." Looking back the way he had come, he screamed frantically at Epps. "Get a med-evac down here *now*!"

Sam wasn't screaming. In fact, he was lying in his bed, in his room, in his house, having recovered just enough awareness to wonder if the events of the previous night had all been a dream. Or maybe the overbearing cop had been right all along and he *had* accidentally ingested one of Mojo's pills.

Better not to contemplate that particular possibility just now, he decided. Not with his mom standing in the open door staring worriedly back at him. She was smiling—that same familiar, comforting smile doting mothers bestow on teenage boys that somehow manages to communicate both their concern and the fact that they still regard their male offspring, no matter how competent and mature they might be, as actually no more than nine years old.

"Hi, honey. Wanna talk about it?"

"No," he mumbled, still half asleep.

"Well," she continued encouragingly, "I'm home if you want to . . ."

"No."

"Okay." The smile faded somewhat, disapproving. "I'm going to the market. I won't be gone long." The implication of that announcement being clear—*Don't do anything foolish while I'm away*. "Can I get you anything special?" He shook his head *no*. She gave it one more maternal try. "Want to talk about it?"

He inhaled room air. "Mom. Seriously. I'm fine, don't worry. Go do your shopping."

"Okay." It was a reluctant acknowledgment that there was nothing more she could do. Or rather, that there was nothing more her son was willing to let her do. "Love you, honey." She turned and headed for the stairs. After waiting a long moment Sam rose from the bed and followed, moving slowly enough so that he would not catch up to her.

The worst of it was that a part of him wanted to.

As intended, he arrived in the kitchen as his mother was backing her car out of the driveway. Thankfully she didn't look toward the house, in his direction, so he did not have to duck back out of view and hide himself as if he really were guilty of having done something wrong. Wiping at his sleep-stained eyes, he zeroed in on the refrigerator. He was taking inventory of the contents on the second shelf when the staccato bark of Mojo strenuously objecting to something unseen interrupted contemplation of potential nourishment.

"Shut up, Mojo," he yelled, too tired to care if the dog actually heard him. Milk, he thought. Milk was good. Milk was safe. Milk was unlikely to turn into something alien before his very tired eyes. Generations of Witwickys would approve of his choice. Also, milk required no preparation. He took out the container, closed the fridge, and staggered toward the stoop on the side of the house. It was always in the shade and would be a nice, cool place to sit and sip the container's safe and sensible contents. Something massive was blocking the view, pressed right up against the driveway door.

His Camaro.

Screaming, he dropped the milk and stumbled backward. Cow juice splattered across the floor. Grabbing a cordless phone from its wall mount, he dialed wildly as he ran. Miles, bless him, was home.

" 'Lo?" his friend's voice responded unassumingly.

"Miles, it's me! I thought maybe it was a dream. It's *not*. It's real. It's *alive*." Looking back over his shoulder he was relieved and almost surprised to see that the den was still empty. He'd half expected to see the car trailing him, pushing and shoving furniture aside like some gigantic chrome-and-steel dog, a big red metal tongue lolling from somewhere in the vicinity of the front grille. "Miles, I bought Satan's Camaro!"

Giving a bath to a two-hundred-pound mastiff is a project on the best of occasions. Trying to cradle a cell phone against one shoulder and maintain a conversation while wrestling said dog, shampoo, clumps of sodden dog hair, and brush in the other hand is truly a task that verges on the impossible. An octopus would have had difficulty attempting to manipulate everything. No cephalopod he, Miles was left to struggle against the soggy reality.

"While I have you?" he replied snappishly, "thanks for

the ride *home* yesterday. You know how many drivers will stop to pick up a lone teenage male hitchhiker after dark? Can you count to zero?"

"Dude, I'm sorry, but *listen*." Pressed against a wall in the hall, Sam kept peering fearfully around a corner in the direction of the kitchen. "My car, it stole *itself*. It went for a walk and now it's back. It's trying to kill me! I think—*it wants my soul*."

Hands full of giant wet dog, Miles still managed to shake his head sadly without losing control of the phone. "Whatever, dude. D'you have my crickets? I don't like the way A-Rod is starting to look at my fingers."

The enormous mastiff let out a proportionate fart. Caught off-guard, a recoiling Miles fought to wave it away. "Mason, *no*! Bad dog! What'd you *eat*? You've been digging up dead things in the creek again. I own a freakin' dog ghoul. Oh my God, *I can't see*. Got an environmental disaster here, Sam—notify the EPA!"

Sam looked to his right. No headlights stared in at him from the vicinity of the front door. The route was clear. For how long would it remain so? He had no intention of waiting around to find out. Steeling himself for the forthcoming dash, he whispered urgently into the phone. "Miles, I'm coming over. *Don't go anywhere*." Before his friend could reply (or object), Sam pushed the phone's OFF button.

He fled from the house. Lawn to the left of him, rosebushes to the right of him. Nothing materialized to contest his flight. Only when he burst out onto the front steps did he remember that his bike was locked up back in the garage. He'd put it there himself. After all, what did a man who owned a '75 Camaro need with a *bicycle*?

The only transportation in immediate reach was his mom's bike. It was pink. There could be no more un-equivocal proof of his desperate state of mind than the fact that despite its damning color he did not hesitate to pick it up, jump onto the saddle, and pedal madly away.

VII

The house was not very big and its location beneath one of the capital's main bridges left a good deal to be desired, but at least it was a *house* and not a cookie-cutter cubbyhole apartment or town house adrift in one of the city's sprawling complexes. The yard could have used some weeding, and a paint job was a couple of years overdue, but otherwise it was well maintained. Better than some of the buildings in the same neighborhood. The taxi that pulled up in front of the modest out-of-the-way structure disgorged a single passenger before driving off.

The fence was unlocked. Maggie could hear the TV braying loudly inside as she hurried up the steps. CNN's coiffure-of-the-month was declaiming sonorously from the deck of an aircraft carrier. She was old enough to remember when it had been a news channel instead of just another commercial-focused entertainment spin-off. Still, it was the best of a bad assortment.

"Jeffrey Abrams reporting, a hundred miles from the Yellow Sea," the reporter was saying. As she approached the front door she decided that he spoke almost as if the news he was reporting was nearly as important as he was. Almost. "Though the North Korean government continues to deny any involvement in the unprovoked attack on a U.S. base in Qatar, they insist that continued aggressive American posturing in what they regard as their immediate theater of interest could lead to war. Meanwhile the Chinese military high command . . ."

An irritated Glen Whitmann did his best to ignore the persistent ringing of the doorbell. He was deep into Warcraft and heavily engaged online with both allies and enemies. The wish-power he had accumulated, however, had no effect on the front door. The bell refused to shut up. Angrily he froze his positions, pushed aside a pile of empty burger wrappers, and headed for the front of the house, determined to see off whatever solicitor or lost soul was so insistent on interrupting his daily recreation.

As soon as the door was halfway open Maggie pushed past him. Though she ignored the fact that he was dressed only in T-shirt and boxers that did not keep him from blushing.

"Maggie, what . . . ?"

"Can I come in?" she asked, halfway to the kitchen.

He whirled away from her, put his hands over his privates, decided that only served to draw further attention to his current state of dishabille, raised his palms, tried casually lowering one to the vicinity of his groin while offhandedly holding the other indifferently upright, and finally gave up and followed her, his escalating indignation outweighing his misplaced sense of modesty.

"No—what? *No.*" He tried to intercept her, failed. "This is my private area back here."

A voice boomed in no-nonsense tones from the rear of the house. "GLEN, WHO IS IT?"

He responded in kind—or at least as near to in kind as

his less-well-developed vocal cords could manage. "HOLD ON, GRANDMA! IT'S NOTHING!" Apprehensively, his gaze returned to Maggie. "What're you doing *here*?"

She pivoted a quick circle, her expression reflecting her instant assessment of her present surroundings. It was not favorable. "You gotta help me with something."

His initial annoyance immediately gave way to a look of fear. He took a step back, his tone wary. "*No,* uh-uh. Been there, done that. I'm not getting fired for you."

"GLENNNN! GLENNY!" a voice for the ages (or at least for the TV age) thundered from somewhere off to the east.

He looked worriedly toward the kitchen. "*Leave,* you're giving the poor old woman a heart attack!"

Clad in a bathrobe of Turkish cotton that only *looked* as if it dated from the time of the Ottoman Empire, curlers in her hair, face cream adorning her cheeks and forehead, the object of his concern strode into the front room. The woman favored the green-haired visitor with a brusque up and down before inquiring curtly, "Who's she?"

"No one, Grandma," he replied soothingly. "Just a friend."

The old woman sniffed succinctly, snapped "Use a condom," and turned to leave.

He did not quite whine. "You're like a scary, old public service announcement. Can't you just go?"

She disappeared into the next room—and just as abruptly popped her head back out. Her expression was dark, like a winter front rolling in off the Chesapeake.

"Are you playing those video games again? You're a grown man! Waste of time."

"It's *research*," he argued unconvincingly. "For my *job*!"

Ignoring his shabby protestations, she nodded sharply in the direction of the TV. "Turn that off, I'll make you a grilled cheese sandwich." Her gaze swung sideways and came to rest on Maggie. "Does your girlfriend want one?"

Glen spun a half circle, helplessly throwing his arms wide. "She's not my—"

"A grilled cheese sandwich would be awesome, Ms. Whitmann," Maggie replied agreeably.

Lowering both his head and his arms, utterly defeated, Glen made a last feeble attempt to assert at least a tiny bit of control. "And, uh, be sure to cut off the crusts."

Maggie smiled at him. "Compulsive-obsessive."

He shrugged weakly. "Maybe so—but it gets me grilled cheese sandwiches."

Behind them his grandmother coughed for attention, nodded in the direction of Maggie's feet, and disappeared into the kitchen. Glen turned to face his guest.

"Take off your shoes and stay on the plastic runners. Grandma's weird about feet touching carpet."

She nodded as she reached down to remove first one shoe, then the other. "Mud?"

He shook his head. "Microbes. Bugs. Anthrax spores." He nodded in the direction of the kitchen. "She listens to too much news. Not good for a woman her age. Too unsettling."

"She doesn't strike me as particularly unsettled." Maggie took a seat on the couch. "Glen, we have to talk. No one's better at signal decryption than you. You're the only one genius enough to understand what I'm talking about."

His brows drew together as he stared back at her. "Did you just flatter me by flattering your*self*? Woman manip-ulator! *Out!* Get out!"

The neon-colored mini flash drive she pulled from her bag all but twinkled in the light from outside. Rising and coming toward him, she held it between thumb and forefinger as she waved it slowly back and forth, taunt-ing him.

"C'mon now, Glenny. 'Fess up. Don't you wanna see something *classified*?"

Hands held defensively in front of him, he backed away from her. "No. Yes. No." He couldn't take his eyes off the drive's bright color. He was clearly struggling with his inner self—and he lost. Halting, he tried to ana-lyze the drive with only his eyes. "Like how classified?" he inquired hungrily.

She grinned broadly, waving it in his face. "Like I-could-go-to-jail-forever-if-I-show-you classified." With-drawing temptation, she slipped it back into her bag and gave a disarming shrug. "But that's cool, whatever. I'll show it to somebody else, get their opinion—"

"Nonono, wait!" he pleaded, hating himself as badly as any addict reduced to imploring his dealer for a fix. "Maybe just a quick look at the file headings—"

"Great," she responded briskly, "let's do it." Batting aside his questing fingers she hurried over to his outsized computer complex and plugged the drive into the nearest USB slot. Eyes bugging, he started toward her, his tone verging on the hysterical.

"DON'T TOUCH THAT!"

Before he could reach her she had moved the mouse and the screensaver had appeared. He stopped dead, she stared. The image filling the screen was her, modeling for a calendar several years before, posing in a bathing suit while cuddling a pug dog. Leaning forward to block his view of the monitor, she turned to glare at him.

"What is that doing on there?"

He swallowed hard, forced a grin. "What? What's your problem? I love pugs! Always have, always will—the cute little fellas. 'Course, Grandma won't let me keep one in the house. Dirt, bugs—you know."

The concentrated bolts of destruction that leaped from her eyes might not have been detectable by ordinary means, but he felt their impact nonetheless. "Get it off before I tell your grandmother!"

Easing her away from his keyboard he hastened to comply, wondering whether a quick death would be preferable at her hands or those belonging to his mother's mother.

Many years had passed since anyone knew exactly how many corridors there were in the Pentagon. It all depended on how you defined *corridor* versus *accessway* or *chamber*. At the moment, Keller was interested only in the one he was traversing, and in his intended destination. Though much younger than the secretary of defense, the aide who was accompanying him had to break into an occasional jog to keep up with his boss.

"One of the special op'rs got a thermal snapshot of whatever it was that hit the base, but the imager was damaged in the subsequent firefight. We're working on trying to recover the content now." Before Keller could comment, they were intercepted by a breathless security agent.

"Sir, we have a serious internal security issue. Severity has not been determined. But circle logs indicate that one of the analysts on site made a copy of the initial network intrusion signal."

Keller looked resigned. "Let me guess. Maggie Madsen?"

The agent was suitably surprised. "Yessir. How'd you know?"

A wan smile. "I'm psychic. It's a secretary-of-defense thing. I suppose you've initiated an appropriate follow-up?"

"Yessir. Standard procedure. As is letting you know."

Keller nodded. "Keep me informed. And please try not to shoot anybody until I've had a chance to talk to them."

Any other time, Maggie's physical proximity as the two of them leaned close together to study the monitor would have jangled Glen Whitmann's nervous system from head to foot. It was difficult to say whether it was to his credit or his detriment that he hardly noticed her nearness as he worked to decipher the information that was coming up on screen.

He was duly impressed. "Never saw anything like this anywhere, ever. Signal strength's through the *roof*. Through the roof and through the ionosphere." He glanced sharply over at her. "Where'd you say you got it?"

Somehow, her reply managed to be simultaneously informative and evasive. "This hacked the Military Air National Guard frequency in less than sixty seconds."

"No way," he shot back.

"Yeah, I know, been there already. No way, but there it is. You're not the only one who's never encountered anything like it. It's driving everybody in cryptanalysis nuts trying to unravel just the core algorithms. Where could it have originated?"

He shook his head in wonderment. "Artoo-Detoo?"

"Seriously," she chided him. "This is serious stuff, Glen."

"Artoo damn Detoo," he reiterated, more forcefully this time. "How should I know?" He waved a hand at the impossibility being served up on the monitor. "I mean, it stinks visually of some kind of assembly code, but there's an elegance to it no programmer could compile. It's like—poetry."

She pursed her lips and considered a moment. When she spoke again her voice was devoid of sarcasm. "Just so one of us finally says it out loud, because it has to be said out loud—are we seriously talking about, like, a kind of alien machine communication here?"

He didn't miss a beat. "Who says life on other planets has to evolve with the carbon atom as its nexus? Why not silicon? Or a synthesis of both? Or something we can't imagine because it's—alien. Wait a minute." Turning back to the monitor, he pushed his face as close as he dared to the continuously cycling recording. "Looks like—there's something embedded in the signal. Chocolate chip in the middle of the cookie."

She joined him in staring. "Maybe it's the file they hacked, locked in sequence. I know you can't do anything with the rest of the noise—yet. But if that's an identifiable human-sourced file, can you maybe open it?"

He was already typing furiously, his fingers machine-gunning the keyboard as deftly as any concert pianist performing Rachmaninoff. He worked without looking up at her. "How'd you get into computers, anyway?"

She shrugged. "Had a stutter when I was a kid. I was afraid to talk out loud. Keyboard did the talking for me. Didn't make fun of me, didn't point fingers, just did as I asked." One cheek was starting to twitch: another memory from childhood. "Whatever, I don't wanna talk about it."

"Too late," he told her. "You shared."

She turned away from him, unhappy with herself. "Well, I take it back."

"You can't." He tried not to sound triumphant. "That's why it's called sharing. Hey . . ." He indicated the screen. Decoded, a file name appeared.

PROJECT ICE MAN—TOP SECRET SCI— SECTOR SEVEN ACCESS ONLY

They gazed at it together. The file title was simple and straightforward, and made not a whit of sense to either of them.

"Project—Ice Man?" Maggie mumbled. It sounded like a title for a new Saturday-morning kids' cartoon series, not something fit to draw the attention of National Security and hypothetical alien machines.

Glen had moved on. "What's Sector Seven? Sounds innocuous enough." Skillfully, he worked the mouse. More information unscrolled on screen. Included among it was, insofar as they could tell from a quick overview, a complete history of Arctic exploration, including foreign sources as well as those in American English. He frowned. He knew all about Peary and Amundsen and Scott and especially Matthew Henson, but he'd never heard of the man who seemed to be repeatedly featured: a slightly addled-looking elder seaman.

Peering over his shoulder, Maggie was equally puzzled. "I recognize the names of some of these other dead guys, but who's Captain Archibald Witwicky?"

Before they could discuss further the apparent importance of the unfamiliar sea captain, the front door flew open behind them and what seemed like an entire division of FBI agents burst into the house. Maggie and Glen found themselves thrown to the floor before they could voice so much as a hello. One agent efficiently secured her wrists behind her back with soft handcuffs as his partner stood over her and recited methodically.

"Maggie Madsen, you have the right to remain silent. Anything you say can and will be used against you in a court of law."

Seeing Glen being treated even more roughly off to her right started her screaming. "He's not a part of this! It's me, all me!"

"What is this?" Glen tried to protest. "Do you have a warrant? What's going on?" A higher voice, stemming from a higher power, reached him where he lay on the floor. It emanated from the vicinity of the kitchen. "Grandma, it's okay, calm down!" Try though he might, however, there was no moderating the agitation in that rising bellow.

"TELL THEM TO STAY ON THE PLASTIC!"

Pedaling furiously on his mom's bike toward his best friend's house, it ultimately occurred to Sam to look behind him. He didn't want to, but he felt he had no choice. It would have been better for his already disturbed state of mind if he had trusted his instincts.

Sure enough, there was the Camaro, trailing him while maintaining a distance of about a block between them.

"Ohgodohgodohgod," he breathed fearfully as he raced around a corner, not daring to look back to see if he had managed to lose his car. Glancing back, he whipped around a second corner.

In the process nearly running over Mikaela as she was coming out of the Burger King with friends. At the last possible instant he managed to swerve, rather neatly avoiding her but alas, not the tree that took her place immediately in front of him. He slammed into it and went down, tumbling off the bike and landing hard on his side. Aware that he was under surveillance, he scrambled to get back on his feet.

Mikaela, thankfully, was more concerned than angry. "Oh my God! Sam?" A wide grin spread across her face. "That was *awesome*."

He took an unsteady step and nearly went down again. "*Feels* awesome."

Her look of admiration turned to one of concern. "You hit pretty hard. You okay?"

Beyond her and up the street the Camaro was easing into view. It stopped partway around the far corner. Idling. Probably sizing him up. Still dazed from the collision with the tree, he felt sure he could hear it growling softly.

"No, not okay! Losing my mind. Gotta go!" Not even trying to hide his terror, he yanked the bike upright and sped off as fast as he could push the pedals. Mikaela's friends began whispering among themselves. She ignored them, choosing instead to follow Sam until he had pedaled out of sight. Something was definitely wrong. It had to be, for him to risk being seen in public on a girl's pink bike.

She wouldn't find out what was the matter standing there swapping giggles and goggle-eyes with her "friends." Her Vespa was parked nearby. Sliding onto the seat, she keyed the ignition and pulled out into the street— barely avoiding being run over by the police cruiser that came screaming past, its sirens howling. Breathing hard, struggling to maintain her balance on the scooter, she found that she was too stunned by the uncharacteristic near miss to hurl insults at the rapidly receding cop car. It had gone by her so fast that she had barely had time enough to catch a glimpse of the forward-facing, expressionless, neatly mustachioed driver.

How Sam ended up in the parking lot under the freeway overpass he was not sure. He knew only that he found himself wishing he had turned right instead of left at the last main intersection. On the other side of the lot a familiar yellow Camaro kept pace easily, paralleling his progress. Straightening and rising out of the bike seat, he used his weight on the pedals, putting everything he had into a last-ditch effort to lose his tormentor.

So focused was he on the Camaro that he failed to see the police car that had parked directly in front of him. The driver's-side door swung open sharply, and he ran right into it. This time he hit the ground much harder than he had in front of the Burger King. Wincing in pain, he slowly peeled himself off the pavement. Fear gave way quickly to anger as he stumbled around to the front of the cruiser, unaware as yet that the vehicle he had run into was a police car.

"That *hurt*. That was *so* lame. This is like *the worst day ever*!" As his vision cleared the details of the vehicle began to register and his mood changed dramatically from anger to thankfulness. "Oh, Officer, *thank God*! You're not gonna believe this, but my car's trying to kill me." The vague shape seated behind the wheel did not move, did not respond. Sam squinted, his perception slightly blurred by the lights revolving steadily atop the cruiser's roof.

"Hel-*lo*? Are you listening to me?" Still no response. Fear and frustration overcoming good judgment, he slammed his fists down on the hood. The police car responded by jerking forward and knocking him backward. Sitting on the ground, the car looming over him, it struck him that he might have acted a tad rashly.

"Sorry," he began, genuinely scared, "no disrespect inten—"

Before he could finish, the headlight covers swung open and the glaring bare bulbs telescoped outward like the illuminated heads of a pair of glassy eyeless serpents, halting only inches from his face. Seconds later they rose skyward as the rest of the car transformed into a sixteen-foot-tall bipedal loosely humanoid robot. Enormous metal fingers reached downward.

Scrambling backward, he somehow skidded just out of their reach as the blunt tips slammed into the asphalt. Pavement cracked, spiderwebbing in all directions away from the metal fingertips. On his feet now, Sam found that he was not nearly as fatigued as he had previously thought. He was running like hell, running for his life. When he looked back over a shoulder, he saw that the thing was coming after him.

"OH SHIT! OH SHIT! OH SHIT!" His repeated exclamations might not have been graded well in debate class, but they fully expressed how he was feeling at the moment.

Swinging around and down in a broad, swift arc, the gigantic hand struck him square in the back and lifted him right off the ground, sending him flying into the windshield of a parked car. Glass cracked underneath him. Badly bruised, Sam slowly turned on the hood as the robot—that was the only definition for it that came to what was left of his mind—stomped toward him. If he'd had any energy left, he would have started crying.

"Bad dream, bad dream," he mumbled over and over. "Pleasepleaseplease lemme just *wake up*!"

He tried to shrink back into the splintered but not shattered windshield as the mechanism that had taken the name Barricade leaned over him. Massive metal fists smashed into the car on either side of Sam, effortlessly mashing fenders and support steel, splintering plastics and shattering glass. This destruction was accompanied by a pair of awful, loud *bangs*—the front tires exploding. Following which Sam was sure he heard a voice. Though the words that reverberated in his ears were perfectly lucid and understandable, they contained not a shred of humanity.

"ARE YOU 'USERNAME' LADIESMAN TWO-SEVENTEEN?"

"What?" His heart threatening to explode out of his chest and make its own way toward the street, Sam had no choice but to meet that overpowering artificial gaze. "I—yeah?"

"WHERE IS EBAY ITEM NUMBER TWO-ONE-ONE-FIVE-THREE?"

"Uh duh wah . . ."

Clearly patience was not among the personality traits that had been programmed into this particular robot. If possible, its tone turned darker and even more threatening.

"WHERE ARE YOUR ANCESTRAL ARTIFACTS?"

"I—I—have n-no idea what you're ta-ta-talking ab-about . . . ," he managed to stammer.

The enormous, mallet-like fists rose into the air again. Sam started to close his eyes. His calf muscles twitched, he swallowed air—and leaped onto the roof of the badly damaged car. Sliding down the rear window and off the lid of the trunk, he hit the ground running. Emitting a metallic snarl, the Decepticon reached down with one hand and contemptuously flung the car aside as it started after its fleeing quarry.

Sam's legs were rubber, his muscles Jell-O, his lungs on the verge of collapsing. He had about one block left in him, he knew. He still had half that left when he staggered around a corner and for the second time in less than an hour nearly collided with Mikaela. Only this time, she was on her Vespa. All three hit the ground together.

"Ow, my arm!" she blurted. Almost at the same time, she recognized who had nearly run her over. "Sam? What the hell's *wrong* with you? What's going *on*?"

"MIKAELA, YOU GOTTA GET UP, GOTTA GET UP NOW! MIKAELA, SERIOUSLY, RUN!"

She might have done so had her eyes not suddenly caught sight of the massive mechanical shape that was lurching directly toward them. Her lungs, however, had no trouble responding. The immediate signal from her brain said *Scream,* and she proceeded to do exactly that.

Sam had just taken her by the arm and was trying to drag her away when another machine roared into view: the Camaro. He barely managed to yank her out of its path as it did a forty-mile-per-hour power slide and smashed sideways into the oncoming metal behemoth, knocking it into a skid across the asphalt. Both passenger doors swung open as the song "Rescue Me" blared from the car's speakers. Adding emphasis to the music's message, the car's horn began honking incessantly.

Across the pavement, the enormous robot was rising to its feet. After everything that had happened this morning, Sam's decision was not an easy one to make, but he felt he had no choice but to worry about it later. If there was a "later."

"GET IN THE CAR!" he yelled at Mikaela.

Entering from opposite sides, they dove into the front seat. As soon as they were in, the doors slammed behind them and the Camaro burned rubber peeling out. Falling behind, Barricade swiftly transformed back into its police cruiser persona and gave chase.

Not-police-car pursued not-Camaro through a manufacturing district that had seen far better days the previous century. The same neglect was evident in the vestiges of tracks and train yard that had once served the skeletal steel remains of now-silent industries. Anyone looking on would have seen an ordinary police vehicle chasing a beat-up old muscle car.

At least the police car was relatively ordinary until the side panels on the cruiser rose up like wings to reveal launching pods beneath each cradling metallic arc.

Explosions boiled up on either side of the Camaro as it swerved and dodged. Inside, Sam and Mikaela did not so much cuddle as get thrown into each other.

"This isn't happening this is *not* happening!" she was screaming.

Try as she might, she could not convince Sam. After all, he'd had plenty of practice not believing in what was happening long before she had even become involved. He tried to take control. But no matter how hard he gripped the steering wheel, it simply slid through his fingers. He was reduced to pounding on it and shouting.

"Whatever, whoever, *wherever* you came from, just goooo!"

If possible, their eyes grew even wider than before as the Camaro approached a very solid-looking dead end. Both teens squeezed their eyes shut in anticipation of the imminent impact. But at the last possible minute the Camaro spun a perfect 180, turning to face the oncoming police cruiser.

Sam opened his eyes, wished he hadn't. "Bad idea, bad idea! Such a bad idea right now!"

Tires squealed as the Camaro lurched forward. The police car did not slow a tick, continuing to launch small and very deadly missiles as it came onward. One sped past the evading Camaro's left wheel as it avoided the oncoming projectile with preternatural nimbleness. Sam's head snapped around as he caught a glimpse of the receding contrail.

"Was that a *missile*?"

"Yeah, I think so!" Mikaela mumbled numbly. A building detonated behind them and came crashing to the ground. Twisting around in her seat she returned her attention forward. Her tone was unchanged. "Uh-huh, yes, definitely a missile."

At the last instant, both vehicles swerved, missing each other by millimeters. It was difficult to say which was louder: the squeal of sliding tires or the screams of the Camaro's two terrified occupants. Screams gave way to grunts as doors opened and they found themselves ejected. They scrambled to stand up and would have run in any direction—except that they found themselves mesmerized by the sight that was unfolding immediately in front of them.

Emitting muted grinding and squealing noises, the Camaro was morphing right in front of their eyes. No changing in the shadows now, no attempt at subterfuge or mechanical dissembling. The robotic shape that emerged from the bulk that had been the Camaro was still the same light-blindingly bright yellow. It even sported, albeit in a radically different configuration, the black racing stripes that had originally caught Sam's attention.

The robot charged at the simultaneously transforming Barricade. Unfortunately for the temporarily riveted teens, they happened to be standing directly between the two clashing machines. As the robots slammed into each other, a section of the erstwhile police cruiser's chest popped opened to reveal an inner compartment. The compartment was not empty.

Springing out and away from the main combat, Frenzy's spidery form clutched at the clothes of the two beleaguered young humans and spun them around. Sam's transformed Camaro interceded immediately to protect them, knocking Frenzy aside while taking the brunt of Barricade's charge, which sent the yellow robot tumbling backward. Rolling onto its feet, it charged straight at the transformed cruiser. As Barricade was knocked askew, one of its massive metal legs swung around parallel to the ground, swooshing through the air just over the ducking humans' heads. Sam and Mikaela rolled and scrambled to put distance between themselves and the battling machines.

At least, Mikaela did. Something was holding Sam back, preventing him from fleeing. Looking around, he found himself eye-to-lens with a mechanical nightmare that had secured a firm grip on his jeans and was pulling him close to its insect-like jaws.

"Get it off, get it off! He's got me, I'm gonna die!" Like Mikaela could do anything, he told himself wildly. The Terminator she was not. His frenzied, rapid kicks glanced off the indifferent mechanical monster. All that kicking did, however, allow him to wiggle out of his jeans. Freed, he managed to get to his feet. In shoes, socks, and boxers he turned to run after Mikaela. Unfazed, the mechanoid promptly leaped onto his back and head.

"HEY!"

Staggering under the weight of the clinging robot, Sam did not have time to wonder where Mikaela had found the power saw. Looking past her, he saw an open chest from which a dozen other tools protruded like metal flowers. Given a choice of the available gear, he would have opted for the oversized hammer. Did that make him less masculine than Mikaela?

Deep psychological issues were not on her mind as she came forward, holding the howling saw out in front of her. "Why don't you come after *me*, you anorexic metal *freak*!"

Responding to the more dangerous threat, Frenzy let go of Sam and leaped at her. Mikaela swung the saw wildly. Since she had no idea where it was going to go, the robot had no way of predicting its arc. Amazingly, it made contact. There was a brief but very loud grinding noise. One of the attacking robot's arms went flying. Having picked up a loose length of rebar, Sam charged the machine from behind and began battering wildly at the bot's head. No one was more surprised than he when the protruding appendage came loose. A couple more hacking swings and it lay on the ground, severed from the main body and twitching spastically. Sucking in air in long, pained gasps, Sam stood over it. He could not have put into words how good, how great, how freakin' wonderful it felt after being chased all day to have finally been able to fight back.

Well behind them now, Barricade had transformed back into a police cruiser. Employing the added velocity of its adopted terrestrial form, it burned rubber and charged. The Camaro-turned-robot waited, waited—and then stepped aside. At the same time it undercut a nearby crane. Hanging from the crane's arm was a solid steel wrecking ball. The crane missed the oncoming Barricade, but the wrecking sphere did not. It smashed square into the roof of the charging cruiser, stopping the vehicle as cold as if it had run head-on into a solid wall. Flashing police lights and their protective plastic splintered and went flying in all directions.

Ignoring the vehicular mayhem taking place behind him, Sam glared down at the twitching mechanical form. "Not so tough without a *body,* are ya?" He took a victorious kick at the head he had just detached.

Both kick and victory turned out to be premature. The metal mouth promptly clamped down onto his foot. Dancing around in a panic, he tried to dislodge the clinging metal skull.

"Get it off, get it off!"

Coming loose, his shoe went flying with the bot head still firmly attached to it. Mikaela came up beside him.

"Sam—*chill*! It's okay, it's off." She leaned around to stare into his face. Eyes met. Chaos and cataclysm receded—a little.

They realized that the sound of metal-on-metal combat had stopped. Both turned toward the place where the two much-larger skirmishing robots had rolled while they had been battling the spider-thing. A shape began to emerge from the dust and wreckage, coming in their direction. Sam held his breath, then slowly exhaled.

The shape was the color of the sun. A black-striped sun.

Standing over the now-silent scene of battle, the robot reached down to pick something out of the dirt. Extending a limb, it offered this to Sam. His jeans. Filthy and torn, but an improvement over his boxers.

"Uh, thanks." Awed by the machine standing silently only feet away, he hurriedly struggled back into his pants. Next to him, Mikaela's stare as she gazed up at the mechanoid was no less rapt.

"What *is* it?"

Sam had already come to a decision. Maybe it wasn't founded on solid science, but it was good enough for him. And there was no one around to contradict him.

"Looks like a robot. Moves like a robot. If it could talk, I have this feeling it would talk like a robot. So I think it's a robot. But like—superadvanced. Way beyond the stuff they use to assemble cars or sell in RadioShack. Probably Japanese," he decided impulsively. "Gotta be Japanese. They *love* the things." Full of wonderment, he took a couple of steps toward the hulking machine.

Mikaela gawked. "*What are you doing?* This thing didn't come out of a cereal box!"

Gleaming yellow, the robot responded by taking a step toward the approaching Sam. The head inclined downward in his direction. Sam found himself smiling. He'd been wrong from the get-go. His car hadn't been trying to hurt him. It had been doing—something else.

"I don't think it's gonna hurt us."

Mikaela's eyes kept flicking between her companion and the massive machine that was now standing within arm's reach. "Oh yeah? You speak 'robot' now? 'Cause this one just participated in, like, a droid *death match*. Maybe it's only intermission. Maybe we're the second round."

"No." For the first time all day, Sam's voice was normal, relaxed. Reaching out, he extended a hand toward the 'bot.

As they stared at the robot and Sam reached out to experimentally caress its gleaming metal skin, they failed to notice the lights that sprang to life within what for the past several moments had been a dark, inert skull. Sprouting tiny centipede-like legs, the decapitated head rose up slightly to take stock of its surroundings. Its attention fixed on an object that had been dumped in the dirt: Mikaela's purse. Skittering over to it, Frenzy's head began to transcan the contents. Lipstick, useless. Glasses, no good. Pen, insufficiently complex.

Sidekick. Limited storage capability, small and decidedly primitive, but sufficiently adaptable. As soon as it completed the transcan, Frenzy kicked the actual device into a pile of rubble and out of sight. Transformation ensued. The result was that it became an exact duplicate of the now-banished device. Unseen, it worked its way into the open purse like a tarantula backing into its lair, withdrew its legs, and went dormant. Like the rest of its fellow Decepticons it had waited for the forthcoming Resolution for thousands of years.

It could wait a little longer.

Sam and robot stared at each other as a still-uneasy Mikaela looked on.

"What now?" she murmured curiously, never taking her gaze from the machine that loomed over them.

"I think—I think it wants something from me." His attention focused on the dark lenses that seemed to stare back into his own eyes.

"Like what?" she whispered. "What could something like this want from someone like you?"

"I'm not sure." He looked over to where the erstwhile police cruiser lay silent and unmoving beneath the heavy wrecking ball. "But the other one kept asking about my eBay page."

As much as she wanted to, she was unable to make sense of his reply. "What's up with *that*? You selling batteries or something?"

Cocking his head to one side, Sam studied the robot's head. "Can you—talk? Communicate? In words we could understand?"

The yellow apparition shook its head from side to side. That, at least, was comprehensible enough, Sam thought. So, too, was the voice of an unknown DJ that suddenly poured forth from within the machine. "XM satellite radio, a hundred and thirty digital channels of nonstop, commercial-free music, news, and entertainment!"

"I think it talks through the stereo," Sam told a staring Mikaela. "Or at least, it can channel commercial broadcasts and try to filter content to convey what it means." In response, applause echoed from the robot.

Nothing to lose by trying to get some more information, Sam decided. "What were you doing out last night? I thought you were being stolen. I followed you and saw you send something up into the sky."

The sound of a radio evangelist's sermon filled the air. "And a mighty voice will send a message, summoning forth visitors from Heaven!"

Sam considered the possibilities. "You were calling someone? Or trying to?"

Mikaela found herself falling for the same notion. "'Visitors from Heaven.'" She cast an involuntary glance skyward. "I don't think it's Japanese, Sam. I don't think it's from anywhere on our world." She looked back at the silent machine. "What're you, like, an alien or something?"

The machine—the individual—nodded and emitted a brief electronic squeak. As they stepped back and looked on, it shrank, shifted, transformed. Moments later, sitting before them once more was a by-now-familiar yellow Camaro. The doors swung wide and the horn beeped insistently.

"I think it wants us to get in." Sam started toward the waiting vehicle.

Mikaela hesitated. "And go where?"

He glanced over at her. "I don't know, but think about it. Fifty years from now when we're looking back on our lives, don't you wanna be able to say you had the guts to get in the car?" Advancing, he put a hand on the open driver's-side door. It looked and felt exactly like a car door. "Besides, if it wanted to hurt us, why transform back and invite us to go for a ride? Why not stay all-robot and stomp us into the dirt right here?" He slipped in behind the wheel. Carefully, he took it in both hands. It remained steady and unmoving beneath his fingers.

Mikaela considered. It was still very empty in the abandoned industrial park. Looking around, she reached down and picked up her purse, then climbed in on the passenger side. The re-formed Camaro roared to life and headed out of the empty lot. As it left it sprayed gravel all over the motionless police cruiser where it lay smashed and unmoving beneath the heavy wrecking ball.

Once back on a busy city street, the Camaro slowed to comply with the prevailing speed limit. Tentatively leaning forward, Mikaela let one hand slide back and forth over the dash in front of her. Stained and sun-bleached, it felt exactly like dried-out old car upholstery.

"Wait a sec." Even as she found herself addressing the car in which she was riding, she worried that somehow, somewhere, someone else might be listening. But the concern did not stop her. "If you can, like, reshape yourself, why'd you pick such a hoopty?" She eyed the scruffy interior. "I mean, you could be anything, right? So why this? Why not a Hummer, or a Ferrari?"

Brakes squealing, the car skidded to an abrupt halt. Both doors swung open, the car tilted sharply from side to side, and its occupants found themselves unceremoniously, though gently, dumped onto the pavement. Sam rose, started to brush at his clothes, and stopped when he realized the futility of the gesture. Plutonium couldn't get his torn jeans clean.

"*Great*. You hurt its feelings."

She stepped back, away from the car. "What's it doing now?"

As they looked on, the car's windshield morphed into a screen. Imaging beams scanned the street, bouncing from car to car, traveling farther than either of the occupants could see. They settled on a brand-new, fully customized Camaro GTO. Simple scanning beams were replaced by more complex transcanner waves. A moment later and the Camaro was transforming again, reshaping itself before Sam's and Mikaela's wide eyes. Metal contorted, flowed, folded in upon itself. But not into the shape of a robot this time. When the process finally concluded, it was a different vehicle that stood before them. An exact duplicate of the distant GTO, except for one difference. It was the same bright yellow as before and sported identical black racing stripes.

Mikaela's expression did a little transforming of its own, changing from one of awe to outright admiration. She took a step toward the freshly morphed vehicle, admiring it openly.

"Now *this* is a *car*."

Sam couldn't repress a huge grin. Other than the fact that he had been arrested and accused of being a dope addict; chased by his own car, which he was sure was intent on killing him; attacked, interrogated, and nearly killed by a giant alien robot—life had never been better.

Mikaela turned to him. "It's waiting on us. Where're we going?"

Walking back to the driver's side, admiring every glimmer of light bouncing off the blemish- and ding-free bright yellow paint job, Sam slid in behind a shining custom steering wheel. "I'm not sure about the final destination, but I think I've found my adventure."

Metal of a different kind blasted from multiple speakers as the transformed car sped off. On the front seat Mikaela slid a little closer toward Sam. Her purse lay between them. Picking it up, she tossed it casually into the backseat.

Intent on each other, on the wicked performance of the transformed Camaro, and on the road ahead, neither driver nor passenger noticed the glowing eyes that peered out over the rim of the purse.

☗ VIII ☗

Except for a Spartan metal table and its attendant chairs, there was little in the room. It had been laid out to accommodate people but not to comfort them. Quite the contrary.

Two of the chairs were occupied by Maggie Madsen and Glen Whitmann. The table was occupied by a plate of doughnuts and other pastries, a pitcher of water, and some glasses. Enough time had passed for Glen to have worked his way through five of the doughnuts. While not his beloved Fruity Pebbles, they had sufficed for a temporary sugar fix.

"Look," he whispered to her, crumbs dribbling from his chin and lower lip as he spoke, "do not say one word. I know how these guys work. It's just like in the movies. They're gonna try and play us against each other. And don't fall for the good cop, bad cop thing. We gotta stick together, okay?" He reached toward the plate. "Bear claw?"

His hand froze halfway to the pastry as the room's single windowless door opened, admitting light and an FBI agent from the hallway outside. The visitor was big, his expression intimidating. His resolve crumpling like a Twinkie, Glen quickly pushed himself and his chair away from his associate.

"Oh, *she* did it!" he declared, pointing. "She's the one you want! *It's all her.* I'll turn state's evidence, wear a wire, whatever you need!"

Maggie whirled on him, outraged. "You freak!"

He was practically blubbering now. Or on the verge of throwing up. Or both.

"I'm not going to jail for *you,* or anybody! I haven't done anything really bad in my entire life!" His voice fell to a self-pitying whisper. "I'm still a virgin! Okay, maybe I downloaded thirty-two hundred illegal songs off Napster and hacked the CIA once—okay, a *lot*—but all I wanted was a free badge, I'll give it back and—"

"GLEN, SHUT UP!" Maggie roared.

Normally that would have worked. In a Starbucks, at work, in a taxi, on the street, he would have complied, would have zipped his lip. Being handcuffed, arrested, and thrown into a government interrogation room without being told what the charges were against him, however, had stiffened his backbone somewhat—even if the stiffening had come about because he was frozen with fear.

"No, *you* shut up! *Criminal!*" He blinked suddenly and had to grab at the table to steady himself. "Whoa, something—in the doughnuts . . ."

She shook her head at the sad sight he presented. "Yeah—*sugar.* You ate like *twelve!*" Without missing a beat she turned to the agent, who had been observing the byplay with the same phlegmatic detachment as the recording device he no doubt wore concealed somewhere on his person.

"Listen *to me,*" she growled dangerously. "They downloaded a *file;* something about some old sea captain named Witwicky. Glen and I found it embedded in the material that was downloaded. I don't know what it means, but if it's that important to whoever's behind all this then it's important to *us*. And while I'm no linguist, I don't think *Witwicky* is a Korean or Russian or Chinese name. You gotta tell Keller before we go to war with the wrong country!" The agent did not respond, and his expression did not change. Next to her Glen was surreptitiously searching his pockets for a pain pill. Her teeth clenched as she regarded him with a mixture of pity and contempt.

"If you throw up, man, it better be in a direction I ain't."

The completely done-over Camaro finally pulled to a stop at a pullout on the highest road near town. Doors opened and the two passengers climbed out. Sam expected the car's intermittently edifying radio to offer up a suggestive song, or at least an informative one. But the speakers stayed silent.

Mikaela stayed close, but not as close as Sam would have liked. He didn't press matters. For one thing, he was afraid that if he took her hand she would take it right back. For another, he was plain afraid to try. Figuring that at this point he was way ahead of the game, he chose to walk alongside her while maintaining a respectful distance. Look but don't touch. For now, at this time of day, that would do. Watching her, he was filled with the same degree of wonder he had felt when his car had stood up on two transformed legs. Just a different kind of wonder, that's all.

Head tilted back, she was staring up at the night sky. "Uh, Sam . . . ?"

Reluctantly, he looked away from her and upward. Blobs and streaks of light were illuminating the clouds from within. There was no thunder, so they could not be caused by lightning. Which meant they had to be caused by—something else.

"That just doesn't look right," he heard himself murmuring.

As they both looked on, what appeared to be a small comet struck the atmosphere sharply, shattering into five pieces. Or perhaps *shatter* was a disproportionate description. *Separate* would have been more accurate. It was also impossible. Comets did not *separate* when they struck atmosphere.

One segment of whatever it was slammed into the hillside atop which they had parked, barely a couple of fields away. Trees snapped, brush ignited, and dirt and rock flew in all directions as the piece of sky ground to a halt. The force of the impact shook the ground beneath their feet. Instinctively, Mikaela grabbed Sam and clutched him tightly. He responded automatically. Only when the piece of comet had come to a complete stop did they realize what they were doing. The same thoughts occurring to them simultaneously, they hurriedly parted and stepped back from each other.

"Sorry," she mumbled, unsure why she was apologizing.

Sam couldn't meet her eyes. Wanted to, but couldn't. The feel of her against him still lingered in his mind. "It's cool," he stammered. As they considered what had just happened and how to proceed, other pieces of the mysterious falling object were drawing attention elsewhere.

From patrons to participants, the attention of the crowd in the packed stadium was drawn away from the game being played down on the field and upward toward the flaming object that seemed to pass directly overhead, to crash into the ground not far away.

In a café in town two teens the same age as Sam and Mikaela were clowning around with each other and with their food as a third friend filmed them with a compact video camera. The background changed radically when the windows imploded as something massive and glowing slammed into the street. While his friends screamed and panicked, the youth with the camera rushed toward the confusion to try to get it all recorded. Instead of flames and fear, his thoughts were filled with visions of network exposure and large royalty checks.

On another, lower hillside in an exclusive subdivision a peculiar thunderclap roused a five-year-old girl from her bed. Walking to the window of her bedroom, she was just in time to see something splash into the family pool, sending chlorinated water and a couple of inflatable water toys flying in all directions. Eyes widening, she whirled and raced back to her bed. From beneath the pillow she pulled out a single baby tooth, held it up, and smiled broadly as she inspected the wayward dentition. Her grin unequivocally revealed the tooth's recent previous location.

This time Sam and Mikaela experienced a good deal less anxiety if no less amazement as they watched the Camaro transform itself back into the robotic humanoid shape. With the mechanoid leading the way, they followed a trail of flaming brush and vitreous scree down the hill until they came to a ditch where one of the falling stars had landed. When they finally reached the site, nothing concealed the still-smoking object from their view.

Mikaela came up close to Sam. "Y'know, maybe we should be walking fast *in the other direction.*"

Pushing aside the few branches that had not been

snapped off or stomped flat by the yellow-and-black robot breaking trail in front of them, a thoughtful Sam disagreed.

"I think if there was any danger, *he* would have stopped us from coming with him."

"Oh, that's fine," she shot back. "I didn't realize you two were on speaking terms now." She eyed the back of the powerful machine. "Especially since it—since he can't speak."

"C'mon," he urged her. "Aren't you curious to see what he is?"

"I'm curious about how an acetylene torch works, too," she murmured tensely. "I just don't go sticking my nose into the flame."

The argument ended then, because they had reached its source. Embedded in the earth at the bottom of the ravine and directly in front of them, a complex knot of steaming metal dripped white-hot silvery beads. Standing yards away, they could feel the heat coming off the object. As they looked on, the globs of liquid metal retraced their path, blending back into and being absorbed by the globe much as a ball of pure mercury would soak up smaller spheres. When the glistening orb began to crack open like a giant metal egg, the two teens stepped back behind the yellow robot they now thought of as a friend and protector.

From within the sphere a metallic leg emerged. It was followed by a second, then by a pair of arms. A silhouette began to rise, higher and higher against the still-flaming, crackling scrub, until it was nearly thirty feet tall. Unmoved by the sight, their own mechanical companion stood nearby, as if waiting for something more. Despite what he had told Mikaela earlier Sam began to wonder if maybe they ought to start looking for some bigger trees. Just in case they had to take shelter behind something other than his transformed car.

The immense shape that had emerged from the silvery egg started to turn toward them. Its attention was drawn away from the two teens by a blast from an eighteen-wheeler barreling down the road above the ravine. Turning in the direction of the sound, the newly arrived alien mechanoid instantly and efficiently transcanned the big truck as it slowed to take a sharp curve. The process did not affect or alert either the truck or its oblivious driver. By the time the night-running transport had sped on past, a second, identical truck was facing Sam and Mikaela from the depths of the ravine.

Okay, he found himself thinking with a detachment that stunned him. *So Camaros aren't the only thing these creatures can change themselves into.* From within the ravine the "truck's" engine growled. It sounded just like a Detroit diesel, only with something added, he decided. It was diesel-plus. Diesel transformed.

Angry diesel.

The downtown street being vacant, there was no one to admire the exotic sports car as it rotated slowly on the turntable in the showroom window. Lumbering up to the glass, the alien exoskeleton was clearly not a potential customer. Not to purchase, perhaps, but in this case to copy. Transcan beams swept over every inch of the low-slung vehicle, recording it down to the last molecule of overpriced paint.

Farther up the street, curiosity having overcome their fright, the teens in the café had joined their cameraman-wannabe companion in rushing toward the place where the flaming object had touched down. It would have been hard to miss the huge fiery hole that had been blasted into the side of an old electronics shop. They arrived at the same time as fire trucks and ambulances. Ever thinking, the youth with the camera was panning across the scene, taking in the confusion, the busy emergency teams, the badly damaged building.

"Hey, maybe it's a meteor!" he blurted suddenly. "Pieces of meteor are worth a lot of money." He would have put his camera aside and gone in search of potentially valuable fragments except that the heat emanating from the building prevented anyone from going inside. Around him and his friends, firefighters were unsnaking hoses and readying protective gear preparatory to searching the interior. *Gonna get all the good stuff for themselves,* the budding cameraman found himself thinking sourly.

One of his friends was pointing. "Something's moving inside. There, *look*."

The shape he indicated was massive and unidentifiable. They caught only a glimpse of it before dark smoke boiling up from the flaming interior of the structure blotted out their view.

"What is it?" the youth with the camera wondered aloud. More movement—something coming *toward* them. He and his friends started to back up. "Oh God," he muttered, "what *is* that?"

It was—an emergency vehicle. Bursting out of the smoke, it hung a hard right and took off up the street. Given the angle at which it heeled over, careening crazily for an instant on only two wheels, all three gaping kids found themselves praying that there were no patients inside. They needn't have worried.

Within that particular ambulance, which was an exact

duplicate of another emergency vehicle that had arrived just a few moments earlier, there was no inside inside.

Warm mist rose from the expensive swimming pool behind the expensive house in the expensive suburb. Oblivious to all the expense around her, a little girl presently short one tooth but full of excitement pushed open a rear door and hurried out onto the concrete patio. That it was presently soaking wet with displaced pool water only added to her anticipation.

Swathed in steam, a dark shape loomed before her, rising slowly and compellingly from the depths of the pool. Straightening its legs, it towered above her. Utterly unafraid, the girl approached with one arm extended to offer up her recently departed tooth.

"Daddy says I get five dollars—but I want twenty."

Ignoring her, the robot's head swiveled to the right. The first mobile mechanism its detectors locked onto was a big black dually pickup truck parked in a nearby driveway. Stepping out of the pool, it pushed aside a pair of mature fruit trees and smashed through the fence separating the girl's property from that of the neighbors.

By the time the girl's parents finally stumbled out the back door, the massive apparition was no longer visible.

Still half asleep, they could only eye their sodden, ruined backyard in shock. Bending, the mother picked up an inflatable inner tube that boasted a bright green horse head and child-sized handles.

"Holy God," the girl's father exclaimed, *what happened to the pool?*"

His daughter turned to him. There was no alarm in her voice, only confusion—and obvious disappointment.

"The tooth fairy drank it!"

A sudden throaty *roar* caused her parents to look up and toward the street—where the back end of an over-sized black GMC pickup was visible screeching toward the first intersection. Even in the darkness they could see that it looked exactly like the one that belonged to the Camberwells next door.

Having climbed back up to the road, it struck Sam that maybe he and Mikaela ought to keep moving—preferably toward town. Or maybe to higher ground. But having climbed out of the ravine with them, their "friend" the yellow mechanoid was now holding his ground, unlike back in the industrial park where he had instantly swung into action against the now-you-see-it, now-you-don't "police cruiser." So despite his uncertainty Sam stayed where he was. It was a long way back to town in any case, and he was reluctant to abandon his car. Even if he did have the awkward habit of sometimes turning into a giant robot. Mikaela stayed, too. Maybe similar thoughts had occurred to her. Or maybe she stayed because Sam did.

Ascending from the ravine, the eighteen-wheeler rum-bled across the road and halted less than a foot from the two teens. Its grille alone was considerably bigger than they were. Sam could have reached out and touched it. He did not because right there, directly in front of them, it transformed a second time.

As he observed the process Sam realized that he had been witness to three other metamorphosing alien ma-chines: his car, the police cruiser, and the crazed spider-thing he and Mikaela had beaten to bits. None of them was anything like the towering, radiant, bipedal mechan-ical life-form that stood before them now.

Wondering what came next, his and Mikaela's attention was drawn down the road in the direction of town. Based on his experiences with the Camaro, the sound of approaching vehicles should have caused it and the giant that had been the truck to seek cover, or at the very least to transform back into their vehicular shapes. Instead they remained exactly as they were, in their natural bipedal forms.

They were soon joined by as peculiar and unrelated a trio of vehicles as one could expect to find gathered together in the same place. There was a beautiful sports car, an emergency vehicle, and the baddest-looking pickup truck he'd ever seen.

That's it, he decided suddenly. *Earth's being invaded by alien car buffs.*

But that didn't explain the Camaro's present bipedal shape, or for that matter the eighteen-wheeler that had turned itself into the colossus standing before him. Considering his and Mikaela's near demise at the hands of the rabid police cruiser–bot, such reasoning was also more than a little too flippant. He excused the frivolous thought by reminding himself that it had been kind of a rough day.

Anyway, he was by now sufficiently familiar with the process of alien transformation, if not exactly jaded by it, for his breathing to remain steady as the three new arrivals simultaneously transformed into upright robotic shapes. He stared harder. Something was happening to the machines' eyes. Or perhaps what he and Mikaela were seeing was the reflection of some complex inner process.

Standing in a silent semicircle, the alien quintet picked up the nearest Wi-Fi broadcast from town and went online en masse. As the two teens looked on, the towering machines proceeded to download nothing less than every piece of information available on the entire Internet.

It did not take them very long at all.

When they had finished absorbing everything there was to know, the monolith that had been the diesel inclined toward the two teens and said something. While not an electronic squeal or an edited radio broadcast, it was still gibberish to a bemused Sam. Not, however, to Mikaela. Banes was full of surprises, he reflected.

"Was that—Chinese?" she suggested. "Classical Mandarin?"

"I dunno, but it would make sense," he agreed. "If I was a new arrival on a new world, I'd start by trying to speak the language used by the largest number of people."

Their brief conversation was all that Optimus Prime needed to identify their modulated verbal exchange as English. He lowered his head farther toward them. Since it was a good deal bigger than the two of them put together, they started to freak out a little. The voice that emerged from the massive head was carefully muted, designed to reassure and not frighten.

"Do not fear. Freedom from fear and all else is the right of all sentient beings. We will never harm humans."

Okay, Sam thought, recovering a little of his previous poise. "Glad to hear it. Excellent policy. Stick to that as much as possible. 'Specially when it involves me." He remembered his companion for what had been an— unusual—day. "Or her."

It was a good thing he remembered to include his companion for the evening. The look she had been giving him until he did include her was capable of doing serious damage of a different kind.

The immense machine straightened, looming high above them. "Samuel James Witwicky? Biological descendant of Archibald Witwicky, captain of the wind-powered liquid water–traversing vessel *Discovery*?"

"Y-yeah." Sam wondered if he was doing the right thing by replying in the affirmative. It was too late to ponder alternatives now: that train of thought had already left the station.

"I am Optimus Prime," the robot announced.

"A pleasure—I guess. Um, you speak English, too?"

"We have assimilated Earth's languages through your planetary information assembly. Your 'World Wide Web,' as it is called." A pause. "We did this just now. It was not difficult. The information is extensive, but the underlying conceptualizations are quite undemanding."

Sam was shaking his head slowly in wonderment. "You *are* aliens. Uh, are you 'biological' creatures, too?"

"No," the robot informed him quietly. "We are independently cognitive mechanical entities from a very distant world—a suitably simple comprehensible identifier for you might be *Cybertron*. Similarly, you could also think of us as autonomous robotic organisms."

Mikaela was murmuring to herself. "Autonomous robots—*Autobots*."

Enormous lenses focused on her. "Just as there are no apposite translations for where we originate or what we are, there are none for our individual nomenclatures."

"You mean," Sam hazarded, "your names?"

"Yes." An immense arm indicated the semicircle of other machines. "For convenience in communication we have selected namings from your vocabulary to approximate a combination of our localized camouflaged shapes as well as our particular temperaments. Though by your definition we are no more than 'machines,' we do possess individual characteristics and personalities as well as abilities and skills. For example . . ." The arm lowered to center on the robot that had morphed from an exotic sports car.

"My first lieutenant: *Jazz*."

The car's high-powered speakers responded agreeably. "Greetings, terrestrial adolescent humans."

Smiling and blissfully ignorant of whatever proper protocol should be followed at such a moment, Sam and Mikaela both waved. Sam felt a little silly. Also over-awed. It seemed to go down well, however. Optimus Prime indicated the thickset bipedal form that had transformed from the black pickup.

"Our weapons specialist, originally forged in the Tri-Peninsular Torus states of Praxus: *Ironhide*."

The robot peered down at his gleaming black shape. "This exoskeleton appears suitable for battle."

Finally, Optimus Prime singled out the mechanoid that had morphed from an emergency vehicle. "Our medical officer, chief emissary to the High Council of Ancients: *Ratchet*."

Emerging from the robot thus identified, a holographic medical beam passed harmlessly over both Sam and Mikaela. Or perhaps not entirely harmlessly. Within the light of the beam, both stood revealed briefly in their underwear.

"*Whoa,*" Sam blurted, simultaneously outraged and—buzzed. Seeing herself revealed, Mikaela had spun away from him, clutching at herself.

"*Hey!* Scanning people like that is *not* cool."

"Uh, yeah," Sam agreed, not entirely convincingly. "It's, uh, not cool at all."

Thus reproved, the medical robot bowed slightly in

Mikaela's direction. "I extend greetings and also apologies for the misunderstanding, immature female."

"*Hey now . . . ,*" she started again, her momentary embarrassment swiftly replaced by something resembling mild outrage.

Ratchet continued. "I am pleased to report that, by your species' customary but inadequate standards, you and your male companion are both in an excellent state of health."

"Oh, well, then." Her indignation subsided. "Thanks, I guess."

Feeling he needed to say something, Sam took a step toward the medical-bot. "Uh, the female's name is Mikaela Banes."

It was Optimus who responded. "Understood and logged. Mikaela Banes." The great mechanical arm gestured one last time at the imposing semicircle of machines, singling out a by-now-familiar yellow-and-black shape. "You already know *Bumblebee,* guardian of Sam Witwicky."

Sam frowned. "Bumblebee? Guardian?" Something unpromising about that. Against what did he need to be guarded?

He was distracted from his concern as Muhammad Ali's voice blared from Bumblebee's speakers: "Float like a butterfly, sting like a bee."

This response caused Mikaela to put a question to the largest robot. "If you and the others can talk, why can't he?"

It was the medical mechanoid who replied. "His vocal-processing symbology was destroyed on the battlefields of Tyger Pax. Despite our best efforts, we have not been able to restore it. There are programmatical complexities involved that you would not understand."

Sam nodded. Whenever the matter of his ignorance regarding these beings came up he was in complete agreement. There was a lot he did not understand—though he desperately wanted to.

"Why—why are you here? Why come to our world? Surely not just to play at changing back and forth between vehicles and your actual forms."

Optimus Prime's voice grew solemn. "You are quite correct, Sam Witwicky. We are not 'playing.' We have come in search of what I will categorize for you as the Energon Cube. This unimaginably ancient entity is the container of a supreme power that imbues us with the gift of—for you I will call it simply 'spark.' This designation is an oversimplification an order of magnitude and significance far beyond your ability to comprehend."

"Another way to explain it," put in the medical mechanoid helpfully, "is to say that it is the life force that exists within all—since you employ the term so frequently in relation to our elastic adaptations you may as well continue to utilize it—within all Transformers."

"We are here in search of it," Optimus Prime continued, "because we must find the Cube before Megatron."

Sam stared. It seemed that every time something was explained to him, instead of becoming more enlightened, his ignorance doubled. "Who—or what—is a Megatron?"

The enormous mechanical paused before answering. Besides providing elucidation, his tone demonstrated that the huge machines were capable of emotion as well as reasoning. Certainly there was no mistaking the regret that underscored his reply.

"We were once brothers, in the sense that you understand the term. But Megatron lost his way. It was no longer enough for him to control himself. He became obsessed with the idea of controlling everything. He turned those he could dominate against those he could not. Instead of builders, they became destroyers. For their betrayal of everything that our kind had always stood for, those who turned now bear the name *Decepticons*."

From his eyes a three-dimensional image appeared in the clear night air: a view of an incredible battle taking place on an alien world composed of metal and other nonorganic compounds. As the view shifted, Sam and Mikaela were exposed to scenes of flaming craters, destruction on an unimaginable scale, mile upon mile of total devastation. The surface was littered with limbs and heads and other pieces of lifeless machines. And everywhere there was fire, and smoke, and death. Though his earlier query had been innocent enough, Sam now felt worse for having asked it.

Optimus Prime and his companions were definitely not "playing."

The view shifted again, to show a ship descending. Its physical appearance was like nothing the two teens had ever seen—or ever imagined. In the process of touching down it *transformed*. Though seen only from behind, the immense outline managed to convey an aura of overpowering menace. Standing over one crippled Autobot, it reached down and plunged a fist into the other's metal chest. Steely fingers yanked back, wrenching out a handful of flickering energy. Alien though the action was, its straightforward brutality caused both Sam and Mikaela to gasp. The pulse of energy rapidly faded to nothingness, as did the light in the lenses of the robot that lay dying on the ground.

"For eons," Optimus continued, "our world was locked in the stalemate that resulted from Megatron's actions. Two equal and opposing forces frozen in interminable battle. The endless combat all but exhausted our resources and nearly extinguished our kind. Those few who survived finally decided the only way to put an end to it was to flee." A deafening bellow emerged from the figure identified as Megatron as the final image faded.

The robot identified as Ironhide supplied further enlightenment. "Only the Cube can reanimate our race, allowing us to repopulate our world, for it alone is capable of energizing Transformers. That is why Megatron desires it. With it in his possession, he will at last obtain the absolute power he has always sought over the future of our kind."

Once more, Optimus Prime took up the account. "In the course of eons of fighting, the Cube was flung out into space. I and my companions as well as Megatron and his ilk have been searching for it ever since. We have finally succeeded in tracing its present position to your planet." Sam and Mikaela exchanged a look as the mechanoid continued.

"When it crashed here it transmitted a signal. That signal took a long time to reach the scattered remnants of our pitifully conflicted world. Megatron was the first to follow it here, pursuing it immediately after it was cast out of Cybertron. Only by a stroke of great good fortune was his arrival imperfect and on a part of your world suitable for delaying him. He succumbed to ever-shifting ice."

Sam's eyes widened with recognition. "*The ice man.* Wow, so when my great-great-grandpa died screaming in that nuthouse, he was telling the *truth*."

"If I follow your inferences correctly," Ratchet responded, "then yes, that was indeed the case. Unfortunately, your ancestor's discovery and subsequent physical encounter triggered a tiny part of Megatron's hitherto dormant internal configuration."

"Your records indicate," Jazz continued, "that the resultant luminal reaction destroyed your ancestor's simple organic oculars. But it apparently left a coded physical imprint as well."

Sam blinked. "What d'you mean 'coded physical imprint'?"

"On his portable prosthetic lenses," Optimus explained.

"His . . ." Thoughts swirled inside Sam's head, finally coalescing into a blinding flash of realization. "*His glasses? The map to this Cube is imprinted on his glasses?* But—how'd you know all this? Or that I was even related to Great-Great-Grandpa Archibald, or that I even *had* them—his spectacles?"

Ironhide explained. "eBay." Snatches of World Wide Web flashed briefly across his lenses.

"*No way,*" Sam exclaimed.

"The Cube still resides on your world," Jazz continued. "But we can no longer detect its signal. It has been—blocked by something."

Mikaela was trying hard to keep up. "Blocked? By what?"

"We do not know." Ratchet managed to sound a bit sorrowful. "But if we find it we will return it to our homeworld."

"If the Decepticons reach it first," Optimus added, "they will use it to rebuild their armies. They will begin this process by transforming Earth's machines. Once that is accomplished, there will of course no longer be any reason or need for your world to continue to provide support and sustenance to irrelevant carbonoids. Megatron will see to it that these wasteful life-forms are extinguished."

"Excuse me?" Sam murmured uncertainly.

"Plants. Animals. You."

A significant silence ensued. It was only broken when Mikaela eventually looked over at Sam.

"*Please* tell me you have those glasses . . ."

♦ IX ♦

The interior of the C-17 was big enough to carry cargo as well as personnel. Among the latter were the remnants of a special operations team who were using the air time to contemplate anything other than their military specialties. Relieved of any immediate duties, at least until the plane landed back in the States, Lennox and his men sat resting or conversing quietly among themselves.

Farther up the belly of the big military transport, a team of a different kind was laboring over a table that was half surgery, half machine shop. The specialists in attendance were similarly equally divided between experts in repairing bodies and those who could take apart and put back together again everything from a muscle car to a microchip. On the table before them, a segment of mechanical tail that had once belonged to the alien creature called Skorponok was slowly but steadily repairing itself.

Leaning slightly over the table, the leader of the research team was watching the process unfolding before him in utter disbelief.

"Unbelievable. It's some kind of self-regenerating molecular armor. A multiplicity of super-refined metals blended with ceramics and a few other components we still haven't been able to break down."

Drawn by the conversation, one by one Lennox and his men ambled over to observe the observers. As the ones who had recovered the tail piece in the first place, he and his men had been given unrestricted access to the dissection. Lennox was the first to arrive tableside. Intently, he scrutinized a torn edge where the artillery round had severed the tail from the rest of the body.

"The scorch marks show where the sabot round hit," he pointed out. "Melted right through."

The research team leader nodded as he nudged a magnifier into position over the spot. Leaning close, the interested captain noticed right away how the burned edge was different from the rest of the slowly regenerating tail. The team leader confirmed what he was seeing.

"It's the only part of the severed appendage that isn't regenerating."

Straightening, Lennox pondered the implications. "Aren't sabots hot-loaded for a six-thousand-degree magnesium burn? An explosive round would generate similar heat, but only briefly. But a mag burn would linger on the site and stay hot for a lot longer. Maybe long enough to overcome the resistance of whatever this thing is made of."

Their exchange was rudely interrupted as the severed tail gave an abrupt, explosive *twitch*. The hypodermic-sharp tip slammed completely through the table as guards and researchers leaped or stumbled backward. One woman fell down close to the table and had to be dragged into the clear, but the danger had already passed. The tail went limp again, and the convulsive reaction was not repeated. For the moment.

A cautious Epps contemplated the newly inert alien relic. "Someone please tell me that was a postmortem reflex."

His tone low and urgent, Lennox turned to the staring tech sergeant.

"Get on the horn to Northern Command. I don't care how you have to get in touch—use smoke signals if that's all that's available. But they have to know something. Tell 'em our effective weapon is high-heat sabot rounds; the larger the volatile magnesium content and the longer the afterburn, the better. Recommend we load 'em in anything that'll handle 'em. *Go.*"

Leaving a curt nod in his wake, Epps hurried to find the nearest functioning communicator. As soon as he had gone, the medical sergeant who had been waiting for their conversation to end stepped toward Lennox. The captain knew the medtech: the man had been working on the injured Figueroa. Instead of speaking, the tech shook his head slowly. Coupled with his grave expression, he needed no words to convey the information he carried with him. Lennox eyed him a moment, then rushed toward the front of the plane.

Figueroa was lying on a pallet in the temporary infirmary area along with other wounded who were being evacuated from the devastated base. The medical staff had made him as comfortable as possible. The chief warrant officer did not look comfortable, however. He looked bad, really bad. Which, after all the treatment he had received since leaving the Middle East, was not a good sign at all.

Stepping into his comrade's field of view, Lennox managed to muster up what he hoped was an encouraging smile. "Hey, *amigo. ¿Qué pasa?*"

Figueroa did not react immediately. Plainly, he was fighting something beyond his control. Something beyond that of the medics as well. Each syllable his mouth formed required a separate, physically taxing effort. His words emerged in weak, rasping gasps.

"Wouldn't have believed any of this if—I hadn't seen it for myself." His gaze focused unblinkingly on his friend. "Just got one thing to—say. You promise me. You're gonna—stop these things."

Lennox tried his best to shrug it off. "Once you're out of that damn bed you can stop 'em yourself."

Figueroa ignored the optimistic suggestion. Both of them knew the captain was lying. *"Promise me."* The warrant officer was as insistent as his debilitated condition would allow. "I don't wanna die for nothing, man. Not with sand in my shoes . . ."

Lennox started to protest again. There were a lot of things he could have said; a lot of things he wanted to say. But it was clear that there wasn't time.

"Promise," the warrant officer persevered.

At a gesture from the mortally wounded man, Lennox leaned closer. Figueroa was holding something small and shiny. He pressed it into the captain's open palm. Looking down, Lennox recognized the Saint Christopher's medal his friend had always worn around his neck. As soon as it was in the captain's hand, the other man's eyes closed. It was impossible to tell whether he was hurting when he died.

Anyone seeing Lennox's face at that moment would have known that the captain was.

It was a singular collection of brand-new vehicles that raced through the network of residential avenues late that night before halting just up the street from the home of Ron, Judy, and Sam Witwicky. Even though they were careful to muffle the noise of their engines, the machines still drew the occasional curious glance out an open suburban window. All that those who bothered to do so saw was a shiny new pickup truck here, an eighteen-wheeler on the wrong street there. A fancy but slow-moving sports car and an emergency vehicle with its lights and siren off. Nothing to be alarmed about. Definitely nothing worth abandoning dinner or a favorite TV show to check out further.

Certainly that was the feeling inside the Witwicky house itself. Ron and Judy sat in the living room eating TV dinners on tray tables as they watched the local late-night news. Though Ron used the remote to surf through multiple channels, it seemed as if every one was playing someone's home video footage of the fiery visitor from space slashing across the sky. Absent any alternatives, he put the remote aside and returned to his food. Sports and weather would be on soon enough.

"Police stations are inundated with calls reporting unidentified lights in the sky," the perfectly coiffed and clad reporter of the moment was declaiming breathlessly. "At this point in time, astronomers believe that it was likely a sizable nickel-iron meteor that broke up on contact with the Earth's atmosphere." She turned to face the screen mounted behind her. "We just picked up and verified the authenticity of this most recent eyewitness video, which appears to show one of the fragments actually striking a building right here in our own downtown."

Ron and Judy paused in their eating to watch as something flashed across the screen. This was followed by explosive noises and the shouts and screams of the three teenagers who had been eating in a nearby café. So absorbed were Sam's parents by the new footage that they scarcely noticed the sudden vibration in the floor that set their dinner trays trembling. Nestled snugly in Judy's lap, a somnolent Mojo suddenly perked up. However loud and garish they were, it was not the sounds blaring from the TV that had disturbed his rest. It was something else. Something much more real.

In the alley behind the house, the eclectic line of vehicles that had carefully worked their way through the neighborhood braked to a stop. Sam and Mikaela exited the shiny new Camaro.

"Stay with 'em," he told her. "I'll be right back." He took a step toward the house, was restrained by a thought, and turned toward the idling convoy. Looking past Mikaela, he addressed the line of idling vehicles with as much sternness as he could muster. "Stay. Stay *here*. Stay." It was all he could think of to say. It worked with Mojo.

Making next to no noise he crept toward the screened rear door. He was convinced he had not made a sound, but that didn't stop his dad from appearing magically in the portal. Mojo appeared between Ron's feet, barking like all hell as he pawed madly at the screen to get out.

Doing everything he could to keep from glancing toward the alley, Sam smiled pleasantly. "Uh—hi, Dad."

Ron let a little time pass. As Sam stood there, each successive second seemed to weigh more and more heavily, until he thought time itself would grind to a halt.

"I bought half your first car, bailed you outta jail, and tonight just kinda felt like doing your chores." His father stared down at him. "Been an interesting day. Not a dull moment. Life's great, isn't it?"

A slight crunching sound drew Sam's attention left-ward, toward a dark part of the spacious backyard. One after another, huge alien robots were stepping over the fence out of the alley and onto the grass. From where he was standing Sam could see them but his father could not. This, he knew straightaway, was a good thing. He uttered a nervous laugh.

"Right—take out the trash cans. I can hear the cats getting into them. I'm on it, sorry."

A master of fatherly facetiousness, Ron smiled thinly at his wayward son. "Don't strain yourself, really. I can do it later. I only have to get up early tomorrow and go to work and make a living. I wouldn't want you to lose any sleep." He started to open the door and come down the steps. Sam hurriedly banged it shut in time to block his dad's exit—but not Mojo's. Still barking wildly, the Chihuahua nearly spun out on his rear legs as he banked right and headed for the section of backyard adjacent to the alley.

"No no, got it!" Sam had to make himself not run after the dog. "Seriously, *my* bad."

Ron studied him a moment longer. Then he turned and, shaking his head dolefully, headed back toward the living room. He didn't want to miss the local sports. As soon as his father turned, Sam whirled and raced toward the alley. He was just in time to see the massive right foot of Optimus Prime turn some patio furniture into Frisbees while the other reduced his father's new and laboriously installed imported stone path into gravel.

"Oh, nono, watch the path! The path, the path!" he yelled frantically.

Consumed in a barking frenzy, Mojo was racing around and around Ironhide's feet, occasionally leaping upward to snap at an alloyed ankle. Peering down, the mechanoid flicked at the dog with one foot, sending the yelping Chihuahua flying into a patch of flowers. One bounce, one roll, and Mojo returned to the attack. A panicked Sam darted forward.

"Whoa whoa whoa, that's my dog! Mojo, off! Off the robot!" As if corralling the dyspeptic Chihuahua didn't present enough of a problem, Mikaela came striding through the alleyway gate. Turning on her, he indicated the yard full of giant robots. "I told you to watch 'em!"

She put her hands on her hips and eyed him challengingly. "Well, I think they're kind of in a *rush*."

"Well," he countered feebly, "you shoulda *done* something."

Lower lip pushed forward, she nodded thoughtfully. "Right. Give me a minute to find the on/off switches."

Ironhide was tracking the unceasingly irritating small mammal that continued to dart in and out between his feet. "I detect that you have a highly localized vermin infestation. Shall I terminate?"

"*Nono*," Sam yelped wildly. "It's Mom's *Chihuahua*." Clearly Ironhide was not the brains of the outfit.

Mojo chose that insightful moment to lift a hind leg and pee on the robot's foot.

Sam rushed toward the dog. "Mojo, *no!*" He looked up at the impassive alien. "Sorry—he's got this male dominance thing." He wagged a finger under the Chihuahua's nose. "Bad dog!" Mojo gave him a lick, then resumed barking.

Still engrossed in the TV, his parents didn't notice as Sam dumped a squirming, protesting Mojo back into the house and then hurried silently up the stairs to his room. The glasses—where had he last put them down? Anxiously he rummaged through the mess that was his daily life: school materials, dirty clothes, game manuals, library books. Behind him, an immense metal hand rose to the level of the open window. Unceremoniously, it dumped Mikaela through the portal and onto the floor of the room. Making a face, she climbed to her feet and straightened her clothes, leaving her purse where it fell on the floor.

"You must help him look," Optimus informed her solemnly.

She threw the robot a dirty look, then moved to lend Sam a casual hand. "They *really* want those glasses."

Instead of motivating him to look harder, her presence caused him to take a breather from the search. Counting his mother, Mikaela was one of only two women ever to set foot in his room. And—the place was a *total disaster*. Junk was scattered everywhere, tastefully decorated with dirty clothes and—underwear. Embarrassed, he started snatching up the most personal items.

"Underwear—underwear—underwear." Having recovered the last of the briefs on display, he hurriedly tossed them in a closet, shut the door, and turned back to his welcome yet disconcerting visitor. "So, yeah. This is my—room."

She was surveying her surroundings. "It's nice. Your whole house is really—big."

"Old house, big lot, lots of room." While he explained, he resumed rummaging through the mountain of fabric on his bed. When the last trivial item had been hauled off and tossed aside, a single used Kleenex floated to the floor in its wake. His expression darkened. He had cleared the bed, but without finding what he had been looking for.

"It's not here."

She stared at him. "What d'you mean?"

"The spectacles were in my backpack. It isn't here."

Her expression turned pensive. "Okay, I understand. Dibs on *not* having to tell the giant alien robots."

"It's *got* to be here somewhere." He resumed searching. Having no idea where to look, she stood off to the side and watched him work.

So did the transformed Sidekick buried in her purse. If there is one quality all mechanicals share, it's patience. Continuing to bide its time, a transformed Frenzy waited eagerly for the human to produce the crucial set of primitive artificial lenses.

Glancing over a shoulder, Sam encountered the enormous, reflective face of Optimus Prime staring back at him.

"Have you found them?" the robot inquired worriedly.

"*Ssssh!*" Sam hissed. Even muted, the robot's voice threatened to resound throughout the length and breadth of the house. "*No,* I haven't. I dunno where my backpack is!"

Outside, the other robots had crowded close around their leader. Optimus scanned the interior of the upstairs bedroom, seeking anything that might give an inkling of glass mounted in metal.

"Did you look within the oblong clothing-storage device?"

Sam gaped at him. "The what?"

"I think he means the dresser," Mikaela suggested helpfully.

"Perhaps it is beneath the four-point floor sheath," Ratchet proposed.

Standing in the middle of his room, Sam pivoted slowly. "Okay, totally stumped."

Mikaela eyed Ratchet querulously. "The rug?"

Sam turned on her. "No, it's not *in* or *under* any of those things. I *know* where it is. It's in a *backpack*. My backpack, the same one I take to school with me every day. The backpack that is definitely *not here*."

Outside, Optimus took a step forward, closing the last remaining gap between his massive bulk and the house. "There can be no 'definite' in this matter. You must continue searching."

"Hey!" Sam exclaimed as he glanced out the window, "my mom's flowers, watch it!"

The enormous mechanoid looked down. Crushed roses splayed outward beneath his foot. "I am sorry," he declared portentously. "The brightly colored weeds will be replaced. But we *must* have the glasses."

"Look," Sam pleaded, "will you just—get outta here? If my parents see you, they're gonna *freak*. *Go!* Hide! I promise I'll keep looking."

Optimus turned to his companions. "Autobots: fall back and cloak."

"And be *quiet*," Sam ordered. "Keep it *down*."

One by one the visitors retreated into a copse of trees. All did so successfully—and, as Sam had requested, quietly—until the preoccupied Jazz backed into a line of wires. The top of his head brushed against a high-voltage line. Flaring in the darkness, sparks arced across his skull.

An involuntary electronic scream erupted from deep within the robot. Convulsing, he toppled over sideways, shattering a small glass greenhouse when he fell. The overstuffed trash cans Sam had promised to haul out front for tomorrow's pickup went flying and rolling, spilling their noisy and noisome contents all over yard, pavement, and one another.

Unsurprisingly, this concentrated calamity did not go entirely unnoticed inside the Witwicky household. As the house shook, Ron was up out of his easy chair and on his feet quickly.

"Earthquake! Judy, under the table!"

She didn't budge from her seat. "It's just a *tremor,* Ron." She gestured at their surroundings. "A few things got knocked over outside, that's all. Probably some of the neighborhood dogs, or maybe that family of raccoons that sometimes comes up from the lake. The house is fine." She paused for a couple of seconds, listening. "See? Not even an aftershock. We'll check the yard in the morning." A hand gestured at his tray table. "Sit down and finish your dessert."

Reluctantly, eyeing the walls as though they might cave inward at any moment, he complied with his wife's wishes. But no matter how hard he tried to shake the feeling that something was not quite right, the defrosted brownie resting temptingly in his plastic tray did not taste as good as usual.

Out back Jazz sat up, shook his head, and gestured upward. "*Do not* touch those! They carry throughout their length the potential for dangerous energy overload."

"It's okay, it's okay." Staring out the window, Sam had been holding his breath. But no one emerged from his house, or from those of any neighbors, to seek the source of the momentary cacophony. He let out a sigh of relief and turned back to Mikaela. In the faint light of his room she looked more beautiful than ever—though at the moment decidedly nonplussed.

Thirty seconds later the transformer mounted on the pole nearest the length of heavy-gauge transmission line Jazz had inadvertently contacted blew up in a shower of sparks and seared metal. Every house in the immediate vicinity promptly went dark.

In the now-dark upper-floor room Sam spun a wild circle, then raced toward the only source of light: the window. The first thing he noticed was the complete absence of light in any other house visible from his room. The second was the complete absence of visiting alien robots in his backyard. In their place was a small fleet of vehicles—including a giant and thoroughly inappropriate-for-the-location eighteen-wheeler. Leaning out, he yelled downward.

"What is it with you guys? Semitrucks parked in the backyard is not *hiding*." He turned back to his room. He still had to find the backpack, and the precious glasses. "You're gonna get me in so much—"

In the darkness he ran into something coming the other way that was simultaneously resistant and soft: Mikaela. Both of them went down in a heap.

Downstairs in the living room, the *thud* from above was clearly audible as Ron switched on a flashlight. Immediately, his gaze and attention turned upward.

"SAM? IS THAT YOU?"

There was no response from above. Husband and wife exchanged troubled looks.

"Stay here," he told her. "Stay *here*."

"No. No, I'm *scared*."

"Well then, come on, but give me room."

"Room?" In the circle of light provided by the flashlight, she stared back at him. "Room for what?"

"Room for . . ." He deliberated a moment. "Room to maneuver."

She nodded and followed him, keeping a couple of arms' lengths back. On the way toward the stairs she spied her son's baseball gear piled in a corner. Picking up the bat and gripping it in both hands, she trailed her husband as he started cautiously up the stairs.

Moaning softly, Sam and Mikaela picked themselves up off the floor. He was a bit dazed, and not just from the force of the collision. She had rather more to say. As she was readying her words, a pair of brilliant beams of light illuminated the interior of the room like an atomic flash. Blinking painfully, Sam tried to turn in the direction of the lights being emitted by the eyes of a helpful Optimus Prime.

"TURN IT OFF, TURN IT OFF!"

Slowly making their way up the stairs, Ron and Judy heard their son's frantic voice at the same time as they saw the incredibly intense light flare from underneath the door to his room. Taking point ahead of them, Mojo was already scratching madly at the wood.

"Sam?" Ron asked hesitantly as he leaned close to the door and gripped the flashlight a little more tightly. "You in there?"

Shit, Sam thought. "Uh, yeah, Dad," he responded, as calmly as he could. "It's me." Whirling on the beam-casting Optimus, he hissed anxiously, *"Turn it off!"*

By now Judy had also halted just outside her son's door. Mojo had calmed down, but only because his jaws were getting tired. Leaning forward and placing her ear close to the door, Judy was sure she could hear voices whispering inside.

"What're you doing in there? You all right?" She glanced downward. "The power's out all over the neighborhood. Where are you getting that light?"

"Big flashlight!" Sam hurriedly improvised. "Borrowed it from Miles." He waved frantically at Optimus

Prime. The robot's eyes obediently went dark. "It's off now. I'm good, Mom, really good!" Looking toward the window, he gasped, *"Hide!"*

Ron tried the knob. It didn't turn. "Why's the door locked?"

It was all becoming too much to deal with. Sam felt like his brain was an old washrag that had undergone its final washing and been hung out to dry for the last time. "I'm just—uh—real good."

His mother considered, not only her son's words, but his tone. She eyed her husband. "Maybe he's m-a-s-t-u-r . . ."

"Judy!" Ron exclaimed. Flustered, he tried the knob again. Definitely locked from the inside. "Sam, open the door!"

"Be right with you!" his son replied, even as he was bugging his eyes out at the now-eye-dark-but-still-staring Optimus Prime. *"Get outta here!"*

The robot replied with damnably single-minded insistence. "But you must find the glasses."

"Open the door *now*." Ron's voice had gone from concerned to curious to borderline angry.

Something fumbled at the knob from the inside. There was a soft *click*. The door opened inward to reveal Sam retreating to stand by the single window, holding up an arm to shield his eyes against the wandering beam of his father's flashlight.

"Hi Dad, hi Mom," he declared cheerily. "What's up?"

Having none of it, Ron swept the light around the room, searching. "Who're you talking to?"

Sam kept his voice carefully neutral. "Talking to *you*."

Beyond suspicious now, his father tried to see past his son. Sam kept shifting his position, as if trying to block any view of the open window. His mother started to take a step toward him, hesitated.

"We heard noises. We thought—"

"Doesn't matter what we thought," snapped Ron, interrupting her. "What was that light?" Stomping into the room, he headed for the window. Desperately trying to look not-nervous, Sam blocked his father's path. When he replied, he spoke more loudly than normal. Loud enough, in fact, for anyone or anything lingering outside to hear.

"*Light?* What light, Dad? Wasn't any light. Oh, you mean the flashlight light. That's gone, isn't it? Why're you looking *outside?* Don't you trust your *son?* That *hurts* me."

Leaning out the window, Ron scanned the backyard. Lights were still out in the neighbors' houses, sparks still sputtered from the ruined transformer, and dogs were starting to bark everywhere. He did not look directly downward or he might have seen several enormous bipedal metallic shapes pressing tightly against the side of the house.

Trying to avoid being seen, they pressed hard enough to make it shudder. Pictures in Sam's room tilted on their hangers as books spilled from their shelves. Ron and Judy stumbled while Sam managed to hold his position.

"Whoa, *aftershock,*" Ron stammered. "Everybody under the door, under the door, under the door!" Arms spread wide, he hustled his wife and son to the presumed safety of the entrance to Sam's room.

Outside, the robots conversed in implausibly concise sonic bursts among themselves.

"Why are we hiding?" Ironhide demanded to know.

"Be quiet," Ratchet commanded him.

The other mechanoid was not placated. "But—*why are we hiding?*"

Jazz proposed an explanation. "If they see us, the boy's progenitors will become alarmed."

"I can neutralize them. It will remove a complication from our quest."

"We do not harm humans. Despite their fragile microbiotic bodies and repeated indications to the contrary, they are sentient life-forms like us," Optimus reminded his colleague.

Ironhide persisted. "I will do it quickly and efficiently. They will feel no pain."

"*Ironhide!*" Optimus snapped.

Thrusting her initial hesitancy aside, Judy had stepped into her son's room and was walking toward the window. "Sam, we *heard* you. You were talking to somebody. We want to know *who*."

Surprising both her and Ron, not to mention Sam, a voice emerged from the darkness. It was followed by a figure. "Yeah, uh, it's just me." She eyed Sam's parents. "Hi. I'm Mikaela."

"Oh," Judy mumbled. A broad smile suddenly spread across her face, completely replacing any previous suggestion of anxiety. "*Oh*. Sammy."

"Sorry to scare you," Mikaela put in.

Ron looked flustered squared. "Scare us, nono, it's— we're sorry we barged in." He gestured inadequately with the flashlight, wishing he were somewhere else. "We just heard noises, that's all. I mean, what with the earthquake and the power going out . . ." His voice trailed away, not entirely unhappy.

Leaning toward her son, Judy whispered encouragingly, "She's very pretty."

Even in the feeble light it was possible to see Sam's face flush. "*Mom,* she can *hear* you."

Judy straightened. "Oh, sorry, *sorry.*"

Sam took a deep breath. "By the way, you guys seen my backpack?"

"On the kitchen table," his mother informed him helpfully. She smiled at Mikaela. "I'll go make some snacks."

The lights in the room flickered, then snapped back on. The power company, Sam speculated, must have done a work-around on the destroyed transformer. He rushed past his parents. Hurrying to recover her purse, Mikaela followed close on his heels.

"Don't worry 'bout it, Mom," Sam told her.

"Nice to meet you, seeya!" Mikaela exclaimed as she disappeared down the hallway. Behind them, Ron switched off his flashlight and eyed his wife meaningfully.

" 'Snacks'?"

She shrugged, smiling halfheartedly. "I didn't know what else to say."

Tearing down the stairs, Sam raced into the kitchen and—there it was. His backpack. Just as his mom had said. It was lying on the table untouched, unopened, and, to all intents and appearances, unmessed-with. As Mikaela set her purse down on a chair and joined him, he walked over and unzipped it. The glasses case, the invaluable glasses case, was right in the inside pocket where he had put it. So intent were both of them on the battered container that neither noticed the spidery shape rising up behind them. Articulated metal fingers reached out and forward to grab—only to retreat rapidly back into the open purse as the front doorbell began to ring incessantly.

Walking through the kitchen past Sam and his friend,

Ron moved to answer the door. It was too late for casual visitors. Probably someone from the electric company, he mused as he reached for the handle, checking each house in the neighborhood to make sure that the power was back on and that there were no problems resulting from . . .

The front yard was full of men and women. Some wore dark suits and busied themselves using strange instruments to scan their immediate surroundings. Others carried even more peculiar devices whose readouts occupied their full attention. Standing by himself on the porch and facing Ron was a tall, skinny, eroded-looking individual who bore an air of seriousness around him like a thick fog. The sort of man who delivered clean white envelopes secured with the presidential seal to women whose husbands and sons were serving in war zones overseas.

"Ronald Wickity?" he asked straightforwardly. Briefly, he flashed an impressively garish badge embossed with an insignia Ron did not recognize and was not given time to study at length. "Name's Simmons. With the government. Sector Seven."

Automatically a mystified Ron responded, "Never heard of it."

"You still haven't," the agent informed him meaningfully. "Your son's the great-great-grandson of the Arctic explorer Captain Archibald Wickity, is he not?"

"It's *Witwicky*," Ron informed the visitor, more than a little put out. Leaning forward, he looked out as the bevy of disparately clad strangers paced and tromped and peered with great intensity of purpose all over his lawn and his wife's flower beds. "What the hell *is* this?"

Simmons was patient. "Your son filed a stolen car report last night. We think it's involved in a national security matter."

"The Camaro? National security?" As a man who prided himself on always being on top of things, Ron had to admit to himself that he was now completely adrift.

His wife, however, had more prosaic concerns. Still holding the baseball bat, she came up alongside her husband in time to see agents plowing through her flowers.

"We got massive hits," one agent called toward the porch, indicating the distinctive instrument he was wielding. Simmons looked back at him, nodding as if the observation was no more than he had expected.

"Get a sample and readings."

The agent and a companion began ripping roses out of the ground. At Ron's feet, Mojo started growling. The dog's reaction was subdued compared with that of an outraged Judy Witwicky.

"Hey, you!" Sam's mother yelled, aghast at the destruction. "Outta my garden!" She hefted the bat threateningly. *"Get!"*

"Ma'am, please," Simmons entreated her, "drop the bat." Blinking, she turned to him. "Are you experiencing any flu-like symptoms?" he asked her politely. "Aching joints? Fever? How are your bowel movements?"

She gawked at him. "I beg your pardon? Who gives you the right to . . . ?"

"Nausea?" Simmons continued without a pause. "Swollen glands?"

"No," she snapped. "Listen to me, you creep—" She broke off and drew back as another agent came close to pass some kind of illuminated wand across her face.

"She's clean." The agent lowered the device and extended a hand. "Ma'am," he asked courteously but firmly, "the bat?"

Sam and Mikaela had come out of the kitchen. As soon as Sam saw the agents standing in front of his mother and father he shoved the old glasses case deeper into his right front pants pocket. The alert Simmons noticed the gesture, but saw only Sam's moving hand.

"You. Sam Witwicky. We need you to come with us."

Sam took a step backward. Reflexively, he put a protective arm across Mikaela's back. She didn't step away from it.

"Dad?" he mumbled uncertainly.

Stepping back into his house, Ron blocked the agent's view of his son.

"I don't know who you are or what's going on here, but 'national security' or not, this is *way* out of line."

Simmons stepped into the house. "Sir, I'm asking you respectfully, please back off."

Balling his hands into fists, Ron let his arms rise deliberately from his sides. "You're not taking my son. I'm calling the cops. 'Sector Seven'? There's something fishy about all this."

"Well, sir," Simmons informed him, "there's something fishy about *you,* your *son,* your little Taco Bell *dog,* and this whole operation in here—and my job is to get to the bottom of it."

This statement was so outrageous that Ron could not even muster the wherewithal to stay mad. " 'Operation'? *What* operation?"

"That's what we're going to find out." Reaching into a pocket, Simmons withdrew a small cylindrical device. Leaning over, he passed it across the face of a snarling, slowly retreating Mojo. "Fourteen on the counter. *Bingo.* Tag and bag 'em."

Straightening, he turned and gestured. From out of

nowhere, agents seemed to pour into the room from every direction. One scooped up the Chihuahua with a catcher's noose. Strong hands came down on everyone else. Wrestled, manhandled, and hustled, Sam's parents were shoved roughly out of the house into the front yard, out onto the street, and into a waiting black SUV. Trapped amid half a dozen other silent agents, Sam and Mikaela disappeared into the one in front of it.

Struggling, Ron yelled toward the other vehicle. "Do not say anything, Sam! *Not a word, till we get a lawyer!*"

One by one the line of cars and SUVs pulled smoothly out into the street, accelerating in the direction of the nearest freeway on-ramp. As the last sped off, the neighborhood descended once more into the calm of late-night silence.

From behind the house and among a cluster of trees, five pairs of deeply perceptive alien lenses stared out to follow the course of the departing vehicles.

☷ X ☷

The Pentagon intelligence center was a hive of activity, a flurry of constant motion as officers and techs and specialist noncoms hurried back and forth or worked intently over individual consoles. On the largest screen two clusters of tiny shapes shifted their position relative to each other with infinite slowness. A closer look would have revealed that each one represented a ship, none of which belonged to Carnival Cruise Lines.

The secretary of defense was staring at the big screen contemplating a limited and unpleasant number of options when the brigadier came up alongside him. Over the previous several days both men had had far too little sleep, and it was starting to take its toll.

"Blue Force tracker has Chinese and U.S. naval task forces approaching within one hundred nautical miles of each other's cruise missile range," the general murmured tersely. Though he had spent decades anticipating this kind of situation, it was one he had hoped he would never actually have to deal with.

Keller kept his eyes on the screen. So many inscrutable dots representing so many men and women. So much unavoidable, seemingly inescapable import. So many lives on both sides, all riding on a very few decisions that he and a handful of others would have to make.

"Tell the battle group commander to wait for orders from Washington. He is *not* to engage under any conditions unless they are fired on first."

The general nodded and vanished back into the hurricane of activity. He was replaced by Admiral Bingham and a Suit whom Keller did not recognize. Cuffed to the Suit's left wrist was a titanium briefcase. The secretary took no particular notice of it: he had seen its like many times before.

"Sir," the admiral began, "this is Tom Banachek, from the White House."

With his free hand, Banachek reached inside his jacket to flash his identification. "Mr. Secretary. I'm with Sector Seven—Advanced Research Division."

Keller glanced at the man, frowned. "Never heard of it. If you don't mind, Tom, whatever brought you here can be referred to me through the usual channels. I'm a little busy right now."

Banachek was not put out by the secretary's response because he had encountered *its* like many times before. "We are a highly independent extra-governmental entity, sir. I'm here under direct order from the president." He indicated the vast, busy room. "Verbal only in here, I'm afraid. A lot of Sector Seven activity takes place in the absence of written records. The president has instructed me to brief you."

Annoyed at the interruption, Keller turned to face the newcomer. "Brief me? *Now?*" He gestured toward the big screen. "When all this is going on? Brief me on what?"

Before Banachek could respond, the statistics being

posted on one screen were replaced by a beeping noise and an accompanying visual FAILURE notification. The screen alongside it went dead next. And then the one beside it, and then three more, and then . . .

In less than a minute every screen in the room had locked up with a FAILURE warning. Conversation and general discussion were replaced by complete pandemonium.

Unable to do little more than stare as the disaster unfolded in front of him, a horrified Keller spoke into his headphone mike. "What's happening?" Almost always under complete control, his voice began to rise. "Somebody talk to me. I need a sit rep—*stat*!"

The general who had earlier reported task force movements appeared at his side. He looked on the verge of utter panic—not a good sign in a general. "Communications are out—the virus, or whatever it is, was coded to shut us down. Our firewall people thought they had a handle on it but—"

Keller interrupted him. "What d'you mean, '*shut us down*'?"

The general swallowed. "It corrupted the entire operating system while hiding itself from view. We thought it had been quarantined, but it was in the background all the time. It's used our own network to both spread right through the secure government web and jump to the public. It's a global blackout—anything involved with advanced communications is dead. Satellite and landlines are dead. Internet is shut down. At the moment, we have *zero* communication, both internationally and domestic."

Keller knew he should say something, should at least comment—but what could he say? What *was* there to say? And even if he said something, according to the general the only people who would hear it were standing within earshot in this one room. His disbelief didn't vanish until he tried his own cell phone. No matter what number he tried, no matter how private or restricted, all he got in return for his several attempts was the same cold, hollow static.

Banachek, however, still had something to say. He hefted his briefcase, his tone urgent. "Sir, you need to see what I have in here—*now.*"

Dazed, feeling more helpless than at any time since he was seven years old and his father had removed the training wheels from his bike, the secretary of defense followed the man from the White House away from the turmoil that had inundated the intelligence room.

Accelerating, the black SUVs swept through night-cloaked Tranquility. In the rear seat of the lead vehicle, Sam and Mikaela were trying not to freak out—and failing. Up in the front passenger seat, Simmons ignored his young charges as he pulled out and flicked open his cell phone.

"Simmons here. We're Code Black, we got the boy. I need . . ."

Pausing, he looked down at the phone and frowned. "You copy? Hello?" On the tiny screen were the words NO SIGNAL. "Must be a bad patch." He shrugged. "Call it in in a few minutes." Hanging up, he turned in the seat to face Sam.

"So tell me, 'Ladiesman Two-seventeen'—that *is* your username, right?"

The seriousness of their present situation notwithstanding, Mikaela couldn't repress a grin as she looked across at Sam. "It is?" she inquired teasingly.

In addition to being terrified, Sam was now also decidedly embarrassed. "It was, uh, a typo."

Simmons didn't pursue it. Instead he pulled out a tiny recorder and clicked it to life. Slightly garbled snatches of the recording Sam had phoned in when he had thought he was going to die filled the interior of the SUV.

"M-my name's Sam Witwicky. My car—it's *alive*. I don't know how, but it's alive . . ."

On the last "alive," the agent halted the playback. "Inexplicable but most interesting. Please enlighten me further." His expression, his posture, his tone: everything combined to indicate that he was dead serious. "I need every word. Everything and anything you can tell me." His eyes all but burned into Sam's. *"Don't leave anything out."*

The SUV stopped at a red light. Other vehicles in the convoy made it and continued on. Sam's right hand was in his pocket, clutching the old glasses case as tightly as any talisman. How much should he say? What did he really know about these people and their ultimate intentions? Simmons was staring over the back of the front seat, waiting on him. Sam had the feeling the agent wouldn't wait forever. The next time he ventured an inquiry, he might not do so quite as politely.

"Listen, this is like the mother of all misunderstandings. You know kids like me—we've all spent too much time staring at the game console. Makes your brain go all fuzzy." He spread his hands. "Someone stole my car, that's all. Maybe I embellished the report a little, but at the time it was, like, the middle of the night and I was kind of panicking. But it's fine, everything's fine now. It came back."

Mikaela jumped in. "Not by *itself*, obviously. Cars don't *do* that, that'd be *crazy*."

Simmons said nothing. Instead he removed a peculiar lens from the dashboard glovebox. "What d'you kids know about aliens?" he asked unexpectedly.

"*Aliens?*" Sam's shocked response was maybe just a bit over-the-top. "Like, *Martians?* Don't believe in 'em."

"Total crap," Mikaela concurred, nodding agreement just a bit too vigorously. "That kind of thing is for fanboys—guys who can tell you what color nail polish some half-naked chick was wearing in the last act of episode twenty-eight of the original *Star Trek.*"

Leaning over the backseat, Simmons jammed the monocle against Sam's face, using it to cover one eye. On the side of the lens facing the agent, the teen's pupil dilated.

"*Whoa.*" Sam drew back into the seat, but he couldn't get away from the lens or from Simmons. "What *is* this?"

"Breathe normally and answer the questions. So: no aliens, huh?"

"Nope," Sam replied brusquely.

"Interesting." Simmons's attention was focused on the tiny round screen. "*Very* interesting. Tell you what else I find *deliciously* interesting, kid: pupil dilation, body language, flushness of your skin. Because taken together they're showing me you're both *ly*-ing." With his free hand he pulled back the front of his jacket to reveal the same badge that had so puzzled Ron Witwicky. "See this? This is like a 'Do-whatever-I-want-and-get-away-with-it' badge. I'm gonna lock you away for-*ev*-er, erase you like you never ex-*is*-ted. And that'll be like a fluffy ball of cotton candy compared with what I do to your *parents.*"

Sam stayed quiet, but not Mikaela. She did not quite spit in the senior agent's face. "And our little dog Toto, too?" she shot back derisively. "Don't listen to him, Sam. He's just trying to intimidate you." She met Simmons's gaze without blinking. "He's just pissy 'cause he's gotta get back to guarding the Mall."

Simmons's tone shifted from threatening to venomous as he glared over at her. "*Hey*. You in the training bra. Do not test me. Not now, not tonight. Especially with your daddy's parole coming up."

Her face paled. All the defiance seeped out of her like air from a balloon. Gaping at her, Sam once again failed to engage his brain before opening his mouth.

"Parole? But you said he lef . . ."

Sunk back in the SUV's seat, she folded her arms and stared straight ahead. "It's *nothing*."

Having started the nail, Simmons had no trouble driving it home. "Grand theft auto, that ain't nothing."

The light changed and the SUV surged forward again. Hating him for exposing her so callously, Mikaela looked daggers at the agent. Having in the course of his career been confronted with far worse, Simmons simply gazed back quietly. Beaten, she turned to Sam. It took her a moment to find the right words to express what she wanted to say.

"Those cars my dad taught me to fix?" She gave the tiniest of shrugs. "They weren't always his."

"Your dad taught you to fix stolen cars?" He stared back at her, unable to think of anything else to say.

Simmons was not similarly afflicted. "Yes *sir*. And she's got her own juvie record to prove it."

This time Mikaela's response was defiant. "I wouldn't sell him out in court, so they charged me, too." She barely glanced in Sam's direction. "I'm just an accessory."

Simmons shook his head in mock sympathy. "Yeah,

anyone can see from your *record* that you're a paragon of youthful virtue. As for your old man, be a shame if he had to rot in jail for the rest of his natural *life*." Having delivered himself of that threat, he turned back to Sam.

"And *you*. Wouldn't be the first time we threw a Wickity in an asylum. See, *my* great-great-grandfather locked up *your* great-great-grandfather. And history's about a walrus snort away from repeating itself."

Doubtless Simmons hoped his words of warning would reduce the younger man in the backseat to a state of cowering submission. Sam's reaction was somewhat different from what the agent had expected. He sat up straight and stared him directly in the face.

"You son of a bitch."

"Not very imaginative," the unruffled agent responded nonchalantly. "Been called lots worse, sometimes in languages you never heard of." His gaze intensified. "No more games. Time to talk. *Now*."

"Okay," Sam shot back defiantly. "You want the truth, I'll tell you. But you're not gonna believe it."

Simmons shifted expectantly against the front seat. "Give it a whirl, kiddo. I'm all ears."

Sam opened his mouth, but nothing came out. Not because he was holding back, but because his incipient confession was interrupted by the sound, sight, and shudder of an enormous metal foot slamming down on the hood of the SUV, crumpling it like tinfoil.

The government vehicle spun to a sudden and violent stop. Repeated pounding indicated the presence of something huge and heavy walking around it. Within the SUV an assortment of sensitive instruments went berserk as blinding illumination filled the interior of the car with light. Simmons threw up his hands. Frantically, the driver tried to accelerate forward. He failed because the vehicle had been lifted into the air and off the road. Shorn of anything to grip, tires spun loudly and uselessly.

There was a metallic *ripping* sound as the roof of the big 4×4 was pulled upward and peeled back like the top of a sardine can. Roughly remade into an instant convertible, the SUV bounced wildly on its shocks as it was dropped back to Earth. Revealed in their own light, several gigantic figures could be seen peering downward at it.

Optimus Prime and his cohorts.

"Oh wow," a juiced Sam burbled in the direction of the car's front seat, "now you a-holes are in serious tuh-*ru*-ble."

Simmons and the driver drew their weapons. These promptly flew out of their hands into Jazz's palm, accompanied by every other device on their persons that contained any ferrous alloy. The driver embarked on a futile attempt to hide behind the wheel.

With every passing second, Sam was feeling better and better. "Gentlemen, allow me to introduce you to my friend—Optimus Prime."

"OUT OF THE CAR, PLEASE," the leader of the mechanoids announced politely but thunderously. Simmons and the driver complied with alacrity. Crouched together on the ground, they recoiled as the massive mechanical head lowered to within a foot of their faces. Enormous lenses focused on Simmons, who would greatly have preferred to avoid the attention. A light from the robot's eyes played briefly over the cringing agent.

"Your nervous system does not register significant shock," the giant observed thoughtfully. "You are not surprised by our existence."

208 **Alan Dean Foster**

"Look, uh," Simmons stammered, "there are Sector Seven protocols that need to be observed here. Okay? I'm not authorized to communicate with you. Except to tell you I can't communicate with you."

A second mechanoid approached. It was bright yellow and black-striped. From an opening on Bumblebee's body a jet of hot lubricant shot out to spray all over the agents.

"Get that thing to stop!" Simmons pleaded as he flailed uselessly with both hands at the dark, soaking stream.

Sam paused long enough in his enjoyment of the scene to query the unhappy agent. "What's Sector Seven? How'd you know about the robots? And *where'd you take my parents*?"

"Wouldn't you like to know," Simmons managed to mumble before a squirt of dark liquid filled his open mouth and he had to retreat, gagging.

Sam had to give the increasingly miserable agent his props. He was still a son of a bitch, but at least he was a dedicated son of a bitch.

Stepping forward, Jazz dropped two sets of steel handcuffs he had taken from the agents in front of Mikaela. "Secure them."

Still a bit stunned by the abrupt turn of events, she picked up the restraints. She flashed a wicked grin as she addressed the two wretched, sodden men. "Take off your pants."

Drenched with alien lubricant, Simmons flicked viscous goo from his fingers. "And for what?"

She sniffed. "Threatening my dad."

"And if we refuse?" he replied, still defiant.

Mikaela glanced up at the car-crushing mechanoid standing alongside her. "Want me to have *him* do it?"

Glaring through the liquid, the agent and the driver obediently dropped their trousers. Both wore boxers that were by now no less fluid-soaked than the rest of their clothes. Simmons's legs, she noted, looked as if they hadn't seen the light of day in years.

"Wow, pasty. Government troglodyte. Vitamin D, sunlight, definitely look into it." She moved toward him. "Legs like that, you don't even have to open your mouth to scare the girls on the beach."

There was a power pole nearby. Working with the skilled fingers of a trained auto mechanic she soon had both agents cuffed securely to the post. Simmons did not take his eyes off her the entire time.

"Little lady, this is the beginning of the end of your life."

Laughing, she retreated to the ripped-open SUV and recovered her purse. "Man, if Trent could see me now."

It was possible that the remarkable events of the day notwithstanding, nothing stunned Sam more than her comment right then. He gaped at her. "Excuse me, what'd you—if *Trent* could see you now?" There was no mistaking the sheer disbelief in his voice. "You're serious."

She blinked at him, oblivious of the fact that she might have said anything in the least unsettling. "What?"

He stood rooted to the ground near the abandoned SUV. "I just—I can't believe this! We contact an *alien race* together and all you care about is what that Neanderthalic jock *thinks* about you?" He shook his head. "You don't think that's a little weird?"

Her defenses were still up from the confrontation with Simmons. "What are you, my therapist all of a sudden?"

He didn't back down. Not now. Not anymore. "This isn't like your average Friday night where we're just hanging out. I mean, a little while ago I had some four-foot little gremlinny alien machine try to cut my legs off!"

"I *know*."

Slipping into a daze of an entirely different kind than the one that had enveloped him on the forced ride away from his house, he looked off into the distance and framed an imaginary scene with both hands.

"Wait, I'm having a vision! We're gonna possibly save the *world* and go back to school Monday morning and *nothing's* gonna have changed. I'll still be the invisible guy in homeroom and you'll go back to being *shallow*." He turned and looked upward. "Optimus, dude, back me up on this."

The robot's tone was profound. "We cannot take sides in your adolescent gender battles."

A furious Mikaela promptly got right up in Sam's face. "*Shallow?* I got a record 'cause I wouldn't sell out my dad! When've you ever had to sacrifice *anything* in your perfect little life? Did you cry 'cause you didn't get the latest Xbox for Christmas? All pouty 'cause you only got an old Camaro instead of a new Corvette?"

They were nose to nose when the rapidly escalating argument was interrupted by the *whup-whup* of several helicopters cresting the nearby hillside. A moment later a small fleet of SUVs arrived, screeching to respective halts on several sides. Robots and escapees alike found themselves suddenly surrounded.

High-intensity spotlights swept across Optimus Prime's massive outline. Taking one giant step forward, he picked Sam and Mikaela up, reached back, and deposited them on his shoulder.

"*Hold on.*"

Merging defensive sonics, the other robots emitted a

collective pulse blast that simultaneously flattened the tires on every one of the SUVs. It was a disabling defense, but not one that was damaging to life. As multiple vehicle chassis hit the pavement, Optimus charged in the direction of the nearest cover. On his shoulders, Sam and Mikaela held on for dear life.

One of the choppers immediately set off in pursuit of the fleeing robot. On the ground, agents used bolt cutters to free Simmons and his driver. Slipping and sliding in the spreading lake of lubricant, Simmons displayed admirable determination, if not balance, as he alternately hopped, slid, and ran toward a descending copter while simultaneously trying to climb back into his pants.

The systems operator in the first helicopter gazed in frustration at his multiple readouts. Given the amount of sensing gear on board the advanced chopper, it should not have been possible to lose the position of one running giant robot. Try as he might, however, he could not locate the alien machine. The chopper cruised low over hills, checked clusters of trees, and even flew underneath a high overpass bridge.

Since every instrument on board was aimed straight down, they did not detect the robot that was clinging to the underside of the viaduct.

Possessing muscles made only of flesh, Sam and Mikaela struggled to hang on to the upside-down robot. They were just barely managing—when the rotor wash from the helicopter passing directly underneath sucked Mikaela downward. Hugging the body of the mechanoid with one arm, Sam reached out with the other and just did catch the loop of her purse.

"Don't let me go!" she screamed, hanging on to the other end of the loop as she dangled over the pavement below.

The strain was evident in his voice as well as his face. "I—I can't hold on!"

A second chopper followed the first under the bridge. Its draft proved too much for the overstressed leather strap. It snapped. Reaching for her, Sam lost his own grip and they fell together, screaming. Swinging out a long leg, Optimus tried to catch them. All the effort did was to slightly slow their fall. The eyeglass case slipped from Sam's pocket and he made a desperate, futile grab for it. Closing his eyes, he waited for the final impact of his body hitting the ground. It came and he winced—and opened his eyes again. The pain was much less than he had expected.

Perhaps because he had landed in one of Bumblebee's hands, and not on the hard pavement beneath the overpass.

With infinite gentleness, the robot set them down on the roadside. Almost immediately, a steel-mesh net launched from one of the circling copters looped his right arm while another whipped around his legs. Working in unison, the two choppers turned north, yanking the robot off his feet and dragging him across the asphalt. Heedless of his own well-being, Sam ran after the entangled mechanoid.

"Stop it! You're hurting him!"

"Sam, you can't—" Mikaela began as she hurried after him. Her words were cut off by the heavy hand that slapped over her mouth. Catching up to Sam, a second beefy agent began wrestling him back in the direction of the waiting vehicles. All the money his parents had spent over the years on good dental work paid off as Sam bit down on one of the restraining hands. The agent cursed and let go.

Scouring the surrounding area, other agents recovered most of what the two teens had dropped during their fall from the bridge. Mikaela's purse and its contents ended up in the back of another vehicle.

Down the road, Bumblebee detected what was happening and redoubled his efforts to free himself from the entangling nets. Around him, camouflage-clad commandos were zip-lining down from a newly arrived chopper. They carried no guns, no explosives. The packs on their backs were filled with a unique supercooled carbon-fiber liquid held under high pressure. Hovering just out of reach, they began spraying the struggling robot from head to heel. Encased in the rapidly hardening material, Bumblebee took a step, a second—and then toppled forward as the substance hardened to form an unbreakable shell around his entire body.

"Get the hell away from him!" Sam howled as he neared the scene. "He's not gonna hurt anyone!"

On the bridge high above, the other robots arrived. Crawling over the side of the bridge, Jazz hung upside down to face Optimus.

"We have to help him!"

The bigger robot's voice was heavy with resignation. "We cannot engage a situation like this without harming humans!"

Racing ahead, Sam reached the place where the commandos had touched down and were continuing to spray the increasingly motionless Bumblebee. Kicking one from behind, he ripped the nozzle out of the startled soldier's hands and pointed it at his leg. The man howled as cold plastic enveloped his lower limb. A moment later agents swarmed Sam and yanked the device out of his hands. They were less gentle this time as they threw him in the back of a different SUV, practically on top of Mikaela.

As the car screeched away, Sam fought to sit up. Turning to look out the back window, he was just in time to see a pair of helicopters lifting the netted Bumblebee off the ground and swinging away to the north. He hit at the window with one fist as he howled in protest. His shouts did not penetrate the SUV's extra soundproofing.

The last of the choppers was gone. The commandos had been picked up and whisked away. None of the black SUVs remained. It was quiet again beneath the bridge. Somewhere, a pair of crickets began calling to each other. Nothing moved.

Optimus Prime dropped from the underside of the bridge to land heavily on the pavement below. Continuing to harden on contact with the air, tendrils of the special liquid plastic coated parts of the street and the nearby hillside. There was also something else. Something the human agents had missed.

Bending low, the robot plucked a small, almost insignificant object from the ground where it had fallen: an eyeglass holder. With the touch of a surgeon, enormous metal fingers delicately opened the case. A pair of shabby old spectacles gleamed in the light from his eyes.

Straightening, the massive robot looked first to the south, then to the north. They had the glasses.

But they had lost something else.

❂ XI ❂

Soundproofed as thoroughly as the best of modern sonic technology could manage it, the conference room had been designed and built especially for holding meetings at the highest levels of government. Nothing could penetrate it: no bugs, no listening devices, no echoes or reverberations from outside. A president could sit and chat securely with a premier—or a useful dictator.

At present the room was occupied by lesser lights: a soft-voiced, enigmatic individual who called himself Tom Banachek and the secretary of defense of the United States of America. As he spoke, Banachek was working to unfasten from his wrist the briefcase whose contents he had yet to disclose.

"You'll have to accept, sir," he told Keller, "that there are many things you won't understand right away. Some will be self-evident, but many will require additional explanation. Sector Seven is a special-access division of the federal government, convened in secret and established under President Hoover. Our jurisdiction, our specialty, is—everything that falls outside every other branch of the government's jurisdiction and specialty. Especially those things that fall *way* outside. By way of introduction, I ask you to remember that President Hoover was trained as an engineer and was therefore comfortable discussing security matters that would have been meaningless to many of our other presidents." A thin smile crossed his face. "I'll cut to the chase.

"Aliens are real. Sir."

Keller started to say something, then stopped himself. Banachek was right. There *were* things he was not going to understand right away. If he kept his mouth shut, he had the feeling many of the questions boiling up inside him were likely to be answered before he could ask them.

From the briefcase Banachek extracted an armored laptop. The secretary looked on in anticipation as the other man turned it on. One after another, a series of security logos ran rapidly across the screen as programs were loaded.

"Self-contained," the Sector Seven agent explained. "Still should function." Sure enough, the appropriate telltales winked to life as he fingered the keyboard. "A few years ago, you may remember, NASA lost the *Beagle Two* Mars rover. Following our analysis of the information that was made available to us from the JPL, my section told them to report the mission as lost, a complete failure."

His fingers danced lightly over the laptop's keys. On one wall of the conference room a screen came alive with light. On it a pixilated video feed appeared. It was blurry and imperfect, but watchable.

"It wasn't lost," Banachek continued. "The *Beagle Two* touched down successfully, the equipment package activated as intended, and as programmed it immediately began transmitting back to Earth. It did so perfectly. For thirteen seconds." He hit a key.

On the big screen a field of rust-red rocks appeared,

protruding from similarly colored sand. Abruptly, the image was darkened by a moving shadow. The view whipped around sharply, as though the camera and its mount had absorbed a severe blow. There was a brief but unmistakable glimpse of something large, regular in outline, and metallic—whereupon the image gave way to static.

Banachek turned to the secretary. "Before it ceased transmitting, the *Beagle* sent back an image of something other than just a pile of Martian rocks. Do you recall the final image?"

A stunned Keller nodded slowly, his tone subdued. "Pretty hard to forget."

"Right. Our analysts had similar reactions. Now here's the image our Rangers were able to retrieve from the attack on the base in Qatar." He tapped a few keys. The screenful of *Beagle* static was replaced by a thermal shape. Additional keystrokes refined the outline, freezing it for close examination. Keller said nothing; he could only stare.

"We think it's the same exoskeletal type as the one in the image returned by *Beagle* before it went dark," Banachek informed him. "Could even be the exact same figure: we simply don't have enough information yet to be able to confirm anything. But one thing we are pretty sure of: neither one is Russian or North Korean in origin."

The secretary swallowed hard as the agent darkened the screen and closed the laptop. "Are we talking about—an invasion?"

Banachek's tone was somber. "Mr. Secretary, we don't know *what* we're talking about—yet. We do know that we've been the subject of hostile action with no attempt at contact. If it is an invasion, it's been a pretty localized one—so far. We have no idea what might be coming next. On a more positive note—"

Keller interrupted. "There's a positive note?"

The agent managed a small grin. "We picked up a message from those Rangers. Our people are trained to fight back even when they're not sure what they're fighting. These things aren't invincible. They can be hurt by our weapons, and now they know it. It's surmised that that's why the virus, or whatever you want to call the synaptic intrusion, shut down our communications. So we can't coordinate against their next assault. Or whatever it is they're planning next. Whatever that might be, I'll bet my inadequate government salary that it's coming soon." He slipped the laptop back into its featureless, impenetrable case. "Usually it's the other way around, but in this case the president has authorized your department to assist *us*."

Keller nodded, beeped for an aide. Stationed outside the room, the woman arrived immediately. "Get word to all our fleet commanders over the National Guard system. It'll take awhile for the information to be relayed, but they have shortwave radio that's still working. Tell them to turn their ships around and come home pronto. The enemy are not the ones they are presently confronting. No combat is to be engaged in, there is to be no exchange of hostilities. Make sure that's understood."

"Yessir." The aide turned and hurried out. As she did so, Banachek closed his briefcase.

The snapping-shut *click* of the metal cuff that kept it attached to his left wrist was very loud in the quiet room.

The room in which Maggie Madsen and Glen Whitmann found themselves was also soundproofed, though not to such an extreme degree as the one in which the Sector Seven agent named Banachek had just alerted the secretary of defense to the crisis facing the planet. While adequate for essential hygienic purposes, the furnishings were also considerably more austere.

Both occupants rose as a cluster of agents entered, followed by none other than Keller himself. His hands secured behind his back, Glen immediately started blubbering.

"Oh God, don't put me in prison, *please* can we call my grandma?"

Throwing Glen a look it was better he did not see, Maggie addressed the agents. "Why are we here? What's going on? I want my lawyer!" Wordlessly, an agent uncuffed each of them.

Keller came up to her. "You don't have a lawyer. You don't need a lawyer."

She glared at the secretary. "Yes I do, because I'm going to sue you, the Department of Defense, and the whole damn United States government!"

"You don't have time to sue anybody," he replied, "because you're going to be my advisor. And if we can't take care of this problem that's come up, there might not be a United States government left to sue." That quieted her. He jerked a thumb in Glen's direction. "Who's he?"

Maggie didn't look in Glen's direction. "*My* advisor."

Though he found the explanation doubtful, the secretary chose not to question it. "Okay. He can come, too." Pivoting, he exited the cell. Maggie and Glen followed, the latter wiping at his eyes. The agents who surrounded them said nothing at all.

It was quiet in the hilly woods above Tranquility. A few birds chirped back and forth as they searched for food or mates. A couple of white-tailed deer strode cautiously between the trees. Movement caused them to bolt, springing off into the nearest cluster of dense bushes.

Having unintentionally frightened the whitetails, Optimus Prime held a pair of decrepit human spectacles up to his face. Two narrow beams of carefully modulated photons shot from his eyes to pass at a particular angle through the lenses of the old glasses. The combination of light, lens, and what had been etched on the glass generated a three-dimensional sphere some distance from his face. Recognizably the world on which they presently found themselves, the slowly rotating sphere was breathtaking in its detail and straightforward in its message: a single pinpoint of light shone unblinking on one of the northern continents. Optimus altered the light, and the view expanded to reveal an irregular body of water entirely surrounded by land.

Less than a second of electronic noise issued from the huge mechanical life-form. "In terms of local measurement, the cube is two hundred and fifty miles from our present position. A distance easily and clandestinely traversed."

Jazz's response took nanoseconds, the sonic alien equivalent of a single Chinese glyph. "They have Bumblebee!"

"Bumblebee is a brave soldier who understands and accepts the risks of our war," Optimus replied solemnly. Sonics gave way to common English. "For the sake of practice and gaining familiarity with idiom, we should speak now in the language of our new home."

"Our new home?" Ratchet was clearly bemused even as he complied with the directive.

Optimus turned to regard his colleague. "I have had sufficient time to ponder all possible ramifications of a multiplicity of actions, and what I have decided is this: if we return the Cube to Cybertron, our war will continue. I postulate eventual victory, but not for a minimum of another thousand years. We have been fighting so long, I can remember nothing else." With a sweep of one great arm he took in their surroundings: quiet, tranquil, and at peace, albeit unsettlingly organic. "The opportunity to live, to exist in a state of being other than perpetual combat, lies here, on this world. The madness ends today."

"But how?" Jazz understandably wanted to know.

Optimus proceeded to reveal that he had indeed thought out the situation in depth. "When we reach the Cube, I will join it with my spark."

Ratchet was openly appalled. "But an energy resurgence of that magnitude will destroy you both!"

"I will *not* allow the humans to become a casualty of our war," their leader declared firmly. "That is not our way. If we have battled so long for naught else, we have fought for that much. It is an immediately achievable goal. To fight to preserve life, however different it may be from our own." He hesitated for a split second. "That is a belief worth dying for."

One by one his counterparts closed in around him. They transformed together, reasserting the aboriginal mechanical forms they had adopted in order to be able to conceal themselves among the humans. Optimus studied his companions. Though still machines, they looked wholly terrestrial. What would be an appropriate indigenous designation for bots of this kind? Conscious of his own directive to utilize local language and idioms wherever possible, he followed through as he voiced his next command.

"Autobots—roll out."

* * *

It was very early and the sun was just raising its scorching self above the sere brown rocks of the desert horizon. These first rays found the three big army choppers traveling low and fast over the desiccated terrain. Each carried a different human cargo. Each component of that cargo had its own perspective on the incredible events of the past several days.

Sam Witwicky and Mikaela Banes sat on the bench on the left side of the middle chopper's cargo hold, Maggie Madsen and Glen Whitmann on the other. All wore advanced radio headsets that for some time now had told them absolutely nothing. They had been exchanging uncertain, uneasy looks ever since they had been loaded onto the copter.

Maggie was checking her minimal makeup in a compact mirror. It was left to Sam to break the silence. He did so with his typical aplomb. "So, uh—this is awkward."

Lowering the mirror, Maggie regarded the younger passenger seated across from her. There was no condescension in her voice because of his apparent age. She remembered all too well what that had been like. "What'd they get you for?"

Sam tried to frame a reply that might make a modicum of sense. It all seemed so very long ago. "Short version? I bought this car. Turned out to be a giant alien robot." If he expected the attractive woman to blanch, he was surprised. He might as well have told her that he was present because he had cheated on his calculus final.

"You?" a curious Mikaela inquired of the woman seated across from her.

Maggie shrugged. "Caught something, maybe one of them, hacking into *Air Force One*."

"Huh" was all Sam said by way of reaction. Like the woman, he was way beyond being surprised by much of anything.

"Man," an unhappy Glen muttered, "me, I was just watchin' television. CNN. I shouldn't even *be* here."

Stretching out across the hold, Sam extended a hand. "I'm Sam Witwicky."

That did get a reaction from Maggie. "Witwicky? You by any chance related to an old sea captain named Archibald?"

Sam nodded. "Yeah. He was my great-great-grandfather. And—a great man."

As the sun rose sharply, its intensifying rays struck gold off the surface of Lake Mead, behind Hoover Dam. Sam, Mikaela, and Maggie sought windows to look out while Glen remained sunk in his funk. All three choppers began to descend.

Along with a couple of agents, a group of seven soldiers emerged from the first helicopter. Coming down the steps, Lennox looked around, shook his head, and muttered to Epps.

"No matter what a soldier does these days it seems he can't get away from the freakin' desert."

Sam, Mikaela, Maggie, and a reluctant Glen exited the second chopper, while the third disgorged the secretary of defense, Sector Seven agent Banachek, and Agent Simmons, the latter looking even more gaunt than usual. As he had been instructed, Lennox held his ground as the secretary came up to him. The two men shook hands.

"We got your intelligence, Captain. Excellent work, especially getting that thermal image."

Lennox nodded in the direction of his friend. "Technical

Sergeant Epps deserves the credit for that, sir." He squinted at the desert sky. Unnervingly, it looked exactly like the sky over Qatar. "What about the gunships?"

"Being retroloaded with sabot rounds now, Captain," Keller told him, "but it's going to be difficult to coordinate much of anything if we can't get military communications back up. The last thing we want is to have to involve civilian authorities in this." He gestured at the woman standing next to him, who seemed unable to keep from shifting back and forth from one foot to the other, as if she needed a continuous outlet for her energy. "This is Maggie Madsen, one of our analysts. And her assistant, Glen Whitmann."

That was enough to bring Glen out of his depression. "Excuse me—'assistant'?" No one paid him any attention as they started toward an art deco entranceway. Mikaela paused to admire the view of the vast lake held back by the dam. As she was doing so, something hopped out of her purse, which had eventually been returned to her, and disappeared among the concrete and scrub.

Scuttling under a barrier, the spider-shape worked its way through passages far too small to admit anything bigger than a large rat. Finally halting beneath a sign, a resurgent Frenzy looked upward.

SECTOR SEVEN ONLY
NO TRESPASSING!
LETHAL FORCE AUTHORIZED

A sonic squeal emerged from the transformed Sidekick. Lasting less than a second, it shrieked in code too dense to be deciphered and too rapid to be picked up by the primitive native sensors nearby.

"Sector Seven located. Follow my signal—and *bring my body*."

On a nearby air force base the engines of an F-22 Raptor suddenly roared to life. Taxiing off the end of a line of identical planes, the interceptor headed for the main runway. Within the nearby tower there was sudden confusion. No one among the air traffic controllers present seemed to know who had requested permission for a takeoff or who had authorized the departure. Their bewilderment would have been worse had any of them been able to see that there was no one in the plane's cockpit.

On the edge of an army motor pool a huge mine-clearing vehicle rumbled to life. It was six-wheeled and heavily armored, and its front end sported specialized steel mine-excavating prongs. There was no one around to notice as it cut quietly through a fence and headed for the nearest highway.

Above a city not far from Tranquility a military helicopter banked sharply and headed north. It was an MH-53. A particular MH-53. Lennox and Epps would have recognized it immediately. They had seen the exact same chopper before. In Qatar.

In a salvage yard two workers were in the process of removing a wrecking ball from the top of a crushed police cruiser. The sight generated chuckles and some especially crude jokes. These were transformed into screams when the freed cop car abruptly morphed into a towering, glowering bipedal shape. As the terrified workers fled the lot, Barricade reached down and picked up the crushed metal body that had been lying next to it. Once the last human had fled, the powerful, thick-bodied Decepticon changed back into police cruiser form. Lights and siren stilled, it rolled quietly out of the lot.

At the base of Hoover Dam, a wheeled platform surrounded by heavily armed Sector Seven agents was being drawn into an access tunnel. Tightly bound to the moving platform, a yellow-and-black mechanical shape struggled ineffectively against its bonds. Mobile platform and its robotic cargo disappeared into the base of the great curved weir.

On top of the dam, Sam and Mikaela were being ushered forward by Simmons and his minions. They were joined by a tall agent with a gleaming metal briefcase cuffed to his left wrist. Banachek glanced at the two youths but said nothing.

"Get your hands off me!" Mikaela growled at the agent who kept shoving her forward. Sam was equally upset. He didn't like where this was going. He didn't like where *he* was going.

"Don't touch me! Where's my car?"

Simmons chuckled under his breath. "Hey, kid—I think we got off to a bad start. You must be hungry by now. Wanna latte? A Popsicle? What do kids eat these days?"

Unmollified, Sam glared at him. *"Where's my car?"*

It was Banachek who responded. "Son, listen to me carefully. Some really bad things have happened this past week. There are some really bad things going on right now. People have died. More people could be killed—maybe a lot more. We need to know everything you know, work together, to stop those things from happening."

Sam calmed down—but only a little. "Not till you promise me you won't hurt him—my car, I mean. It's the only way I'll talk."

Banachek nodded understandingly. "Agreed. There will be a few passive scans only. Nothing intrusive, no—dissection. Deal?"

Sam nodded, albeit reluctantly. "One more thing." He indicated Mikaela. "You gotta let her dad outta jail." He eyed Simmons, smiling as he remembered. "Like, for-*ev*-er."

The other agent's expression was unreadable. Mikaela's, on the other hand, was not. She was looking at him gratefully. As the two of them eyed each other, they were joined by a group of soldiers. Soldiers with grim expressions and very good tans, Sam noted thoughtfully.

"Ladies and gentlemen," Banachek exclaimed as soon as the troops had joined up with the rest of the group, "follow me. Time is of the essence."

Having once been forced to sit through a dated black-and-white presentation on Depression-era government construction projects, Sam recognized the massive turbines in the vast room at the base of the dam. He had never expected to see them in person, though. As Banachek led the group past the humming generators, Simmons was finally able to unburden himself of some classified information.

"Here's the situation insofar as we have been able to determine it," he told them. "We appear to be facing war against a highly advanced technological civilization far superior to our own." He nodded at Sam, then Mikaela. "You're here because in one way or another, you've all had direct contact with the NBEs."

"Which, like it or not," Banachek told them, "makes you the world's foremost experts on the—visitors. In this situation, age is of no consequence. It's your individual experiences that are important and that interest us as a matter of national and world security."

Epps looked uncertain. "NBEs?"

"Non-biological extraterrestrials," Simmons told him. "Try and keep up with the acronyms."

"Oh," Epps shot back challengingly. "Like CQ, Vector Delta, Niner-Alpha—*that* kind of acronym?"

"Maybe," Simmons admitted, realizing he might have overstepped.

"In our language, they can be called 'Transformers,'" Sam put in helpfully. Banachek looked sharply back at him.

"They told you that?"

Sam put a little more hip in his step. "They told me a lot. We're tight."

A massive door loomed ahead. It would not have been out of place fronting an airline hangar—except that it was hundreds of feet underground. Though out of time, Banachek still tried to prepare them.

"You're about to see something few people know about and even fewer get to experience in person. Don't forget to breathe."

Rumbling, the door began to move aside. As soon as enough of an opening had appeared, Banachek led them inside.

The underground silo was immense. Multitiered gantries and girders leavened with strands of tubes containing liquid nitrogen surrounded something frozen in blue-tinted ice. Something huge, ominous, and—bipedal. Another robot. As big as if not bigger than Optimus

Prime, an awestruck Mikaela decided. She could not take her eyes from it as they were led inside. Neither could Sam.

Such a spectacle was completely new to Maggie and Glen. He simply stared, nervously rolling a last trio of Fruity Pebbles back and forth, back and forth, between his fingers.

"Oh my God," she murmured as she gazed up at the mechanical colossus. If it was any consolation, the secretary of defense was no less flabbergasted than she was.

"I'll be a son of a bitch," Keller murmured as he regarded the metal leviathan.

Aware that he was privy to information denied to all but the highest level of government, there was a note of pride in Simmons's voice as he joined Banachek in leading the group forward.

"This baby's the first we found."

Banachek offered more detail. "We think that when it approached our world, it came in too low over the North Pole. Maybe there was an especially active aurora at the time, or maybe it miscalculated the strength of our gravitational field, or maybe a sudden solar flare screwed up its navigational instrumentation. Though we remain ignorant of the cause, it was fairly clear from the position and attitude in which it was found that it did not make a controlled touchdown. We surmise that it crashed into the polar ice, was seriously incapacitated, and subsequently became frozen in place by a series of active cross-current pressure ridges." He looked over at Sam. "Not unlike the fate that befell your great-great-grandfather's ship."

"We call him NBE One." Simmons glanced at Epps. "Acronym."

"I *got* it," the tech sergeant snapped irritably.

Eyes fastened on the gigantic frozen form, Sam stepped forward. "I don't think that's quite all of it, sir." He nodded at the towering shape. "That—is *Megatron*. Leader of the Decepticons, as we would call them."

"Basically, the bad guys," Mikaela added helpfully.

Lennox eyed her admiringly. "Yeah, I kinda got that from the name."

As they conversed, a tiny mechanical spider-shape was working its way around the perimeter of the enormous open space. When workers threatened to come too close, Frenzy merged into the background until they had continued on past. None of the passing humans noticed anything out of the ordinary. How could they, when the slender Decepticon could transform itself to become an indistinguishable part of their surroundings?

A tight-lipped Keller was glaring at Banachek. "I guess no one thought I might, as secretary of defense, need to *know* that the government is keeping a hostile alien robot frozen in the basement of Hoover Dam?"

The agent waxed apologetic. "I'm sorry, but it's always been that way, sir. Presidential discretion. Roosevelt never told Truman we had the atomic bomb, and he never told him about this, either. Being a military man, Eisenhower was informed. He understood the need for continuing the secrecy. Other presidents have maintained the practice, wishing above all to avoid anything that might cause a general panic. And until now, we had no reason to believe that there might be others like it—much less that they might show up here and pose a direct threat to national security."

"That's a question." A curious Lennox spoke up. "Why 'here'? Why Earth?"

"The Energon Cube."

Wherever else they had been looking, whatever else they had been thinking, all of them now turned to stare at Sam. He'd always wanted to be the center of attention—but not necessarily here, and not necessarily now. He indicated the towering, frozen shape.

"The way it's been told to me, Mr. NBE number one here, aka Megatron, is like the harbinger of universal *death*. Pretty much wants the Cube so he can transform all machine 'life' and take over the universe one technologically oriented world at a time. Starting with ours." He turned a slow circle, the look in his eyes a bit wild. "Can I get a Coke?"

Banachek and Simmons exchanged a fleeting glance. Sam was no trained psychologist, but the meaning behind that look was easy enough to grasp. He gaped at them both as comprehension dawned.

"You know where it is!"

☙ XII ☙

Though not as vast as the silo that contained the frozen body of Megatron, the chamber that held the Energon Cube was just as impressive. The Cube itself hung in the center of the brightly lit room, swathed in a web of umbilicals that both supported and monitored the alien artifact in their midst. Visitors and technicians alike could observe the Cube from an observation deck walled with panels of transparent, double-thick polycarbonate. As his charges moved close to the panels to examine the interior of the chamber, Banachek filled them in on some of what was known.

"Carbon-dating of organic debris recovered near the Cube and from the same frozen strata puts its arrival here around ten thousand BC. We didn't find it till 1913. Its actual age is unknown. A few years ago we managed to obtain a tiny sample of the outer coating utilizing a high-energy industrial laser." He shook his head. "We couldn't make a determination on anything, much less radioactive decay. We couldn't find any potassium-40 and there are no uranium elements. We thought we might have detected traces of thorium-232, but that turned out to be a false positive. As far as datable isotopes go, the recovered alloy sample continues to drive our people crazy.

"It was stored nearby in a deep salt mine in Utah until President Hoover had the dam built around it." He pointed straight up. "One hundred football fields of concrete thick. Perfect way to mask the energy it's leaking from being discovered by anyone on the outside."

"It's not perfect," Sam corrected him with assurance. "Optimus Prime says it calls to them every thousand years. That's why they came. I guess all the necessary conditions were finally right for making contact."

Maggie tore her gaze away from the Cube and looked back at Banachek. "Wait a minute, back up. You said the dam hides energy that's leaking from the Cube? What *kind* of energy, exactly?"

"I could give you a thick file to read through. There are more equations than words. Come," he told her quietly, "and I'll show you."

The next chamber they entered was barred by a thick steel door that opened to reveal a laboratory that must have been founded some time in the 1930s. While much of the equipment and technology on view was state-of-the-art, some that had been pushed aside or stored near the back hinted at experiments that had been conducted much earlier. The slender tentacles of electrical and other cables spread out in all directions from a central transparent box mounted on a high dais. Or maybe, Sam thought, the cables ran to it. A couple of uniformed technicians were waiting for the visitors. Busy preparing instruments and checking readouts, they spoke hardly at all.

"Everyone step well inside, please," Banachek told them. "They have to lock us in."

Lennox looked unhappy. "Why do they *have* to lock us in?"

The vault-like door swung shut behind them with a loud, decisive *boom*. This was followed by a series of metallic clicks as heavy bolts were slammed home. Unlike the visitors, Simmons looked like he was enjoying himself.

"Kind of a tricky bit of science they do in here. You never know how things might develop." He grinned humorlessly. "Could turn out to be a bad day."

Epps gestured toward a series of deep parallel gashes that scored the far wall. "Who did they have in here? Freddy Krueger?"

Simmons indicated a sign that proclaimed WE HAVE WORKED 322 SAFE DAYS, then pointed to the gashes. "Those happened three hundred and twenty-*three* days ago." Now even his severe smile vanished. "That was a *real* bad day." He nodded to one of the techs who was working nearby. "Charlie was a good man." The tech nodded back.

"Anybody have any advanced electromechanical devices?" Simmons asked them. "BlackBerry, key alarms, flash drive, cell phone?"

Remembering that he had seen Glen with a cell phone, Banachek walked up to the programmer and confiscated it. "For essential demonstration purposes," he explained. Having been shuttled gruffly around the country like an accessory to one of the computers he so loved, Glen was in no mood to be accommodating.

"Demonstration purposes my ass—anything happens to that, I want every song that's on it *replaced*—and I've got a list!" His voice fell when one of the techs handed him a pair of heavy-duty industrial safety goggles. "Hey, what are these for?" The tech didn't reply, moving along to hand goggles to everyone else.

"Ohhh," Simmons was murmuring knowingly as he considered the device, "cell phones can be *real* nasty."

Banachek passed the phone to one of the technicians. Opening the box, the man placed it inside and proceeded to attach to it a couple of cables no bigger than wires. He then stepped back, closed the box, and locked it down with enough seals to secure a rampaging wolf.

"Goggles everyone, please?" Banachek advised them. No one saw fit to argue with him by not donning theirs. Once everyone had proper protection in place, he moved to a console and thumbed controls. Energy flowed into the transparent box—a minuscule bit of energy channeled from the Cube in the next room.

Sam and Mikaela leaned forward. Was the phone shaking? It began to vibrate violently, trembling on the platform inside the see-through box. Without warning it sprang to loud life, blasting music into the room. The box, clearly, was not soundproofed.

Then the phone began to transform.

Lacking intelligence, without anything to guide it but with the Cube spark to animate it, the device went mad. Legs and arms sprouted in all directions. Impelled by the powerful but aimless life force with which it had just been imbued, the trembling, jerking, writhing mechanism threw itself violently against the side of the transparent enclosure, fighting to break out. Every one of the newcomers instinctively jumped backward, away from the insanely flailing machine. Looking on as it all but beat itself to pieces against the unyielding transparent polycarbonate, Maggie thought it entirely appropriate that the music that was blasting from its outraged speaker was thrash metal.

"Mean little sucker, ain't it? Kinda like the Energizer Bunny from hell." Fearlessly, Simmons approached the container. Sensing his presence, the transformed multi-limbed phone began battering rabidly at the transparency that was all that separated him from the soft-fleshed human. Leaning toward the box, the agent studied it phlegmatically. When he had seen enough, he nodded at Banachek. "Better zap the little freak. Before it figures a way out."

Removing a small cylindrical charge from a standing container full of them, the other agent slipped it into a straightline tube that pierced one side of the container. Patiently, he waited until the struggling phone was directly opposite the tube before pushing a switch. The box was filled with a blinding flash. When it cleared, everyone could see that the insane shrieking mechanism had been torn apart. Emitting a horrific electronic squeal, it flipped onto its back. Everyone could clearly see the hole in the center of its body where frame and components were melting away. The steaming circle continued to widen as they looked on.

Stunned silence filled the room. One by one, the numbed spectators removed their protective goggles and handed them wordlessly back to the waiting techs. Simmons grinned, contentedly this time.

"Well whaddya know: sabot rounds work. Even mini sabot rounds." Reaching out, he gave Lennox an approving smack on the shoulder. "Nice work."

The Ranger captain took a deliberate step away from the agent. "Don't touch me." His tone was not hostile, just very matter-of-fact. Nonetheless, there was no mistaking the implication that underlay it.

Steel and bolts notwithstanding, Glen promptly rushed the lab's vault-like inner door. "Okay, Grandma needs her insulin. I'm *out*. You hear me? Find somebody else to help you. Go ahead and shoot me if you want to, but I'm—"

The floor rocked beneath them. Not enough to knock anyone off their feet, but sufficient to indicate that for a locality that was supposed to be tectonically inert, something was badly wrong. If they could have seen the approaching transformed bots, from the F-22 Raptor to the MH-53 assault helicopter to the eclectic assortment of oddly perfect vehicles that was presently rushing the dam, Sam and Mikaela would have felt considerably worse.

A lack of familiarity with Decepticons and their capabilities did nothing to still the tide of dread that was rising inside Maggie. Moving to the port that overlooked the Cube suspended in the larger room nearby, she gazed anxiously at the alien relic. It was completely covered in static alien glyphs—except that some of them now seemed to have acquired a slight shimmer. Nothing more than a trick of the artificial lighting—she hoped.

Lennox was looking upward. "Those are concussion blasts. Could be terrorists—or something else."

Keller bit his lower lip. "Terrorists could never get this close to the dam. Security is too tight. Has to be something more than that. Bigger than that." The secretary did not have to further identify the unstated "something." Everyone in the lab knew who he meant. Knew *what* he meant. Turning, he looked toward the chamber that held the silent, pulsing Energon Cube.

"They know it's here."

High above the canyon of the Colorado, a pilotless F-22 swooped in low and dragon-like over the dam. The missiles it unleashed struck the main aboveground electrical distribution complex. Immediately, significant portions of the city of Las Vegas went silent and dark.

In the old laboratory far below, lights exploded and instrumentation went crazy. The lab went black, but only for a moment until battery backup power kicked in. Lennox didn't know about the others, but he for one was not about to wait around toothless for the next strike. Terrorists or Decepticons, he was not about to go naked into the good day. Turning, he put himself right in Simmons's face and demanded:

"Where's your security armory?"

Meanwhile, in another room that was much larger but not very far away, power to a special cooling system failed. Emergency backup immediately came online. Initial panic among the technicians began to subside. It resumed full-bore when backup power, too, suddenly vanished. Essential readouts were frantically checked, vital monitors scanned. The junction where the flow of backup power had been cut could be located, but could the key failure be repaired in time?

Not if the spidery mechanoid called Frenzy had anything to do with it. Unseen and unchallenged, it roamed through the most sensitive concatenations of circuitry and linkages, snipping cables, frying microchips, and generally wreaking nonstop havoc with the intricate system that maintained the vast room at a specific predetermined temperature.

That room was beginning to warm up.

With the power to them now cut off, clamps and cables holding the huge mechanoid steady and stable in the center of the room began to retract. Some of the technicians began to flee the observation deck, running like mad for the elevators.

Lennox and the others had no time to flee. But the security armory was close by. The captain felt much better as soon as he was cradling one of the high-tech handheld rocket launchers in his arms. Together with the few Sector Seven agents Banachek had been able to round up, Lennox and his men began feeding the weapons dozens of recently arrived compact sabot rounds. As loading continued, everyone present spun possible options.

"Nellis Air Base is fifty miles away," Keller remembered. "They can have air support here in ten minutes."

Maggie had been employing every kind of workaround she knew to try and coax a response from her phone—to no avail. "Everything's still out." A distraught Glen eyed her meaningfully.

"You wouldn't get a signal down here even if they were working." He gestured upward with an index finger. "All those football fields' worth of concrete, remember?"

"I thought there might be embedded relays . . . ," she began. Ignoring the others, the two of them fell to discussing possibilities for communicating with the outside world.

Sam, on the other hand, felt he knew exactly what had to be done. "You gotta take me to my car!" He was doing everything but kicking Simmons in a frantic effort to get the agent's attention. "He'll know what to do with that Cube!"

The agent finally deigned to notice him. "You nuts?" Simmons gestured back in the direction of the lab they had just fled. "You saw what just a drop of that energy can do to even a small machine. We have no idea what might happen if we let one of these more advanced Transformer-things near it."

Sam met the older man's gaze without flinching. "You wanna find out what'll happen if we *don't*?"

Another concussion coursed through the ground under their feet. Lennox confronted the agent. "I've seen what these things can do. If whatever is here now is anything like the ones I and my people had to deal with in Qatar and they get hold of that Cube's energy, we're dead anyway."

Glaring at both of them, Simmons protested loudly. "He's a delinquent! You expect us to believe a—"

Grabbing the agent by the front of his jacket, an enraged Lennox lifted him off the ground and slammed him up against the wall. Immediately the Sector Seven agents in the armory drew their weapons. So did the captain's men.

Lennox's tone was low and tight, his words careful and distinct. "Listen to me. I got a wife who's wasting away waiting for me to come home and a baby I've never even seen and I promised a good man as he was dying in my arms that we'd waste these things and you haven't got an idea in hell what to do next, *so take the kid to his damn car!*"

The tension in the armory was thick enough to cut with a knife, except that it would have upset the shaky balance of power. In the ensuing silence, Keller took a deliberate step toward Banachek.

"I'd do what the captain says. Losing's really not an option for these guys."

Torn between several options, none of them promising, and unsure how to proceed, Banachek continued to hesitate. "If the boy is wrong, we could be unleashing hell."

Holding his recently acquired weapon at the ready, Epps let out a short, scornful laugh. "We've already been in hell."

Simmons's expression changed from natural defiance to a resigned sneer as he relaxed in Lennox's grasp. "All right, sure, why not? Hey, you wanna lay the fate of the world on the goodwill of a kid's Camaro? That's cool."

While the soldiers, agents, and visitors in the lab tried to decide how best to proceed, the now-unclamped and fully defrosted monster in the silo not far away was starting to awaken. Electronic synapses pulsed with renewed energy. Permanently self-lubricating joints began to stir. Enormous limbs ran checks on the condition of their long-dormant extremities. Dark irises expanded. Consciousness was returning to Megatron, and the cosmos would be the worse for it.

Optics began to focus. On the floor and within the observation deck techs and scientists and maintenance personnel were now fleeing in all directions as they scrambled to reach the nearest exits. Behind them, the first electronic utterance to emerge from the gigantic long-quiescent mechanoid was accomplished with the expenditure of a barely measurable amount of energy.

"INSECTS."

Contemptuously shaking off the last of the restraints that had held it in place for so many years, the first of the great metal limbs began to move forward.

In a separate containment area, Bumblebee remained secured to an examination slab. Lights of different wavelengths bombarded both the platform and its imprisoned occupant. Mists that had been treated with various chemicals drifted over the struggling subject and were drawn into multiple collection tubes. The venue was loud and unpleasant.

Sam had to yell at the top of his lungs as the door to the examination area burst open and he rushed in, followed by his companions and the two groups of armed agents and soldiers.

"Stop! You gotta let him go!"

Banachek had hurried over to the researcher in charge. Flashing a badge, he nodded agreement. "It's okay, release it. My authority."

Despite the racket, Sam overheard. "*He's* not an 'it'!"

Puffing, Keller came up alongside Banachek. If the agent's security clearance was not sufficient to justify the release of the mechanoid currently undergoing examination, the presence of the secretary of defense certainly was. Feeling covered, the lead researcher relayed the necessary orders.

Study lights winked off and the cloud of sensing gas began to dissipate, sucked away by concealed fans. Bindings and clamps were withdrawn. When the last of them had pulled away, the robot on the rack sat up as Sam raced over to check on his—friend.

"You okay?"

The Transformer looked down at the young human. The song that emerged from within the metal body was perfectly appropriate to their reunion.

"Yeah, yeah," Sam responded, "it's great to see you, too, *but listen to me.* The Cube's here, so is Megatron, and we're pretty sure the Decepticons are coming for both of them!"

Instantly the yellow-and-black robot was on its—on *his*—feet and racing for the access door. With shorter strides and considerably more apprehension, the growing knot of humans followed. Fresh shocks passing through the surrounding concrete knocked lines and supports, old plaster and paneling from the ceiling as they ran.

Halfway to the exit, Keller spotted the secret installation's central research room. He started to tell his idea to Banachek, reconsidered, and instead found himself making the suggestion to the attractive young woman with green streaks in her hair who was running alongside him.

"National Guard radio may still be up and functioning. We can try and get word out over rudimentary frequencies."

She considered, nodded approval, and turned to Glen. In the absence of his usual Fruity Pebbles fuel he was having a hard time keeping up.

"Can you hotwire some old gear to transmit simple Morse?"

Panting hard, he replied while shaking his head. "I dunno, I dunno. Maybe. I'm a coder and a decrypter, not an electrician."

"Bull," she shot back. "I've seen you build portable drives out of crap RadioShack throws out as unsalable. I know you can do something this uncomplicated."

"All right, yeah—get on it!" Pacing effortlessly nearby, Lennox drifted over to the two youths. "Make contact with Nellis if you can. You get our birds in the air, then when we get wherever we're going we'll find some kind of transmitter and Epps can vector 'em in." His expression was feral. "Put 'em right on top of these Decepticons of yours."

Simmons stared at him. "How the hell're you gonna do *that*?"

Lennox grinned over at the agent. "Improvise."

Keller leaned close to Sam. At that moment he was not the secretary of defense of the United States, one of the most powerful men in the world. He was merely an older man urging on a younger one.

"Never, never give up, son. Do it—*go!*"

Sam responded with a nod as the group separated, with Keller, Maggie, Glen, and Simmons heading for the research room.

Having been informed via runners about what was happening throughout the complex, the researchers in the Cube-holding chamber were not startled when the group of soldiers and youths burst in. There was a moment of confrontation during which the guards who had arrived in small military vehicles had to be convinced to place themselves under Lennox's orders. Having Banachek present as a leader of Sector Seven and taking the captain's side greatly facilitated the hasty handover of command.

It was much harder to convince the technicians charged with monitoring the Cube to step back from what for many of them had been their life's work and let an alien robot take control. Lennox and his men felt no such restraints. Having been witness to the deaths of many of their comrades at the hands of malevolent versions of such machines, they were eager to have one on their side for a change.

Another explosion shook their surroundings. Shielding his head from falling debris, Epps shouted at the advancing Bumblebee, "Do your alien thing fast, big guy. I don't like enclosed places. Remind me too much of coffins."

Bumblebee reached the Cube. For an instant he hesitated and simply stared. The artifact before him was, after all, the original source of all life energy for his kind.

It was not quite like a human confronting God. More akin, Mikaela found herself thinking as she looked on, to a sentient laptop being offered a battery that would never run down.

No one asked Bumblebee what he was thinking.

As the robot extended both hands toward the Cube, the ceaseless hum that emanated from it began to rise and fall, to stutter rapidly as it responded to the proximity of a Transformer. Tendrils of energy suddenly arced between the Cube and Bumblebee's fingers. Some type of contact had definitely been made, Sam was sure as he raised a hand to shield his eyes from the flashing, flaring lights, but it was contact of a kind that could never be known to mere humans. The robot and the Cube were talking with light.

Contact came to an end. There followed a moment of silence that was shocking in its tranquility. Then both Cube and robot began to transform. Sam and Mikaela and the captivated soldiers looked on as Bumblebee bent and twisted before their eyes, first contorting in upon himself, then thrusting blades of metal out and forward, until finally where the robot had been standing there stood nothing more complex and alien than a simple car.

Well, maybe not so simple, Epps thought admiringly. The tricked-out Camaro was pretty slick.

As for the Cube, it had begun the process of transformation by folding in on itself, sides and glyphs and symbols shrinking and contracting, becoming a steadily reducing succession of concentric squares, until at last it had shrunk to something that was no bigger than a football. Resting in the backseat of the car, it presented an appearance that was both harmless and unimpressive. A seat belt rose up seemingly of its own accord to lash it down. Doors snapped open, and the car's horn honked anxiously.

Sam and Mikaela exchanged a glance. Looking back, Sam saw that the army captain was waiting for him to take the lead, to issue an order—to do *something*.

Well, why not? he thought. It *was* his car.

He got behind the wheel while Mikaela climbed in on the other side. In the backseat, something a lot bigger than it looked lay snugged up against the brand-new upholstery. Before either of them could say anything they were thrown back in their own seats as the Camaro peeled out, heading for the exit tunnel. Joining the recently arrived security troops in their compact vehicles, Lennox and his men followed.

Behind them, deeper within the complex, the immense figure of Megatron continued to step clear from the last of his trailing restraints. Cables and smaller wires tore away from the gargantuan body like thread. Conduits that continually replenished the material in which he had been frozen broke free, spraying supercooled liquid in all directions. By now the vast silo was almost empty of its human occupants.

The Cube, he thought. The Energon Cube had been close—very close. Now it was gone. He sensed its presence, its power. Both were receding steadily from his current location. But it was not far. After so many millennia, the delay in recovering the Cube would be as nothing. No time would be involved, little effort would be required.

Tilting back, the enormous metal skull peered upward. Acute sensors detected other presences. To his right was the long tunnel through which he had originally been hauled in so many years ago. Cowering behind stacks of barrels whose thick white exteriors were enlivened by stencils of skulls and crossbones, one tech who had been unable to escape looked on in terror as the huge mechanism began to change before his eyes. He need not have feared for his life. Even if he had been in a mood to kill, Megatron would not have wasted his time with such inconsequentialities.

He had a rendezvous to make.

The bipedal shape contracted, flexed, flowed, and expanded. What condensed in its place was something like a plane, something like a jet fighter—but unlike anything the tech had ever seen before, except perhaps in the illustrations on the covers of certain magazines to which he subscribed.

Growling to itself, the alien aircraft pivoted on the debris-filled floor. Purple fire emerged from one end. Turning away from the sight, the tech shut his eyes tightly and covered his eyes as the machine smashed through the towering blast door and disappeared down the access tunnel, leaving only a thunderous echo in its wake.

After performing a perfunctory reconnaissance of his former prison and its immediate surroundings, Megatron circled slowly downward to land among the rocks at the bottom of the dam. Transforming back into his natural bipedal shape, he walked up to a second machine. Awaiting its master, the other mechanoid sat perched eagle-like on a massive jutting finger of granite. Their greeting was brief and incomprehensible to humans.

"Starscream," Megatron rumbled coolly. "It has been a long time."

"Long even by our standards, Lord Megatron," the other Decepticon readily agreed. "Many things have changed, yet much remains the same. The essential absolutes are unchanged. The passage of time is nothing more than a delay. Today the inevitable finally achieves fruition." A hand swept toward the dam and, by inference, everything that lay beyond. "This world called Earth by its inhabitants now belongs to us. It swarms with primordial machine life awaiting only our touch to jump to the next stage."

"The insects," Megatron growled, "must be cleared."

Starscream gestured concurrence. "Once we have transformed Earth's machines, the purification should take less than a day."

"It will be a joy to observe such a cleansing," Megatron replied. "Following which we can then—"

He broke off. In the distance something was calling to him again. After all these eons. It was a calling that superseded all else: transformation, the coming gathering of allies, even the intended return to war-racked Cybertron. Starscream felt it, too. Before anything else could be done, it had to be dealt with. A last dealing, Megatron knew. A final reckoning. Everything else could wait, including the cleansing of this useful but currently diseased planet.

As he had already determined, it shouldn't take long.

⚛ XIII ⚛

There was the usual traffic on the highway leading to Vegas, but not enough to dangerously inhibit the convoy. Flanked in front and behind by the shepherding army vehicles, the Camaro purred northward away from the dam and the Colorado River. They were headed for the complex of military bases located just outside the city. Once there, they would be far better equipped to protect the Cube and deal with anything the Decepticons could throw at them. In the vehicle he was riding in, an expectant Epps kept his sabot-loaded launcher close at hand. Donnely was alive in his mind, and so was Figueroa.

One shot, he kept repeating silently to himself. That was all he wanted, all he wished for. Just one shot, within range. Blow a freakin' hole right through one of the soulless metal bastards. Watch its guts melt and leak out all over the road as he stared back into its empty plastic eyes and waited for it to die. Catching a glimpse of the Camaro ahead of him, he felt that he had to revise his scenario somewhat. Alien machine or not, he decided, maybe, just maybe, some of them were not quite as soulless as the rest.

Inside the Camaro, Mikaela turned to look into the backseat.

"Is the Cube okay?" Sam asked her. He could have turned to look himself—he was only feigning driving—but habits die hard.

"Yes," she reassured him. "It's wearing its seat belt." Turning to face forward again, she caught him staring at her. There was a touch of wonderment in his voice when he replied. Not because they were transporting an elemental alien device that was the source of unimaginable power, not because they were riding in a self-driving car that could at a word transform itself into a giant alien robot, but because of something considerably more mundane.

"Wow," he murmured in disbelief, "just then, we just sounded like *parents*."

Riding in one of the army vehicles, Lennox tensed as an exotic sports car suddenly appeared in the passing lane and accelerated to slide in beside the Camaro. He relaxed when one of its side-view mirrors twisted up and around to flash him a sculpted Italian-designed equivalent of an automotive wave. Any other time, any other day, such a sight would have caused him to question his own sanity. Not this afternoon, however. Not after everything that had transpired this morning. Back inside the dam the kid had mumbled something about other robots, about the Camaro he called Bumblebee having friends who might well come looking for him. Evidently, this sports car was one of them. The captain wondered what it would look like transformed into its natural state. As a car, it was pretty sleek.

It was not alone. Other escorts soon made their appearance. Expecting more cars, Lennox was surprised when the sports car dropped back behind the Camaro to allow an emergency vehicle to take up a flanking position. He might have anticipated the tricked-out black GMC pickup that showed up next, but the blaring eighteen-wheeler that rolled in behind the entire convoy constituted still another surprise.

Oh well, he told himself. *Every robot to its favorite bilocation.* When he and his wife went out for an evening she was pretty surprised at some of the things he chose to wear, too.

They had reached the outskirts of the city when a new disturbance drew his attention. There was trouble on the highway behind them. His fingers tensed on his weapon as he rose and waved an arm, raising the alarm.

The siren and the whirling lights atop the police cruiser that was a revived Barricade cleared much of the unsuspecting civilian traffic from the Decepticons' path. What didn't get out of their way was thrown aside, one car at a time, as the mine-clearing steel mandibles of the gigantic Decepticon known as Bonecrusher scooped up slow-moving vehicles and tossed them out of the way. The fact that each of the vehicles so callously and violently disposed of happened to contain live human beings hardly registered on the single-minded Decepticon. Without slowing down, Bonecrusher transformed into his natural state. Metal feet slammed down onto the highway, cracking concrete and sending shards flying. The screams of those caught in destroyed vehicles were not ignored by the onrushing Decepticons so much as they remained beneath notice. No matter how loud or piteous they might be, one could not take the time to pause to acknowledge the protestations of insects.

Pickup/Ironhide and the big diesel that was Optimus Prime dropped back to confront the challenge. As Bonecrusher propelled himself forward, Optimus transformed.

The sound as the two robots collided in midair was thunderous. Locked together arm in arm, they crashed down from the freeway's upper level to land on the access road below.

A mother driving a van full of kids barely had time to react to the impossibility that suddenly appeared in front of her. As she wrenched the wheel over hard, the heavily loaded vehicle skidded sideways toward the separating robots. Bonecrusher leaped over the van—not to avoid damaging it, but to try and put the local machine between it and the larger robot. He could not, however, escape the concentrated full-force pulse blast that Optimus unleashed in his direction.

The full strength of it struck home, sending the Decepticon smashing into a cement-lined river basin. Arriving alongside, Optimus walked warily around the unmoving pile of metal. Bonecrusher did not move, not even when Optimus kicked hard at the crumpled form.

He sensed rather than saw Barricade as the second Decepticon landed on his back. There followed a flurry of furious action that ended only when Optimus flipped the machine clinging to him against a steel-and-cement freeway pillar. The impact cracked and bent the column. It did worse to Barricade, who lay twisted and unmoving. Two Decepticons dealt with in only a few minutes. Things were going well. Resuming his eighteen-wheeler form, Optimus pumped exhaust and blared his horn as he accelerated to rejoin the others.

The loss of two of their number caused the pursuing Decepticons to slow and reevaluate their strategy. This gave those they were pursuing time to exit the freeway and enter the city. There being no direct access to the military complex on the other side, the convoy would have to negotiate some of the city's poorer outskirts before clear access and additional freeway allowed them to enter the air force base. The alternative was go a dangerously long way around.

As they entered an area of the city speckled with small stores and family businesses, Lennox directed the driver of his vehicle to pull over and park. While pedestrians gaped at and commented on the decidedly odd mix of military and civilian vehicles, Lennox raced around to the driver's side of the idling Camaro. Epps was close on his heels while Sam looked up at him in confusion.

"Gimme a second to find an old radio!" Lennox yelled in at the two youths. "We need to be able to relay our position."

Sam was no military strategist, but he had played enough games to know what the captain was talking about. "What if no one's been able to call out your air strike?"

Lennox almost grinned at the kid. "Well, that would suck."

"Yeah," Epps added unnecessarily.

Mikaela leaned toward the officer. "Shouldn't we keep going toward the air force base on the other side of the city?"

Lennox shook his head. "Not good tactics to split up, miss. Not here. Please, just a minute."

Sam was still uncertain. "Where are you gonna find an old radio?"

Lennox turned and pointed. Following his lead, Sam and Mikaela saw the old pawnshop that had drawn the captain's attention. The barred windows were crammed with an impressive assortment of cast-off junk, some of it fairly recent. That was hardly surprising in a city like

Las Vegas, where sometimes it seemed like every other piece of personal property in town had at one time or another been pawned to pay a gambling debt.

If they found the right piece of old junk, Sam reflected, it might just save their lives.

The research room and library dated back to the construction of the dam. As if the architecture and 1930s art deco décor were not confirmation enough, row upon row of bulging cabinets straightaway caught Maggie's attention.

"Ohmigod," she murmured in disbelief. "*Paper* files."

"Welcome to the Mesozoic," Simmons told her. "The information stored here goes all the way back to 1913." He picked one thick wad of papers off a table and held it up. "Handheld file, circa early twentieth century. Access is slow, but on the other hand you don't have to worry about accidentally deleting the contents."

Off to their left, an agitated Glen was already ripping the back off a computer. Keller joined Simmons in searching for a tool kit, soldering equipment—anything that could be used to join wires and unfried microchips. As he worked, Glen was muttering unhappily.

"I'm feeling, like, *real* anxious here, Mags. Better keep your distance—I might throw up on you."

She smiled encouragingly. "Perfectly understandable reaction, Glen. Feel free to upchuck, but at least try to aim first." She indicated the rapidly unfolding guts of the computer he had chosen. "Try to give the electronics a miss, too."

He managed to grin back. "Hey, I'd puke on you in a minute, but *never* on gear."

"That's all right." She put a reassuring hand on his shoulder as he worked. "I know my place in the hierarchy."

Keller dumped some tools on the table beside him. Picking up a small screwdriver, Glen stuck his tongue out the side of his mouth as he went to work in earnest on the computer's interior.

"I'd kill for a Red Bull right now," he muttered.

"No Fruity Pebbles?" she teased him.

Adept as those of a surgeon replacing a fleshy heart with one made of metal and plastic, his fingers were a blur as they manipulated the components inside the computer casing. "Need both hands," he told her pithily. "Can't suck Fruity Pebbles when I'm working like this. But don't tempt me."

Simmons did not know how long the old antenna wires had lain in the back of the research room and didn't care. Choosing one set, he began stripping away the cracked and flaking protective outer covering and the underlying insulation to reveal the clean copper underneath. He was making good progress when something slammed into the metal door that led to the access tunnel outside. Everyone stopped what they were doing except Glen. For the first time in days, he was in his element.

"What the hell's that?" Holding the shredded antenna wires, Simmons stared at the door.

"Didn't sound good, whatever it was," Keller commented uneasily.

The banging and hammering resumed with methodical ferocity. Ignoring it, Glen wired the antenna Simmons had found directly into the hastily revamped guts of the old computer.

"I'm *really* gonna barf," he mumbled as he worked.

Leaving his side, Maggie rushed in the direction of the noise. "Help me with the door!"

Simmons came up alongside her. "Lady, back away! We have protocols for this!"

Whatever was on the other side of the barrier kept pounding. Metal hinges started to bend inward. Maggie's gaze kept shifting from the buckling door to the agent.

"What the hell kinda protocols?"

"We do a drill every Thursday," Simmons informed her.

"Yeah, great," Glen called over to them from where he was working furiously. "'Alien invasion Thursdays.' That should *really* help."

Leaving Simmons to contemplate proper procedure, Maggie moved to help Keller. The secretary was shoving a heavy cabinet toward the doorway. All those heavy paper files, she reflected, still had some practical use after all. Depending on the situation, there was a lot to be said for sheer deadweight.

A portion of the door bent toward the inside and a skinny robotic head and upper body managed to wedge their way through the gap. Swiftly scanning the room to evaluate its contents and occupants, Frenzy flexed its torso.

"Get down!" Keller yelled. He might be a civilian now, but he had done his stint in the active military.

A trio of silvery discs shot from the robot's chest. Keller tackled a startled Maggie as two of the discs whizzed over her head to rip into books and files. The third disc shot over the keyboard of the computer Glen was modifying, nicking one of his fingers before smashing into the computer behind him. He all but jumped out of his chair, nearly abandoning his work as he whirled to gawk in the direction of the slowly deteriorating door.

"*What is that freakin' thing?*"

Recovering, Simmons stumbled over to a glass case filled with Sector Seven emergency equipment. "Awright," he snarled, "*screw* protocols." Pulling out a riot gun and a box of twelve-gauge shells, he handed both to Maggie. She fumbled with the box as Simmons took out a small, very portable device whose compact tank was filled with jellied gasoline under pressure.

A flash of sparks caused Glen to flinch back slightly from his work. He was not displeased by the effect. "*Got it!* We can transmit."

Keller looked upward. "Through all this?"

"The network must still exist," Simmons told him. "It's the transmitters and terminals that went down.

"When this setup was built, every room in the complex was equipped for radio transmission. When more advanced means of communication came along, they took out the radios but left the wires behind. More trouble to pull 'em out than just leave them." He gestured upward. "Same with the old antennas on top of the dam buildings and the canyon rims. Easier and cheaper to leave 'em be. As long as they haven't completely corroded, this should work. Our signal's going to go out over a wire. Simple but straightforward. Morse ain't advanced, but a code is a code. All we need is for the dips and dashes to get out into the ether. Somebody'll recognize it and pass it along, even if it's only a ham operator or two."

Nodding his understanding, the secretary turned to Glen. "*Send exactly what I say*. This is Secretary of Defense John Keller calling NORTHCOM. Authenticate emergency response Blackbird one-one—"

"—nine-five-Alpha," Glen finished. For someone used to typing well over a hundred words a minute—blindfolded—it seemed beyond prehistoric to be using only two keys of the keyboard, one finger on each, to send a message. He'd set up one key to send a dash, the other to send a dot. One long, one short. It sure was a long way from programming in C++ or Java.

The secretary stared at him. "How'd you know my ID?"

"Look," Glen told him as he tapped away at the two keys. "I *told* your people I got this hacking problem! I know a whole buncha codes. I know *your* codes, the *president's*, NASA's—I even know how many times you voted for the last American Idol!"

Keller ground his teeth. A year ago he would have had this smug nerd locked up forever for what he had just confessed. Now thousands, maybe millions of lives depended on him being intimately familiar with what he had just confessed to having stolen.

"Just type the message!"

"Okay, okay." Glen paused, his fingers hovering indecisively over the two reprogrammed keys. "Uh, I'm having a brain fart. Can't remember all my Morse. It was so long ago . . ."

"Oh God," Maggie stammered, "me neither."

"You people gotta be kidding me!" Having relieved himself of that observation, Simmons proceeded to assuage his frustration by unleashing a column of concentrated flame in the direction of the rapidly failing door.

Maggie came up to Keller. "You're the secretary of defense! Didn't you learn Morse in the navy?"

"Sure," an agitated Keller told her. *"Thirty years ago."*

She strained to remember something she herself had learned long ago. Or maybe someone had just told her about it. "There was a song, the one they make you learn for the NSA field test." She started humming to herself as she loaded shells into the riot gun. Driven back by the heat from Simmons's miniature flamethrower, Frenzy had been forced to retreat. Now it was back, and the angry pounding on the barrier had resumed.

"A dit is a dot, a dot is a dash." Eyes shut tight, Maggie was struggling to remember the relevant mnemonic. "Al-pha: dit-dit—it's like that."

"Yeah." Keller's expression brightened. "Yeah, that's right. Bra-vo: dot-dit-dit-dit—it's all coming back!"

Sparing the briefest of glances for them, Simmons raised his voice above the roar of the flamethrower. *"Great. Sing faster!"* Every time a flailing metal limb tested the opening in the damaged door, he bathed it in fire and it hastily withdrew.

But if the door came down, he had already decided, they would have about thirty seconds in which to kill the thing before it started ripping into them.

Lennox banged furiously on the pawnshop's gated door. The sign outside said BIG RHONDA'S.

While being skilled and highly experienced in field visual recognition, the captain suspected that none of those abilities was necessary to identify the woman who came lumbering toward him as the eponymous owner of the establishment. Flashing him a warning glare, she wrenched open the glass-fronted door that backed up the grates.

"Hey! Don't be bangin' on my door! I ain't open right now."

Lennox struggled to compose himself. "Ma'am, we got a *serious* emergency. D'you have a shortwave radio?"

She studied the uniform and the face that went with it. "I told you: we closed."

"Ma'am, please," Lennox entreated her. "If you have a radio—"

"No, but I got a CB. You payin' cash?"

He ground his teeth. "*It's a matter of national security*. Open the door!"

"Don't you be takin' that tone with me, boy. This here door's a matter of Big Rhonda security. I know my rights. Hey, you happen to know why none of my cell phones ain't workin'?"

Stepping back, Lennox unsnapped his holster to reveal his service pistol. "Ma'am, let us in or I'll have to *shoot this lock*."

Edging to one side, the pawnshop's owner reached down. When she straightened she was holding a shotgun. Big barrels; not fancy, but efficient.

"G'head," she retorted, "and I'll have to be shootin' *you*!"

He raised both hands. "Okay, okay! Ma'am, we don't have time for this!"

She gestured at him with the shotgun. "I'm closed—I got plenty o' time."

"Look." He slowly extended his left arm toward her and pulled back the shirt sleeve. "See this? You can have my watch. Military Ranger issue. Tells *perfect* time by the atomic clock in Geneva—that's in Switzerland."

She glared at him. "I know where Geneva is." She nodded brusquely toward the back of the shop. "I got three cuckoo clocks back there, no atomics, and they all work just fine."

A frantic Lennox continued his sales pitch. "You can even scuba dive with it. Watertight down to a hundred meters."

She drew herself up. The action was both a definition and a warning. "Do I look like I'm goin' *scuba diving* to you?"

"LADY, FOR THE LOVE OF GOD, TAKE THE WATCH!"

Still gripping the Mossberg, Maggie shoved hard against the cabinet with her shoulder, leaning all her weight into it to keep it wedged against the badly damaged door. She was joined in the effort by Keller and Simmons. Behind them, a preoccupied Glen was leaning toward one of the jury-rigged computer's speakers. An electronic stutter suddenly made itself known above the low-level static.

"They're responding!" he yelled excitedly to his companions. He met Keller's gaze. "They've accepted your authorization code!"

The secretary's spirits soared. "Call in the strike! Tell them what's happened here, put it in your own words, but tell them what to look for in the immediate area and to respond accordingly!"

Glen nodded and bent back to the keyboard. As he did so, the deteriorating door finally buckled enough to allow Frenzy to squeeze through. Leaping into the room the Decepticon instantly appraised its surroundings and began unleashing one lethal disc after another.

Maggie juked to the side as one disc cut right through the barrel of her riot gun, taking another couple of inches off its already reduced length. The damage didn't seem to affect its functionality, however. When she pumped it and fired, the shell struck the homicidal robot dead-on. The mechanoid emitted a crazed electronic squeal as the sheer force of the shot knocked it backward. Recovering its footing, Frenzy looked around and sprang straight up as Maggie fired again. The robot disappeared through a gap in the ceiling where an insulation panel had been removed to allow maintenance access.

"Send the message quick, Glen!" she shouted at her friend as she patrolled beneath the ceiling, trying to listen for movement overhead as she gripped the shotgun tightly.

He was tap-tapping furiously on the two keys. "I'm doing my best here, Mags—the killer robot's *really distracting*!"

Halting, she listened intently, then raised the Mossberg and fired upward. A section of ceiling came crashing down, followed by the robot. Whipping limbs sent Keller spinning to the ground as she screamed. Stepping up beside her, Simmons unleashed his flamethrower. Displaying reflexes no human could have matched, the robot dodged the gout of flame and fired another disc. Only Simmons's exceptional training saved him as he twitched to one side at the last possible instant. The flying disc sliced away some hair, but nothing essential.

Having sidetracked the agent, the crazed machine spun on Maggie. She fired once, twice, *click*.

Empty.

Using the gun as a club, she swung madly at the oncoming robot. Her eyes were fixed on the place on its torso that emitted the deadly discs. When it fired again, she crouched down as low as she could. The discs bounced all around the room. Most embedded themselves in equipment. Only one of them ricocheted several times before returning to take a reverse swipe at its intended target. Ready for it this time, she ducked a second time. It shot over her and—cleanly decapitated the machine from which it had been launched. As Frenzy's head fell to the floor the multilimbed body swiftly crumpled. Breathing hard and still clutching the empty shotgun, she straightened and glared down at the twitching body.

"Ha! What goes around comes around!"

Setting aside the flamethrower, Simmons searched until he found a tool suitable for grasping at a distance. Avoiding contact with the squirming, spastic hunk of alien metal, he got a good grip on it and began dragging it across the room.

"Make way, coming through! Garbage pickup!" Unexpectedly, he smiled across at Maggie. Even more surprisingly, she smiled back. Then she turned to confront an exhausted Glen.

"Did you," she asked apprehensively, "get the message out?"

He slumped in the chair. For a moment he didn't respond. Then he turned to her and a wide grin broke out across his face. Holding up both index fingers, the ones he had used to tap out the Morse, he blew on the tip of first one and then the other, nodding as he did so.

It didn't take long after Lennox rejoined the others for Epps to make relay contact with the scrambled flight from Nellis. It was a strange way to communicate—CB radio to field relay to base to aircraft—but it worked. If there was one thing the military was good at, it was battlefield improvisation. Especially when not too many officers were involved.

"Aircraft circling city, this is on-site. How copy? Can you track our position?"

The only reply was static. Then a low whine became audible. Coming in low and fast, the F-22 Raptor passed directly overhead, a lot lower and closer than anyone in the FAA would have countenanced. As it thundered past, Lennox turned to follow its progress.

"The air force *has* arrived! Confirm our position."

A couple of the soldiers fired flares. It was immediately evident that they had been observed, as the jet began to circle back. Cheers erupted from the troops in the line of vehicles.

"Raptor flight," Epps said into the CB, "we're five klicks south of the tallest building passed on your recent flyover. We have you visual—your heading returning to our position, over." He clicked the switch on the CB, hopeful of a response and verbal confirmation this time. But there was still only—static. The fighter kept coming, dipping lower as it approached.

Within the convoy, shapes shifted, bodies morphed as pickup and eighteen-wheeler, sports car and Camaro and emergency vehicle swiftly transformed. They did not need to consult with the humans in their midst to know that something was wrong.

"Jazz, Bumblebee," Ironhide rumbled, "flanking positions!"

Jazz loped to one side as the Raptor came on, impossibly low, and—unleashed missiles straight at the convoy.

"Nooo!" Lennox howled as he dove to one side.

Starscream fired several times as its targets scattered for whatever cover they could find. Heedless of their own exposure, Bumblebee and Ironhide picked up and flipped a nearby heavy truck in front of the convoy to shield the unprotected humans. One missile struck the truck and sheared it in half. Bumblebee was catapulted backward, his torso bouncing one way, his legs the other. The hideous squeal of metal sliding over cement accompanied him as he finally tumbled to a stop.

Knocked free by the blast, the Energon Cube went bouncing onto the asphalt. The combination of the impact and the concussion from the missile strike caused it to release a short-range shock wave that swept over everything within the wave's effective radius—including any and all electromechanical devices.

Having looked on in shock at the ongoing chaos, two young men abruptly fled from their car as the energy wave from the Cube swept through their vehicle. As they stumbled away, every piece of electronics in the tricked-out sedan was transformed into a miniature multilegged horror, as if a pregnant metal spider had suddenly given explosive birth to a bevy of unspeakable offspring.

Rapidly losing intensity as it dissipated outward, the wave still retained enough strength to shatter the windows in a nearby superstore. Rushing through the aisles, the energy burst swept over one shelf after another. Soon panicked shoppers were fleeing in all directions. One employee pushing a cart piled high with game consoles screamed as metal arms suddenly thrust out of every box, ripping at the cardboard in a frenzied desire to escape. Elsewhere, legs appeared beneath flat-screen televisions and blaring stereos as they dislodged themselves from their mounts and stumbled aimlessly about, drunk on Energon energy.

Among the stores situated on a street a block farther away was an extensive gun shop. Within the single, heavily barred window a single rifle put out hesitant tendrils and started to rise before collapsing back onto its display mount. The Energon wave had lost its potency nary a yard too soon. There was no envisaging what bedlam a second, stronger discharge might set loose on the already chaotic streets.

Out on the pavement, Lennox dragged himself out of the debris. His gut instinct was to find a weapon and start fighting back. But seeing the two teens who had been put in his charge, he instead hurried over to help Sam and Mikaela climb free of the wreckage.

Around them the street had turned into a war zone. Water fountained from a broken fire hydrant. Lying off to one side and close by, Bumblebee's shattered lower torso trailed twisted metal. His legs were nowhere in sight.

"Bumblebee." Sam's eyes widened in horror as the full extent of the damage to his friend became apparent. "Oh, God, somebody, *help*!"

Fighting, digging at the ground with his hands, the yellow-and-black torso struggled to drag himself over to where the Cube lay exposed and unprotected on the bare pavement. Under Lennox's direction, soldiers who were able to do so spread out to form a defensive cordon around the vital artifact. Recovering the CB from the wreckage, Epps hurriedly ran a check on the primitive device. It was beat-up, but intact. The question was— was it still functional? Only one way to find out. Turning a knob, he was rewarded with a crackle of static. He put the mike to his lips.

"This is an air force combat controller on-site southern city suburbs; we're under heavy fire here from rogue aircraft. *Anyone copy?*"

More static. Epps was sick of static and heartily sick of the archaic CB. His mood improved dramatically, however, when a garbled voice came back at him over the device's clunky speaker. It was barely comprehensible.

"Yes, army Black Hawk—inbound to your—copy . . ."

Much of the transmission was unintelligible. "Say again," Epps growled at the mike, *"over."*

". . . lay down," the voice was saying, ". . . your coordinates . . ."

Static and mayhem, Epps thought edgily. Nothing for it but to reply—and hope.

"From IP Alpha two-seven-three degrees, ten miles November Victor one-two-four-three and three-four-two-seven, NA one-point-two-six klicks north."

"Copy th . . . respo—ETA two minutes."

Two minutes. Moving as fast as he was able, Epps ran to pass the information on to as many members of the convoy as he could. It wasn't easy. There was—interference.

Two blocks away, Blackout appeared, perching like a hawk on top of an undamaged building. The ground shook as a previously undetected Decepticon came rumbling around a corner. Cloaked in the persona of an Abrams tank, it flattened unoccupied cars beneath its massive treads as it trundled forward. Transfixed and with nowhere to run, Sam and Mikaela could only crouch and stare.

A couple of the small-armed Sector Seven vehicles charged at the advancing tank, firing their mounted weapons. Instead of artillery shells, pulse blasts erupted from the armored behemoth. Both charging vehicles were hit, knocked engine-over-exhaust, to explode when they hit the ground. Looking on, Lennox could only grind his teeth in frustration. Commandos formed a tight, protective group around the two teens. With only small arms to defend themselves there was little they could do against the oncoming Abrams—but they were determined to do what they could.

They did not have to deal with the tank. As everyone looked on, the Abrams tank known as Devastator *transformed,* rising upward on two massive legs. But the head remained a turret. This pivoted toward them. Sam grabbed Mikaela and this time, she clutched him back.

Something low and fast appeared behind the transformed tank, morphing even as it skidded forward. Transforming in midslide, Jazz leaped onto the hostile robot's back and wrenched its torso backward as it fired. The pulse blast shot skyward, missing people and buildings alike. Spinning free, the smaller but more agile Jazz slammed the robot Devastator into a nearby structure just as Ratchet and Ironhide arrived. Transforming together, the three robots began to pound the single powerful Decepticon in their midst.

They were not alone. Seizing the opportunity, Lennox led soldiers and Sector Seven commandos forward. Launchers were lifted and carefully aimed so as to avoid robotic allies. Miniature sabot rounds sped toward their target.

A massive pulse blast from an unseen source struck Jazz, knocking him to the ground and out of the fight. Looking upward, Lennox and his men retreated as rapidly as they had just advanced. Something truly massive was coming around the corner.

Megatron.

Bending over the injured Jazz, the dark metal monstrosity zeroed in on the damaged robot's torso, reached down, and with piercing fingers *ripped out* a flashing, flaring sphere of energy. His spark brutally extracted, Jazz went instantly immobile.

A moment too late, a second colossal machine arrived. Tearing through the fences that separated several of the surrounding buildings, the big diesel was transforming even as he raced forward.

Megatron saw Optimus Prime coming and transformed in reverse. But as the alien aircraft started to rise, Optimus stretched out both arms, took a single tremendous leap, and locked onto his ascending counterpart. The weight was too much. Both machines plunged downward, smashed into one building, and plunged to the street. Optimus rose immediately. As he stood, the enraged Megatron transformed again, back to his innate, intimidating, bipedal self.

"Hello, Brother," the giant hissed.

Holding his ground, Optimus gazed evenly back at his peer. "Hello, Brother."

Nothing else was said. There followed no further words, no elaboration, no nanosecond burst of sonic communication. There was nothing more. It was as though all the millennia that had vanished into time since their last physical encounter had never passed.

They charged simultaneously, and collided.

Using his hands, Bumblebee had managed to drag himself over to the softly pulsing Cube. Recovering the device, he then pulled himself over to where Sam and Mikaela crouched holding each other. When Sam turned at the gentle metal touch, the robot placed the Cube in his hand, clearly urging Sam to flee.

"No." Moisture began to well up in Sam's eyes. "*I'm not gonna leave you.*"

As had already been explained to them, they knew that the yellow-and-black robot did not have much to speak with. But by rechanneling an electrical impulse here, recalibrating output elsewhere, he managed to work around his long-destroyed vocal symbology. Managed to utter two words.

"Ggggooooo Ssssammmm . . ."

Above the hiss and roar of sabot rounds being fired and exploding, colliding metal, and crumbling infrastructure, the sudden *thumping* of multiple rotor blades suddenly made itself heard. Lennox looked up. Army Black Hawks, several of them. Better late than neverland, he told himself. He hurried over to where Sam was still standing next to the severely damaged Bumblebee.

Reaching into a pocket, he pulled out a compact cylinder. "Here's a rescue flare." He indicated the nearest building. "Get up on that roof and signal one of the choppers—they'll pick you up. Do not stop, do not look back—just go."

Sam shook his head. "But—what'm I supposed t'—"

The captain cut him off. "Look at me, son! You're a soldier now. Everybody's a soldier until this is—over. Get that Cube outta the city. As far away as you can. Or a lotta people are gonna die here!"

Sam looked over at Mikaela. A lot passed between them then, without a word being spoken. She moved closer to him. "No matter what happens," she murmured, "I'm glad I got in the car with you."

He smiled back. He had nothing left to say that he had not already said with his eyes. Holding the Cube like the school football he had never been allowed to carry, he turned and ran. A shadow loomed over him. Ironhide, providing cover. They hurried past cars that had been abandoned, past others that had been destroyed or were burning noisily.

A pulse blast struck Sam's bulky escort. The force of it blew Ironhide off his feet and into the side of a building on the far side of the street. Though Lennox's words echoed in Sam's brain, the captain's admonition was unnecessary. Sam had no intention of stopping.

But when the F-22 came rocketing down the avenue toward him and transformed on landing back into Starscream, Sam had no choice. His path was blocked, and not by rubble. Changing direction, he turned and raced up a narrower street. Behind him, the huge robot fired in his direction. Brick and rock and asphalt erupting all around him, Sam could only yell wildly.

"You're not gonna get me! You're not gonna get me!"

Crowded up at the front of a nearby restaurant,

trapped patrons looked on as Decepticons continued to tear up the adjacent city block. Their attention was momentarily distracted by the sight of a red-faced seventeen-year-old carrying a glowing cube as he came running toward them, dodging nimbly in and out between parked and abandoned cars. A pile-driver of a metal foot slammed downward, just missing him. Screams erupted inside the building as a car thus crunched came spinning and flying into the restaurant's front window.

In the narrower street Sam's smaller size worked to his advantage. Blackout's foot came down hard, only to miss him again. He had to find a place to hide, a place to wait until he could make a dash for the top of the building the army captain had pointed out. But where?

Far down the street the battle of titans continued unabated. Stepping back, Megatron's arms morphed into an enormous piece of alien artillery. The pulse blast they produced sent the stunned Optimus hurtling backward the length of a full city block. Virtually ignored in light of the larger battle, Lennox had time to grab Epps, spin the tech sergeant around, and point to a nearby building.

"Tell 'em to rendezvous with the kid on that roof!" *If he makes it,* he added, but only to himself.

Epps obediently worked the still-functional CB. "Army Black Hawks: request immediate critical evac for civilian boy carrying vital cargo. Subject headed to rooftop of highest structure in immediate vicinity of active combat. *Expedite, expedite!*"

Ignored by soldiers, agents, Decepticons, and Optimus's robots alike, Mikaela searched for some way to contribute to the ongoing battle. Parked in a nearby towaway zone, a tow truck beckoned. Smashing the window with a chunk of concrete, she climbed inside. Hoping for keys, she found none. The same piece of broken roadway that had secured her entrance served to batter loose the ignition assembly. Expert fingers and agile teeth stripped wires and brought them together, generating sparks.

"Come on, *come on*," she muttered anxiously.

More sparks were followed by a throaty rumble as the engine finally turned over. Straightening in the seat, she looked over a shoulder and threw the truck into reverse.

The handsome old office building was in the throes of reconstruction. Because of that and the concurrent absence of furniture, there was only construction detritus to block Sam's way: gallon cans of paint, half-assembled scaffolding, yards of plastic sheeting, rolls of fiberglass insulation, bags and packages, and stacks of refuse. No use looking for a functional elevator, he saw right away: that was also undergoing renovation. The main stairs beckoned and he bolted upward as the building shook from the shock of nearby explosions.

This wasn't so bad, he told himself. No worse than running the bleachers at school, and this time there was no red-faced coach to yell at him and tell him he was slacking, holding back, you'll never make the team this way, Witwicky, you'll never . . .

A gigantic metal skull crashed through the floor he had just surmounted. Turning to look upward, it shone dark lenses on Sam's minuscule ascending form. Five massive fingers thrust upward, reaching. He leaped for the next landing as the hand smashed into the stairs he had just vacated.

The roof was empty, deserted, and undamaged. His fingers fumbled with the flare, nearly dropping it. Halfway to the edge of the building it suddenly ignited.

By great good fortune it happened to do so as it was pointing upward. The bright ball of light soared skyward, an unmissable, unmistakable beacon that screamed *Here, I'm here!*

The Black Hawk chopper appeared at the side of the building before the flare had fallen halfway back to Earth. Standing on the skid facing the roof, an army commando reached out and down with one arm, extending himself as far as he could.

"Grab my hand, kid! My hand!" he yelled.

Sam leaned out, the gale from the hovering copter buffeting him, threatening to blind him with his own windblown hair. It seemed a long, long way between him and the chopper. It was certainly a long, long way to the pavement far below. Easing himself forward and holding tightly to the Cube with one hand, he reached out with the other.

The world blew up in his face.

Stunned and thrown backward by the force of the explosion, he struggled to see through the rain of flaming copter debris landing all around him. Scrambling to the building's edge and peering out and down, he was just in time to see an F-22 go thundering past.

It looked up at him, electric with menace. Starscream again.

A distraught Lennox tracked the wreckage of the flaming Black Hawk as it spiraled downward. "No no no!" He turned away as it slammed into the street and exploded. When he looked up again, his eyes encountered a massive pair of lenses—questioning, not threatening. Whirling, he pointed to the top of the tall building.

"The boy, he's up there, he's in trouble!"

The head of the enormous mechanoid tilted back to follow the captain's lead, and considered.

In the heat and confusion of combat there was someone else besides her no one was paying any attention to, Mikaela knew. Bringing the tow truck around, she hurried out and around to the back. She found the tow chains stored and waiting where they ought to be. Pulling them out as she had done with other car chains so many times before, she dragged them over to the recumbent Bumblebee and began draping them around the metal shoulders. The procedure didn't take long. *Not much difference,* she reflected as she searched for the external crane control, *between shoulders and fenders.*

Locating the correct lever and pushing it down drew the chains taut and hauled the yellow-and-black shape erect. But all the seriously wounded robot could do was sit upright. Both legs were missing. And in his present badly injured state he could not properly transform. Not that a Camaro with both rear wheels missing would have been much help in any case.

Just as she was trying to decide which street to flee down, another shape appeared. The transformed tank, Devastator, had recovered sufficiently to rejoin the battle. Firing in her direction, its first blast knocked her off her feet. Dazed, she struggled to recover her senses. If she did not, and didn't do something quickly, both she and the robot Bumblebee would be reduced to mush. And unlike the robot, she would not last long if she was compelled to sacrifice something of importance—like her legs.

Using the truck for cover, she hurried forward and managed to slip into the cab. Flooring the accelerator, she abjured the chaotic streets in favor of heading into a narrow parking lot that occupied the space between two buildings. Another street loomed ahead, at the end of the angular lot. Approaching the exit, she slowed. A foot at a time, she eased out into the crossroad.

It was quiet. Dead quiet. No strident sabot rounds sending flaming magnesium flying everywhere. No giant robots slamming into buildings and one another. She could go left, she could go right. Whichever way she chose, she could accelerate away from the area of conflict. Behind her, buildings shook from the concussions of the ongoing war.

Several choice curses took turns running through her mind. Uttering the most damning of the lot, she wrenched the wheel hard over and headed not north or east, but back around the block. Back the way she had come.

Back into battle.

Taking cover in a badly damaged building, Lennox and his troops had to sprint and dodge to avoid one strike after another from Devastator. Given a brief respite as their hulking hunter sought their latest hiding place, the captain called a squad of Sector Seven commandos to him.

"We're three stories here," he told them, breathing hard as he indicated the surrounding structure. "Get up on the top floor and try to get a better angle on this thing. We'll keep it busy down here." The squad leader nodded his comprehension and gestured at his men. They rushed for the stairs, leaving Lennox and the others behind.

Screeching around the last corner, Mikaela found herself back on the periphery of the ongoing mêlée—and

behind Devastator. In front of the tank she could see soldiers popping up and down inside a building to fire in the
direction of the transformed tank, and the robot responding by unleashing periodic pulse blasts in their direction. Devastator gave no indication that he was aware
of the presence behind him. Taking a deep breath and
gripping the wheel tightly in both hands, she floored the
accelerator, dragging Bumblebee between abandoned
cars, the robot's wide body snapping off doors as the tow
truck gathered speed.

"I'll aim, you shoot!" she yelled back out the open
window. Appropriately angry music—the heavy metal
was not unexpected—blasted understandingly from the
robot's torso as he readied an arm cannon.

"Bumblebee," she howled as the transformed tank
loomed larger and larger in the windshield, "blast that
mother . . . !"

The rest of her sentence was drowned out as the precisely aligned shot from the injured robot screamed past
her. It was followed closely by a second. Both pulse
blasts slammed into the rear of the transformed Devastator, splintering the air intake while lifting the back of the
tank completely off the ground. The robot landed, ruined and smoking, in the street.

"Nice shot!" she yelled out the window. She had
driven for her father in demolition derbies, but never in
one where the opposing vehicles shot back at you.

As Sam huddled on the rooftop wondering what to do
next, an enormous shape erupted from the stairwell behind him, shattering the roof and sending chunks of it
splattering in all directions. Through the flying debris he
saw a dark form rise up, and up.

"CLEVER INSECT." Megatron was looking directly

at him. Sam could only look back. There was nowhere left to go. A huge hand extended in his direction. "IT IS OVER. GIVE ME THE CUBE."

Scrambling to the edge of the roof, Sam took a look over the side, nearly vomited, and hung on to his small glowing burden.

"No, I won't do it—"

"I ADMIRE YOUR ARMOR. BOLD WORDS FROM SUCH A TINY, FRAGILE ORGANISM. WORDS ARE PRAISEWORTHY. METAL IS BETTER." The fingers gestured. "THE CUBE. NOW."

Chest heaving, Sam crawled a little farther, until his head and part of his upper body were hanging over the drop. "I. Am. *Never*. Giving it to you." Rolling suddenly to his right, he sprinted toward the opposite edge. Through the settling dust he had spotted a double loop of metal there—a fire ladder, hanging over the side.

Out in the street where he and his men had fled from the building, Lennox's gaze locked on a parked motorcycle. In his panic, the driver had abandoned it. The key was lying by the kickstand: good. Picking it up, he turned to yell back at the trailing technical sergeant.

"Epps, I'm gonna see my little girl, you understand?"

The sergeant grinned back. "What, like I don't wanna see mine?"

"Then bring the rain!" Unlimbering the launcher from his back, he positioned the tube he had been carrying against the bike's handlebars as he gunned the powerful street machine forward through the flaming wreckage. Epps followed him with his eyes for a moment, then spoke clearly and distinctly into the CB.

"Nellis Raptors, you are cleared hot! Choose your targets!" Having delivered that message, he joined the rest of the Sector Seven troops in searching for someplace deep, dark, and solid in which to bury himself.

The two planes came in low and angry at the top of the street—and did not transform as they vectored in on the rampaging Blackout. The Decepticon turned to face the oncoming human threat. As it did so it did not see the lone human buzz in underneath it, grab the launcher it was balancing on the front bars of its two-wheeled vehicle, slide the bike it was riding between both towering legs, and fire just as Blackout was preparing to bring down both oncoming aircraft.

The mini sabot rounds tore into the Decepticon's body and limbs, melting metal, leaving behind ugly spreading lesions in the alloy. They were not serious enough to bring the robot down, but they were more than distracting enough to divert it sufficiently for the two diving fighters to have time to unleash their own missiles. Missiles that had been hastily fitted with oversized sabot warheads.

They ripped into the glowering robot, tearing off an arm, blowing great white-hot holes in its chest and lower torso. Shrieking electronically, the mechanoid shook, wavered—and, as Lennox scrambled clear, began to disintegrate.

The ladder, Sam thought wildly as he ran toward it. If he could just reach the ladder. Then what? A chance, maybe. Not to climb all the way to the ground—too far. Megatron would be on top of him long before he could reach the street. But break open a window, disappear into the depths of the empty building, dodge and hide— let the big chunk of murder find him then!

He did not have to.

A huge hand slammed downward, digging into the

roof and blocking the way between Sam and the beckoning ladder with a wall of metal. A terrible arm rose up, cannon-tipped. It fired, once, striking the section of roof just in front of Sam. Intended as a final warning, the shot had an unforeseen secondary effect. The rooftop crumbled, breaking away beneath him. The robot had underestimated the force of his own pulse blast. Tottering near the edge of the gap, fighting to retain his balance, Sam felt himself falling, falling, accompanied by broken statues from another decade and other rubble dating from the 1930s. As he tumbled from the crumbling building he reflected on what a pity it would be that he would not have a chance to appreciate all the elegant architectural refinements in their infinite and no doubt pleasing detail. Perhaps one or two, close up before he smashed into the ground. He closed his eyes . . .

And hit. Hard, but not nearly as hard as he had expected. Sooner than he had expected, too. Opening his eyes he saw that he was lying in the palm of an enormous hand. Something about the color was familiar—he looked up, and found himself gazing into the lenses of Optimus Prime.

They were falling toward the street together. Leaping from above, a furious Megatron plunged downward after them. Even if they landed in one piece, Sam realized, they would be crushed between the ground and the colossal mass of the hurtling Decepticon.

Cradling Sam protectively against his chest, Optimus whirled as they fell. His other arm morphed into a huge gun. A first shot missed, but the second struck home, blasting the pursuing Megatron off to the side. The leader of the Decepticons would hit the ground with tremendous force, but he would not land on them.

Extending both legs, Optimus jammed his feet into the side of the building. They ripped through successive floors of concrete and steel, slowing but not stopping the robot's fall. When he finally struck the street, the concussion rattled every building nearby. A cloud of dust and debris geysered from the point of impact.

More F-22s from Nellis Air Base appeared overhead, cruising low and slow, searching for targets. Rising from his place of concealment, Epps was happy to help out.

"Restricted attack, heading west, main target is mobile," he barked into the CB. "Expedite!"

Landing on his feet nearby, Megatron recovered immediately from the shock of contact with the street. As he did so, Lennox and his soldiers appeared out of holes in the ground and began plastering the immense mechanoid's armored body with a fusillade of mini sabot rounds. These were far from lethal—but they were distracting. Not unlike insects.

"Laze targets!" the captain shouted. "Hit 'em, hit 'em—*hurry,* Epps!"

"I'm on it—rain's coming, get out your umbrellas!" the technical sergeant yelled back over the din of handheld launchers repeatedly unleashing their contents.

As the dust cloud cleared from the small crater Optimus's landing had made in the street, the robot lowered one hand and uncurled his fingers. Still somehow clutching the Cube, Sam slid off the slick metal and back onto solid ground. Understandably wobbly, he stumbled backward and would have fallen if not for the metal finger that gently caught his back and helped keep him upright.

"You would give your own life to protect the Cube?" Optimus was quietly incredulous. "But it is not the source of your kind's spark."

Standing away from the supportive finger, Sam summoned a smile from the depths of exhaustion. "Hey—no sacrifice, no victory," he barely managed to mumble as he wrapped both arms tightly around the softly glowing Cube.

The ground shook as Megatron came flying around the nearest building to slam into Optimus, knocking the other robot backward.

"IT'S MINE! THE CUBE IS MINE!"

Shaky but aware that there were still legs under him, Sam whirled and half stumbled, half ran away from the renewed struggle.

Diving jets unloaded missiles at the unmissable target that was Megatron. Several punctured the layer of extreme outer armor. They slowed the giant but did not stop him as he reached for Sam. The human-inflicted wounds meant nothing to the huge mechanoid. All that mattered was the Cube, the Energon. The Source. Recover that and all else would follow inexorably and effortlessly. He bent forward, arm extending, fingers open and reaching . . .

Swinging around sharply in an arc parallel to the ground, Optimus's leg screamed through the air above Sam's head as he dove beneath it. The heavy metal limb hit Megatron hard, driving him back but not knocking him down. The blow was a diversion, not a killing strike.

"Aim the Cube at my spark!" Optimus yelled at Sam. *"The merging will overwhelm both power sources and destroy it!"*

Battling to stay on his feet, Sam looked across at the supine mechanoid. "But—what about *you*?"

"DO IT NOW!" the robot thundered.

Sam hesitated, then raised the Cube in one fist and advanced on the recumbent mechanical form, approaching Optimus's chest. Seeing the movement, a shocked Megatron immediately divined the human's intention. Gathering itself, the Decepticon lurched forward.

"NO!"

A massive hand descended as Sam thrust the Cube toward Optimus's torso. He moved forward—and then darted to his left and took one, two, three steps *up* the inclining robot's extended arm. Who could have guessed that all those boringly repetitive agility drills he had participated in on the football field would actually turn out to be worth something?

Insects can be easy to smash, but hard to catch.

As a startled Megatron reached with his other hand for the human who was unexpectedly running straight *at* him, Sam half closed his eyes. With no idea what to expect, he slammed the Energon Cube straight at the center of the Decepticon's chest.

The blinding flash that resulted blew him backward as Megatron's overloaded spark exploded. Tendrils of unconstrained energy erupted in all directions, lightning crackling from the disintegrating ventral armor. The giant straightened and stepped backward, clutching at his chest. Inclining downward, the awful head sought and found Sam where he lay helpless and dazed on the ground. A hand reached toward him—and halted. Megatron took a step forward, another backward, shuddered once—and fell.

In the sky nearby, the transformed Starscream let out a shriek of dismay, whirled, and fled. Not to any point of the terrestrial compass, but upward into the clouds and beyond, speeding toward a destination where the human-piloted F-22s that pursued him could not follow.

For the first time in a long while, quiet descended on the city's southern suburbs.

With each of them supporting the injured secretary of defense under one arm, Maggie and Glen helped Keller stumble forward along the road that led from the base of the dam to a service area beside the river where a medevac chopper was descending. Simmons walked alongside, his step almost jaunty as he tossed Frenzy's severed head easily up and down, from one hand to the other.

"Little memento for my trophy case." He winked at Maggie. "Nice workin' with ya, Ace. Might have an opening in the Sector, if you're interested. Our HQ is outside D.C., out in the country, and a long way from Langley. A lot quieter. Woods, deer, running stream, lots of perks." He smiled encouragingly. "The work is always interesting." He saw Glen eyeing him and shook his head curtly. "Not you—just her. You panic."

Keller grimaced at him, smiling through his pain. "Get in line. She's already on my staff." He looked back at Maggie. "You wouldn't object to a corner office? Nice views, close to the Pentagon and a brand-new Chevy Solstice."

"Nossir," she admitted truthfully. "A corner office would be swell. But if I could get a little advance on salary, I owe my landlord a lot of . . ."

His smile tightened, but only a little. "Don't push it."

"Yessir."

Emerging from the copter, army medics relieved her and Glen of the secretary's weight and helped him toward the waiting craft. Standing alongside Maggie, a hesitant but determined Glen did something far more difficult than rewiring an old computer or hacking restricted government websites: he took her hand in his. Her expression flat, she immediately shook off his grip—then smiled as she took his hand in *hers*.

Emerging from the wreckage that until that afternoon had been a bustling southside city street, Lennox searched the rubble until he found Epps. Officer and tech sergeant regarded each other for a long moment. Then hands rose up. The *smack* of a loud high five being exchanged echoed across the devastated street. Both men smiled.

Within an hour, Epps was complaining again.

Elsewhere, Ratchet and Ironhide came trundling up another street in search of their leader. The lifeless, sparkless Jazz lay cradled in Ironhide's arms. Gently, he set his brave fellow robot down on the ruined pavement. Bending low, Optimus studied the metal corpse. Nothing was said. No words were spoken, no communication exchanged, not even electronically. It was not necessary. Each of them felt the appropriate words without having to speak them. The moment was shared.

Turning away, Optimus walked the few steps to where a deep crater had been gouged out of the main avenue. A shape lay in the bottom, crumpled, broken, inert. Megatron.

"You left me no choice . . . Brother. For the Energon to be dealt with, one of us had to die. I was willing for it to be me." He pivoted. "Better it was you."

A much smaller shape approached tentatively, leaned forward to peer into the crater, then straightened to consider the standing robot. "All I remember is a bright light and being picked up and dumped across the street. What happened to the Cube?" Sam inquired hesitantly.

"It is destroyed," Optimus told him.

Sam looked up at the giant. "But you need it to go home and bring your world back to life."

"Without the Cube there is no going back. That purpose is ended now. That home is closed to us." The enormous, gleaming metal head tilted downward to meet his gaze. "Our home must be here now. Among your kind. Among humans." And with that, he bowed, the entire immense upper body inclining in Sam's direction until it was directly over him and parallel to the surface. To his considerable credit Sam held his ground as tons of metal hovered just over his head.

"I owe you my life," Optimus Prime told him. "Humans do not always think rationally, but you can think fast. I did not anticipate what you did." Straightening, he looked toward the crater. "Neither, thankfully for all, did Megatron. We are all of us in your debt." Gathering around him, the surviving robots formed a towering circle of glistening metal. Emulating their leader, they, too, bowed toward Sam. Looking upward, he turned a slow circle to regard each of them in turn. The sight was impressive, inspiring, almost overwhelming.

"Ah, geez—you guys," he muttered, unable to hide his embarrassment . . .

It was a normal morning on an ordinary day. Or maybe an ordinary morning on a normal day. Either way, it was comfortingly afterward. Subsequent to tragedy and confrontation, life goes on: across the planet, across the country, even in the town of Tranquility. Even in Tranquility High School. The hallways were filled with color and noise and subdued (according to regulation) music.

Sam and Miles were just one pair among the milling crowd that was busily engaged in walking and talking, laughing and gossiping. They stopped when Sam caught sight of Mikaela heading his way, surrounded by her usual retinue of friends. Glancing up, she looked in his direction, met his stare, and looked—past him. Turning, he saw Trent DeMarco standing with his buds from the football team. Inside, he slumped. Why should he be surprised? he told himself. Didn't history, as he had learned in Mr. Dockweiller's class, have this lousy stinking tendency to repeat itself?

Striding past him, she continued on down the hall and stopped next to DeMarco. Trent had the body, Trent had the money. Trent was a player, Sam realized. No matter what had transpired the previous week he, Sam Witwicky, was not. For once Miles didn't offer up a wisecrack as the two friends headed for the main exit.

DeMarco saw Mikaela coming, grinned contentedly. "Apology accepted. I'll take you back."

"No." She eyed him speculatively. "Just answer one question. What's the fuel-injection rate of your daddy-bought Escalade when you're going up a hill in second?"

He gaped at her, confused. "What're you talking about?"

"Nothing you'd understand." So saying, she resumed walking—right past him. DeMarco and his buddies followed her with their eyes. It was all they could do.

Out in the school parking lot Sam bid good-bye to Miles, who had finally managed to scrounge enough money to buy his own junker. It wasn't much, but it was perfectly adequate for transporting crickets, and at least he was no longer beholden to Sam for a ride. Which was just as well with Miles. Sam was his best friend, sure, but—frankly, Sam's ride *scared* him.

As Sam approached the Camaro—beautifully restored and refinished, gleaming like new thanks to the combined efforts of Lockheed Martin Corporation's supersecret Skunk Works and Tranquility's Zero-Gee Bob's Racing and Custom Auto Body Shop—he was greeted with the words to "All by Myself" humming from the stereo.

He halted next to the driver's-side door. "Hilarious. Really. Thanks so much for the moral support." He reached for the handle.

A voice stopped him. "Hey, Ladiesman . . ." He whirled.

Mikaela. Coming across the lot, looking—spectacular. Coming—toward *him*. She stopped close. Real close. Grinning. Sam opened his mouth to say something but he never had the chance to get the words out. It was all her fault. Those damn lips, clamping down hard over his, not letting go. Barely letting him breathe.

Oh, well, he mused as all other incipient thoughts died aborning. He could complain later. He would really, really bawl her out. Let her know how he felt about her doing . . . about her . . . about . . . ab . . .

Music purred from the speakers of the shimmering yellow-and-black vehicle at his back—Aerosmith's "Young Lust" . . .

It was a lovely clear day in the capital. Even the usual back-and-forth catcalls and name-calling of partisanship debate seemed softened by the weather. In a downtown office the secretary of defense of the United States stood at one end of a long conference table and regarded the individuals seated before him. Their expressions were expectant, their attention absolute.

"In an effort to limit awareness of the extent of the situation and its true import, the president has ordered Sector Seven to be dissolved and the remains of the deceased aliens to be secretly disposed of. He and his administration will take the heat for what will officially be called 'a civilian-military experiment gone bad.' There will be a storm of questions from the media. Given that 'alien invasion' is among the least likely explanations to be believed, we think it should be possible to manage the consequent fallout. Public relations–wise, containment will not be perfect, but I am assured that it can be spun."

Turning, he indicated a wall screen. It showed the bow of a huge freighter surrounded by escort vessels. As the remote camera looked on, the twisted, gnarled remains of lifeless Decepticons were pushed through an open railing and over the side of the ship, to disappear beneath white-topped waves.

"To prevent any chance of unforeseeable environmental fallout resulting from possible degradation of the, uh, bodies, they are being dumped into the Laurentian Abyss. At the disposal point it is seven miles to the sea bottom—the deepest point in any of the oceans. The programmed detonation at the location will be buffered by the massive depth, pressure, and water column above it. Worldwide sensors will register it as nothing more than a small seismic disturbance, typical for an area where the seafloor is spreading. Additionally, the exact site that has been chosen lies within a sunken caldera. I am assured that sufficient kilotons are being employed to implode this geological feature, thus burying everything beneath the resultant rubble."

The government officials and high-ranking officers exchanged looks around the table. When someone finally spoke, it was an assistant secretary from another department. Given the somberness of the occasion, his words could have been anticipated.

"Wonder what's for lunch?"

The farm was set in rolling countryside. The old truck and battered sedan that were parked out in front of the house were joined by a gleaming black GMC pickup truck that pulled up and parked in the dirt. Lennox stayed behind the wheel for a long moment: staring at the house, drinking in the surrounding yard, the nearby barn and shed. Nothing new, nothing very special, but to him it was Xanadu. As he exited the truck and stepped down into the dirt, the front door of the house opened and a woman ran out, coming toward him with a baby in her arms. Her smile was as wide as the country that stretched off toward the sunset and as warm as the sun that was setting. They melted into each other's arms. Then Lennox took the baby, holding her for the first time. The little girl stared up at him in wonderment, and burped. For once, a perfect day.

Unnoticed, the black pickup gave a little shake, doglike. All the dirt fell from its sides, right down to the dust that had accumulated in the multiple wheel wells . . .

The hill crest wasn't exactly Everest, but it was the best one could do without driving a long way from Tranquility. Sam and Mikaela sat on Bumblebee's hood gazing at the same sunset that was presently casting its magic over a small farm. Unoccupied by driver or passenger, an emergency vehicle sat parked nearby. It looked as out of place on the hillside as did the giant eighteen-wheeler that loomed over it.

As Mikaela rested her head on Sam's shoulder and he fought hard not to slide off the slick hood and act cool at the same time, Optimus Prime mused to himself.

"For now, the Decepticon legions are vanquished, and fate has yielded its reward. A new world to call—home. We live among its people now, hiding in plain sight, but watching over them in secret. Waiting. Protecting. I have been witness to their capacity for courage and sacrifice. Though internally and in many other ways we are literally worlds apart, as with us there is more to them than meets the eye."

Except for the two young humans, the odd assortment of vehicles was alone on the hill. Optimus felt safe in raising his hood—his head—slightly off the ground and aiming it skyward. With that look, and an undetectable burst of energy, a final message flashed outward toward the sky and the stars beyond.

"I am Optimus Prime, and I send this message to any survivors of my kind who may be taking refuge among other systems, other stars. You are not alone. You have a home here, among others of your kind.

"We are waiting."